I0630770

Cover Design: Deranged Doctors

Editing: Tamara Mataya

ISBN: 978-1-7350961-3-1

❀ Created with Vellum

Finally Falling
book two

FORGET
about it

JESSIE HARPER

1

Cassie

"And here's to many happy years!"

I lift my glass and toast the happy couple for what seems like the millionth time. It's only 9:30 and already I've reached my engagement celebration limit. I'm going to claim my right to be annoyed. After all, how many people can say they've had their best friend lap them *twice* when it comes to walking down the aisle? Yes, Julia is headed to her second happily ever after and I've got the dubious distinction of being her maid of honor. Again. Not that I want to be getting married. I'm a certified wedding hater. I love a good true love story, but do we have to slather the whole thing in white icing and release a bunch of butterflies every time someone decides to commit? I'm happy just the way I am— free to do what I want when I want with whomever I want. I'm not a relationship girl. And marriage? That definitely counts as a relationship. I can barely handle a second date with most men let alone the rest of my life, so I empty my pint glass in honor of Julia and Zach and make my way to the bar for a refill.

Julia's been my best friend since middle school so I'm not all gloom and doom about her upcoming wedding. She's managed to find love again after not only enduring the death of her first husband, but the later realization that he wasn't who she thought he was. That's enough to make most people want to crawl in a hole and never come out. The fact that Julia's here tonight surrounded by friends and family celebrating her engagement to the world's nicest guy is something that does warm my cold, black heart. But another wedding? I wish I didn't have to keep raising my glass to toast this shiny happiness, especially since I keep finding it empty. By the end of the night I should be well on the way to excessively happy, myself, if I keep drinking like this. Weddings are the worst and engagement parties are coming in a close second right now.

I slide in front of the cantina style bar and make eye contact with the only person who might be feeling less excited about this wedding than me: Julia's ex-boyfriend Graham. He's sitting at the end of the bar with the worst fake smile I have ever seen plastered on his face. Under normal circumstances I would be enjoying his pain—we've been enemies since middle school, after all—but I'm pretty sure my own face has a very similar look to it. Graham pulls out the bar stool next to him and pats it with his gigantic paw.

"You wanna sit?" He turns his face toward me and lets the smile slide from his mouth. The grim line that replaces it looks more like what I would have expected. "We can talk about all the crap we have to plan."

The last thing I want to do is sit with Graham and discuss wedding stuff, but as the two members of the wedding party on the bride's side we do have a ton of stuff to organize. Yes, that's right, I'm Julia's maid of honor and Graham is her other bridesmaid. It would be funny if it wasn't so horrible. Not only do I have to spend more time than I'd like with the boy who tormented me in middle and high school, but I have to do it in taffeta. He can't be having an easy time of it either, having agreed to watch the love of his life get married for the second time to someone else. But he's the one who promised to be in the wedding party when Julia asked him. He's the one who would have been able to say no. Not that he's ever been able to say no to Julia, but at least as a hulking football dude, and her ex at that, it wouldn't have looked strange for him to have refused to stand next to her at the altar. He could have wriggled out of this obligation way easier than I could have. Yet here we are, toasting the bride and groom and drowning our sorrows at the bar where Zach and Julia's relationship got its start.

"Are you sitting or not, Cassie?" Graham's impatient bark cuts through my indifference.

"Fine, I'll sit if it means you stop grimacing like you have been. It's creeping people out." In reality, I'm sure no one's been paying as much attention to Graham's discomfort as I have. Maybe Julia's parents have noticed since they love Graham like a son. I'm sure they were hoping the two of them would end up together after she moved back to our hometown. Everyone else, however, is focused on Julia and Zach and the happy little bubble they're floating around in.

"Is it that bad?" he asks. "I just hate events like this." He reaches for his drink and finishes it in one gulp. "You empty? Up for another round?"

I settle myself on the stool next to him and catch a whiff of his cologne. Why do the guys who are the biggest jerks always smell so damn good? There should be some karmic retribution for jerkiness that prohibits guys like Graham from smelling like I imagine Superman smelling.

"Oh, I'm getting another drink. That's the only way I can keep smiling through this."

"Upset about always being the bridesmaid and never the bride? Afraid of becoming an old maid, Mama?" There's the caring commentary I've come to expect from Graham. And he threw in my old nickname from when I was the fat girl. Extra points for that.

"Hardly. I'm just not excited to do all this wedding stuff another time. How about you? Getting used to having your girl swiped out from under you again? I would think you'd be a pro at that by now."

Graham ignores me and motions for the bartender.

"It can't be easy to watch your dream girl get married to someone else. Again. Did I say that already?" I can't help but poke a little at what I'm sure is a soft spot.

Graham doesn't give me the benefit of a reaction; he's used to my biting remarks by now. The only reason we ever hung out was because of Julia and now we're stuck together again. I have no idea how she put up with him when they were together and no idea why she does it now. Obviously we're at each other's throats.

"She hasn't been my girl for a long time." Graham goes back to ordering drinks. Julia considers him more like a brother now, not that she tells him that. The thought of actively choosing to make Graham an honorary family member makes me gag.

"But she still managed to convince you to be a bridesmaid," I remind him. "She asked and you didn't even think about it, just said yes."

"Old habits, I guess." Graham slides a tequila shot over.

"And I thought we agreed to drop the 'bridesmaid' thing. She asked me to be in the *wedding party*."

"No matching dresses then?" I feign disappointment. "But you would have looked so nice in something frilly."

Graham gives me a slight smile but doesn't fight back. Instead he motions to the salt shaker. "You salting up or just drinking?"

"Who said I was drinking tequila?"

"This situation. If you and I have to sit here and deal with all this then we're getting drunk."

From the back corner of the room one of Zach's friends starts another toast. I can barely hear what he's saying, but the repeated *aahs* from the crowd let me know I'm going to be drinking to that for sure. I lick the back of my hand and sprinkle it with salt before giving it another lick. Graham does the same and we lift our glasses, clinking them together.

"Then here's to making sure we don't remember any of this happy night," I say.

"I'll drink to that."

We both knock back our shots. I shove a lime slice in my mouth to combat the burn of the tequila. "Keep 'em comin'," Graham tells the bartender and she sets us up again.

"And here's to the best set of bridesmaids anyone's ever seen," he jokes, giving me a wink. Maybe spending all this time with Graham won't be nearly as bad as I thought.

There is nothing worse than the sound of jack hammering before the sun's even up. Scratch that—there is nothing worse than the sound of jack hammering in the morning when you have a raging hangover. I can feel actual throbbing in my temples as the noise starts up again. Isn't there a rule against construction so early? And on a Saturday? I pull the pillow over my head to block it out. This proves to have zero effect on the overall noise level in the room. What time is it anyway? I thrust my hand out to grab my phone from the bedside table.

Instead of the cool surface of the nightstand my hand hits something else entirely.

Something decidedly warmer. Something bulkier.

The noise stops and I realize it isn't the sound of construction at all, but rather, the bulldozer-like snoring coming from the massive dude still asleep next to me.

I freeze. *Shit, Cassie.* I barely remember the rest of the night—once Graham convinced me to start on the tequila things got a little fuzzy—and I definitely don't remember coming home with whoever this is. I lift the tangled sheet high enough to see that, yep, I'm totally naked and so is my new friend. I let my eyes travel down his muscled back to the curve of an impressively toned ass. Even in the dark I can tell this guy is built. At least the liquor didn't keep me from picking wisely in the body department. Still, unless I want to make some seriously awkward introductions this morning I'm going to need to sneak out of here, and fast.

Luckily, I haven't brought Mr. Mystery back to my apartment. That would require me waking him up in order to convince him to leave. This way I can get my stuff together and be out the door, hopefully before he even notices. I'd like to do this walk of shame without an audience.

I slide to the edge of the bed, noting the silkiness of the sheets. The high thread count would most certainly have impressed me had I been in any state to notice details last night. As it is, I don't even have time to really appreciate what is turning out to be a very impressive bedroom. It isn't thrown together like most of the places single guys end up living. Stuff matches. There are a few pillows thrown on the floor next to my side of the bed. Pillows that imply this bed was actually made when we fell into it and suggest an interior decorator. Did I sleep with a married man?!

Although, maybe I haven't slept with him at all. Naked doesn't automatically mean sex, right? I keep my fingers crossed as I make my way across the king-sized bed to freedom. My friend stirs a little and grunts as I work to ease myself off the mattress. I hold stock-still, barely breathing, until he settles back down again.

Any hope that my visit was purely platonic evaporates when I see the condom wrappers on the bedside table. Wrappers *plural*. At least I don't have to obsess over whether or not I've exposed myself to some horrible STD. I mentally kick myself again for being dumb enough to go home with some idiot from the bar.

Some idiot who has the money to buy some genuinely gorgeous bedroom furniture.

I run my fingers over the edge of the lamp on the table, avoiding the pile of wrappers as I go. The possibility of finding a wedding ring on this guy's hand is becoming more and more likely. Looking over at his sleeping back, his face pressed into a pillow, I resist the urge to move around the bed to get a glimpse of his face.

I bend over to pick up my discarded panties. I would say it was lucky that I had on sexy underwear last night, but I always wear sexy underwear. And I wear it for myself, not because some guy might see me in it. Still, I hope this snoring pile of muscles appreciated my lacy black bra before he launched it up onto the edge of the blinds currently covering his extremely tall windows. I shimmy into my panties before I try to jump high enough to reach the rest of my underwear. Silent jumping is harder than I imagined—my pounding head does not appreciate it and neither does my roiling stomach—and manages to get my bed buddy stirring on his side of the bed. The rest of my clothes seem to make a trail out of the bedroom and toward what I'm hoping is the front door. I could leave the bra where it is and make my escape, but I hate to leave such a pretty—and expensive—reminder of this evening here. I don't want to leave any evidence or any reason to meet up again. Not that I could—I don't even know who this guy is. But there's the chance he wasn't nearly as drunk as I was last night. He could have my name and number in his phone for all I know. *Damn you, Graham and your tequila shots.* Hopefully he's feeling as awful as I am this morning. Not that I'll mention this part of my morning to him or anyone else. Ever.

I make one last attempt to free my bra from the lip of the blinds. The strap is clinging to the sharp corner of the edge, refusing to slide free. There's a chair strategically positioned in the little alcove across from me, if I could stand on that I could easily liberate the rest of my underwear. I try to lift it, but it's too heavy to move without lots of huffing and puffing. Pushing it makes the floor creak and I curse whoever decorated this room. The wood floors are beautiful, but don't muffle any of the sounds of my struggling. I go back to my original plan, throwing my arms around in the hopes of getting my bra down. I grab the part of the strap I can reach and give it a tug. I can see the fabric straining, but still it hangs there, taunting me. I jump again, accidentally slapping the slats and grabbing an edge. I hang there for a second, as the bolt slowly pulls from the wall. The blinds come crashing down, flooding the room with light. They swing back and forth, banging into the window frame as my eyes squeeze shut, protesting against the light.

My secret lover groans, rolling over in bed. I hold my breath, keeping my back to him. I try to think like a rabbit. Should I drop to the floor? Try to scurry away? The bra's free now, of course, but it's not like I can put it on, or get into any of my other clothes either. Even if I could make it out before he wakes all the way up, I'll still be standing outside basically naked. Can you call an Uber and expect them to let you dress in the backseat? There's a question I never thought to ask.

He's groaning louder now, the sheets rustling as he moves. Yep, he's awake and obviously not all that happy about how it's happened. I'm destroying his bedroom along with my ability to flee the scene.

"Jesus, Cassie. What the fuck are you doing?"

That voice. Not a stranger at all. A voice I've known for years. I spin to face him, hoping by some miracle I'm wrong.

"If you wanted the blinds open you could have just opened them, Mama. You didn't need to rip the whole thing down." He's using my old nickname from middle school. The one I hate. He's calling me that name as he rises up, letting the sheet slide down, exposing his chest as he sits up in bed. He's looking at me in only my thong as he tries to block some of the sunlight with one of his giant hands. The sheet settles low on his hips. I take in his square jaw, the massive span of his shoulders against the headboard. "Do you want breakfast?" he asks me, amused, rubbing across his nipples with the other hand.

Like a flash of lightning I suddenly remember those hands in places they shouldn't be. Snippets of last night come rushing back, flooding my head with all sorts of Xrated images. I gape at him, my brain refusing to process what I've done.

I've slept with *Graham*.

I've slept with my childhood nemesis, the boy I'd vowed to hate for all eternity. My best friend's ex. An egomaniacal professional athlete. The worst choice ever.

I've slept with Graham Stevens. *Fuck.*

2

Graham

How did I manage to get myself into this mess? From the moment I woke up—or was woken up, actually, by a nearly naked Cassie—I've been scrambling to fix things. Anyone could have predicted that bringing her home last night would be a colossal mistake. Obviously, I wasn't thinking things through after she and I consumed a vat of tequila. By the end of the night the bartender had just left us the bottle and we made short work of it once we were in charge of pouring our own.

I'm not sure when things changed from adversarial in a friendly way to ending up naked in my bed, but somewhere during the evening, there was a definite shift. Cassie went from giving me her usual barbs and irritated looks to resting the full length of her thigh along mine. Laughing at my jokes. Giving me that look she's probably given countless guys before when she's been out on the prowl. I shouldn't have let things get out of hand, but in the end, I let my baser instincts take over. It's been a while since I've been with anyone. I'll admit that I was weak.

For all the talk of professional athletes and our revolving door of fuck buddies, I've never been able to really convince myself to go that route. Sure there are willing women, but I haven't been one really to indulge since college. Not since I screwed everything up with Julia because I thought that would be better than what I had, that I would be missing out if I didn't take advantage of the perks of being a football star. It turns out I like the steady stuff, commitment and all that comes with it. It also turns out I'm an idiot because by the time I figured that out Julia had moved on. And she never looked back.

And now I've gone and slept with her best friend. A woman who I would have thought hated me until she jumped in my lap as I unsuccessfully tried to get us home from our drunken evening at Mamacita's. Well, I succeeded in getting us to *my* home, something Cassie regretted this morning if her crazy behavior is any indication. She ran out so fast I wasn't able to say anything at all. And she and I have to pretend to be the best wedding party ever over the next few months. Her unhappiness at waking up in my bed is going to become a major issue if I don't get to talk things through with her. Luckily, I know exactly where Cassidy Blake goes when she needs to forget about her problems. After downing copious amounts of water and enough ibuprofen to tranquilize a moose, I get in my car and head in her direction.

Sure enough when I push through the glass doors of the weight room at Fantastic Fitness, there she is with a bar loaded heavy enough to put most guys to shame. I watch Cassie go through her squat routine and try to gather my thoughts. There has to be a way to go back to before, right? Some sort of a reset she and I can negotiate in order to get through the next few months until Julia's wedding is finally over. Then we can go back to only seeing each other when we absolutely have to, just the way we like it. Or at least the way I liked it before because right now I'm having a hard time remembering what it is about Cassie that I don't like, especially when I catch a glimpse of her ass in the tights she's wearing. She bends to adjust the weight on the bar before hoisting it up again and I can see every muscle in her legs flex. My hands twitch involuntarily, remembering how soft the skin under those leggings felt under my palms, how warm. Great, now I've got other less convenient body parts twitching. *Down boy.* I'm not here to convince her for a repeat. I'm here to make sure she knows it'll never happen again.

Cassie catches a glimpse of me from across the room and narrows her eyes. I give her a smile and a wave. She answers me with a scowl. The girl who always gets under my skin is back. So much for starting out playing nice. I set my shoulders and stride over to her as she slides onto a weight bench. I clear my throat and stand there, waiting for her to at least acknowledge my presence. She ignores me and gets set to lift the barbell positioned over her head. It's loaded up fairly heavy and I instinctively move closer. I don't want her to drop it on herself or something.

I clear my throat again. "Do you want me to spot you?"

Cassie's scowl deepens. "No."

"Are you at least going to talk to me? Or are you going to pretend you don't see me standing here?"

Silence.

"Fine, then I guess we'll just work out."

"No, I'll work out and you'll leave me alone. Actually, you'll just leave." She blows out a long breath as she raises the bar. "How did you get in here anyway? I know you don't have a membership."

I shrug. Cassie knows how I got in here. I worked my magic on the girl at the front desk. Took a few selfies with the rest of the staff and told them I was here to see my friend. They basically begged me to come in, already posting their photos to social media. When I need to use what I've got left of my celebrity, I do it.

Cassie rolls her eyes. "Damn it, now I've lost count," she gripes, still holding the bar up.

"That's twelve." Her face contorts again in silent fury. "What? Habit. If someone's lifting then I'm counting."

Cassie rises from the bench, keeping her back to me. When she stalks off to the free weights, I follow her at what I think is a safe distance. I'm not entirely sure she isn't about to turn around and try to pummel me with a piece of equipment. She grabs a set of hand weights and I do the same, positioning myself next to her in the mirror for curls. She moves two steps away from me, shooing me away with a wave of her hand. She looks so frustrated that I laugh and immediately regret it when Cassie's fierce face locks eyes with mine in the mirror. If we weren't in public she would definitely kill me.

"We have to talk about it." She continues to ignore me. "There's no way to avoid it. Not if we have to spend time together for all this wedding shit."

I try to convince her as we move our weights up and down. I'm keeping my voice low, but Cassie's acting like she can't hear me, her eyes focusing straight ahead, arms rhythmically pumping. She's one of the most stubborn people I know, always busting my chops for stupid shit. Having her ignore me would be a dream come true in any other situation, but today I need her to listen to me. I don't want to cause a scene, but she's not giving me many options.

I drop my weights and let them bang onto the floor.

Several sets of eyes turn our way and when Cassie finally whips around to face me none of them turn away. This isn't exactly private, but I'm willing to have an audience if it means she and I can hash things out.

"The whole point of coming here this morning was to forget about what happened last night," she hisses at me, dropping her weights next to mine with a colossal thud. "This is my space. My place. Not yours. I'm not talking about this here."

She points a finger toward my chest and I will her to touch me. Her anger's doing funny things to me. Making parts of me perk up in ways they shouldn't. An image of her face positioned over mine from last night flicks through my brain. I consider reaching out for her, pulling her to me and pressing my mouth on hers. I shake the thought away, but lean in toward her accusing finger. She moves her hand away and points her defiant little chin up at me. I look down at her and am startled by how pretty she is. Her angry, flushed face competing with her red hair. Green eyes glittering under long lashes. She's slightly sweaty, definitely hungover, and without a stitch of make-up on. Still she's beautiful. How have I never noticed this before?

"Mama, we can either talk here now or we can talk somewhere else later but we're talking about this."

Cassie plants her feet and pulls her hand up in front of my face, giving me the finger. "Fuck you, Graham. You come in here and call me that name? Fuck you."

She's getting loud now, attracting more and more attention. I'm not sure why her old nickname sets her off, but now she's furious. Out of the corner of my eye I see one of the gym's personal trainers shuffling over. I'm guessing he's drawn the short straw here because from the look on his face he'd rather be doing almost anything other than being in charge of telling us to cool it.

"Is everything all right here?" he squeaks out before clearing his throat. "I'm going to need you to—oh, Graham Stevens?" The poor guy does a double take, looking me over. "I'm a big fan. I mean I was. I still am. God, sorry about your knee." He looks down at my right knee and I feel it twitch.

"Thanks, man," I manage. "It's all good." It isn't, but there's no use in talking about it. For a normal person my knee is fine; I'm here working out, right? But for a professional football player? My knee is a disaster. The kind of disaster that gets you put on injured reserve and eventually puts your career in the crapper. The kind of disaster that leaves me figuring out what to do now that I can't do what I love anymore.

"I do need to ask you two to keep your voices down. And I can't have you throwing the equipment around." He hesitates. "If that's alright with you."

"We understand." I clap a hand on his shoulder. "My friend and I were just having a little disagreement but we've worked it out. Right, Cass?" She's still shooting daggers at me with her eyes, but she doesn't contradict me. "I promise we'll keep it together over here. No more yelling."

"Okay," the poor guy says, rubbing the back of his neck with his hand. "Could I ask you a favor?"

"Sure."

"Can I grab my phone real quick and get a photo?"

One hour later I'm waiting in a coffee shop down the street for Cassie to grace me with her presence. She agreed to meet only after I continued to shadow her every move at the gym for a good thirty minutes. Between her annoyance with me and the constant interruptions from people wanting to talk football, she'd finally given in and sworn she wouldn't stand me up if I left her alone and gave her a chance to shower. I'm still determined to convince her that we can both put last night behind us and go back to the way it was before, but if today is any indication, I'll be lucky to go back to her previous level of hatred. Somehow, sleeping with Cassie Blake has made her hate me even more than before.

From my seat by the window I can see her as she makes her way up the sidewalk. She's got her hair piled on top of her head, strands of it sticking out everywhere, and the way she walks swings her hips just enough to make more than one guy on the street turn around to look at her as she passes by. For some reason this makes my fists clench up. I work on getting my fingers to uncoil as I watch her pull the front door open and scan the room. She looks relaxed, happy even, until her eyes settle on me—then her top lip curls up into a sneer that would look fitting on a damn cartoon character. It would be funny if there wasn't so much on the line here. If anyone finds out Cassie and I went home together, there's bound to be trouble. I've got enough going wrong in my life without this extra drama adding to it. I'm here to shut this thing down.

Cassie slides into the booth, folding her long legs under the table. I've had to push the table forward to fit in on my side so she's squished up against the edge of it once she gets settled. This only makes her more irritated and she gives the tabletop a shove, sending the thing slamming into my midsection.

"Cassie, what the fuck?" I rub a hand over my middle.

"Let's get one thing straight here, okay? Last night. That's never happening again. As far as I'm concerned it never even happened. I've already put all of that"—Cassie gestures in my general direction with her hand—"in the vault and I'm expecting you to do the same."

"O-Okay," I stutter out. I hadn't expected her to be as adamant about things. I'm supposed to be laying down the law to her, not the other way around. "But we should still debrief so we have our stories straight. Do you want coffee or something?" I move to signal the waitress but Cassie slaps my hand back down. She pulls a napkin from the metal dispenser on the table and makes a show of wiping her hand. "Give me a break. You touched way more than that last night," I remind her.

Cassie shudders, deliberately exaggerating the movement. "What part of 'never happened' are you not understanding? If anyone ever found out that I slept with you..." She lets her disgusted face do the rest of the talking.

"Please, if people found out they'd be high-fiving you all over town." I puff up a bit because I know that this is partly true. Some people would think Cassie had picked the golden ticket getting to roll around in my bed. Other people... not so much and we both know it. Julia. Her parents. Our shared friends. None of them would be celebrating. They'd all be thinking we'd lost our minds.

"Look, you and your ego can add last night to your spank bank, I guess. But I don't think we need to hash out the details. We shared an Uber. No one needs to know that you dragged me back to your lair instead of taking me back to my own apartment."

I look across the table at Cassie in disbelief. "Excuse me? I didn't drag you anywhere. You're the one who jumped all over me. I couldn't even get you to keep your seatbelt buckled! The poor guy driving us almost threw us out of the car. You had your hands *down my pants*."

"That's not how I remember it," Cassie tells me flatly, crossing her arms over her chest. Her breasts spill over the top of her V-neck T-shirt, distracting me.

"Well, how do you remember it then?"

"I remember you trying to get me drunk and then waking up naked. That's what I remember."

"Are you kidding me?" I run a hand through my hair. I sincerely hope she's lying here. We were both pretty drunk, but I never would have done anything to take advantage of her. I'm starting to feel my chest getting tight. "God, Cassie. I don't even know what to say right now. You don't remember the ride home? The rest of it? I mean we were at it all night. That's a whole lot of orgasms to conveniently forget."

Cassie's face flushes and I know she remembers. She remembers everything.

"Lower your voice!" Cassie leans forward in the booth.

I lean forward to meet her half way. "How many times did you come last night, Cassie?" Her face is inches from mine and I can see the blush rising on her neck. "How many times did I get you off?"

She glares at me before turning her head and mumbling something under her breath.

"What? What's that?" I cup my hand around my ear. "I couldn't hear you."

"Five," she spits at me. "Five times. Happy now?"

I lean back into the cushion behind me, unable to keep the smug grin off my face. "Not as happy as you were last night. You're welcome."

3

Cassie

Stupid fucking Graham.

Actually, stupid me for fucking Graham. Yeah, that's more like it. I slam the front door to my apartment so hard it rattles on its hinges. I'll probably get a noise complaint from one of my elderly neighbors but I don't care. I'll just add that to the rest of the shitty things piling up on this already monumentally shitty day. I swear I hear Mrs. Duthie's door creak open. Luckily, she doesn't try creeping down the hall to see what's happening. That's the problem with living in an old building—you can hear everything. The floors groan, the windows rattle in the breeze, and the old duct system carries every secret argument through the building. But there's no place with character like this one. I fell in love with the old mantle around the fireplace, the high ceilings, and the giant trees in my front yard. It's like a park with birds singing in the morning and squirrels scampering around. And it's only ten minutes to downtown and my job at the hospital, giving me the best of both worlds: tranquility and convenience.

But right now I'm not feeling very tranquil at all. And my situation is far from convenient. I've slept with Graham and he refuses to just forget about it. I'll admit it wasn't fair of me to try to pretend I didn't remember what happened. After my acrobatic routine this morning with his window blinds everything came rushing back into my foggy brain. Even if it had been gratifying to make him squirm a little, I can't let him take responsibility for all of this. Especially when I know I'm the one who started it.

The seatbelt thing?

True.

Mauling him with my mouth in the Uber?

True.

The hands down his pants part?

Also, mortifyingly true and surprisingly interesting. Graham is built *everywhere*.

He tried to be a gentleman, but I wore down his resolve and I'm not even sure why. There were plenty of other willing participants at the bar last night so why did I pick Graham? Why did I flirt with him instead of someone even marginally more suitable? And I've got no excuse for the number of times we, um, forgot all the reasons we hate each other. I mean, once is a drunken mistake, but over and over again? We were the definition of screwing our brains out. In the morning we were both definitely idiots. I know I have fewer brain cells today and it isn't all from the tequila.

I try to zero in on the reasons I would make such a stupid decision when my phone pings. Julia's name lights up the screen, texting me from somewhere in her perfect house with her perfect family. I'm not jealous, but I get a familiar twinge. Loneliness. I was feeling it last night too, watching my best friend smile up at yet another adoring face. I don't want a husband, babies, and a white picket fence, but sometimes I do wish I had some of what Julia has. Here it's just me, running the show the way I like it but occasionally wishing there was someone here to share it with me. Of course, setting myself up to keep a giant secret from Julia isn't the best way to keep your friends close. And who am I supposed to talk to about any of this? Graham? I certainly can't ever tell Julia. At least Graham and I agree on that. If I'd been looking to hurt her, sleeping with her first love is a pretty good way to do it. But I don't think that's what I was trying to do last night. I don't think I'd been thinking about much at all except having a man's hands on me. Too bad I had to pick the biggest asshole in the place to make that happen.

Julia: Did you make it home safe last night?

I let my fingers hover over the screen.

Of course! Graham and I got a ride together!

Delete.

Sure did! Nothing interesting to report!

Delete.

Exclamation points? What is wrong with me? Julia's not even standing here in person and I'm ready to spill everything I've just sworn I'll never, ever tell her.

Yes.

Send.

Julia: Good. Didn't see you leave. Did u have a good time? Thought maybe you'd found someone new to hang out with. Any new prospects? ;)

If only you knew, Julia. Then there'd be no cute little winky face blinking at me. There'd be some sort of middle finger emoji.

Nope. Went home alone. You know me and Zach's gym buddies—not a good match.

Only fifty percent lie. I do hate most of her fiancé Zach's meathead gym friends.

Julia: Are you working today?

Me: No.

Thank God. I can only imagine how much worse this day would get if I had to work a twelve-hour shift at the hospital.

Julia: Can you stop by? I have wedding stuff to talk about. I'll make you dinner...

Knowing the contents of my refrigerator I should immediately take Julia up on her offer. Tonight will probably be another night of me wishing I had gone to the grocery store while eating a sleeve of crackers. But between work and my extra special run in with Graham, I'm starting off the week without any of my usual planning. I should spend the rest of my weekend getting back on track: cleaning my apartment and food prepping for the week, getting to bed early so I won't be dead on my feet when I have to go into work on Monday. But the thought of someone else taking care of dinner makes me forget all those other concerns.

Me: Sure. What time?

Julia: Great! Can you come over around 6?

Me: See you then.

I walk up the sidewalk to Julia's house with a bottle of wine tucked under my arm. I can do this. I can look her in the eye and wipe all traces of Graham from my mind. I straighten my spine and ring the bell, noticing the planter full of flowers spilling over onto the porch. I've barely got the capacity to raise a cactus and here Julia's growing not only kids, but flowers. I'm sure somewhere in her house is a fish swimming happily in its little bowl. They'll probably get a puppy next.

Julia throws open the front door and greets me with the kind of hug you reserve for long-lost relatives. I can barely breathe in her python-like grip and do my best to wrestle away before she strangles me.

"Shit, Julia. Not so tight. We just saw each other last night." I thrust the bottle of wine forward to put some space between us.

"Sorry! I'm just so excited you have tonight off. Zach and I have been doing wedding stuff all day, but I need fresh victims. He's gotten tired of the planning already."

"Victims?" I ask, emphasizing the plural. I don't like the sound of that.

"Sure. You and Graham," Julia tells me as I catch a glimpse of his broad back on top of a ladder behind her. "He was over helping my dad with a few things so he walked down. He and Zach are replacing the ceiling fan. Fingers crossed they don't burn the house down." She raises her hand to cross her fingers and I am blinded by the sparkle of her new engagement ring.

"Graham was at your parents' house?" I don't know why I even bother asking at this point. Of course he was. He's embedded so tightly in Julia's family that I wouldn't be surprised if he had his own room over there. He and Julia's dad have developed the kind of bromance I love to make fun of. Graham and Steve could be father and son these days and he's always hanging around their house, helping with stuff and generally making them wish he and Julia had never broken up. If it was a diabolical plan I would give him credit for executing something so brilliant, but I know that having grown up without a dad of his own Graham's not in it to win Julia back. Steve's truly been like a father to him since high school. Hell, I would have loved to be able to find a great surrogate dad for myself conveniently hanging around after mine hit the road.

"Are they even qualified to put that thing up? Shouldn't you call an electrician or something?" I poke my head through the doorway and see Zach handing pieces up to Graham. You'd think it would be awkward—Julia's ex with her new almost-husband—but it turns out I'm the only one feeling awkward here, a feeling that only intensifies when Graham turns a bit to face us and I convince myself I can almost see his nipples through his T-shirt. Nipples that I now remember having between my teeth a few hours ago.

"Have a little faith, Mama." He lets his eyes rake over me. I make myself ignore him, but the skin on my neck starts to burn. "Zach and I are trained professionals. We can install a ceiling fan."

Zach gives me a thumbs up, still looking at the directions he has spread out on the coffee table.

"I made them look at those," Julia whispers conspiratorially. "And I'm having the electrician come to check their work in the morning. Come on, help me in the kitchen."

I follow her over toward the stove where she's got multiple pots going at once. I lift the lid on one and am rewarded with a face full of steam. So much for my mascara. Not that I should care what I look like for dinner with friends, although I'm glad I at least changed out of my sweats and into a pair of jeans that I know make my ass look fantastic.

"You didn't tell me Graham was going to be here," I say more accusingly than I intend to. "You could've given me a warning."

"I just assumed you'd know he'd be here. I mean he's

also wedding party, right? And I know he can be an ass, but I thought you two were getting along better. You went home together last night, didn't you?"

My face flames. "What? We didn't go home together."

"I thought you shared an Uber. That's what Graham said." Julia's brow knits a bit in confusion.

"Oh. Oh, that. Yeah." I make a show of looking for the corkscrew and pulling down wine glasses from the cabinet. I know the drawers' contents almost as well as Julia does, having spent many a night here in her house once she moved back to town. Back then she was a recently widowed single mom trying to figure out what to do next and now she's got me here to talk about wedding plans. Things definitely have changed.

"Fuck!" Graham yells from the living room, reminding me that some things will never change.

"Where are the boys?" I ask Julia, hoping neither of her elementary-school-aged sons are about to appear and start repeating the colorful language Graham's so loudly spewing.

"They're at my mom and dad's. We thought it'd be easier to talk without them interrupting every five seconds. Zach's going to walk over and get them in time for bed." One of the many benefits of Julia being able to move a few blocks away from her parents, I guess. I'd hate to be this close to my mother, but they're making it work. Julia goes back to stirring, dipping the wooden spoon into the pot and offering me a taste. "Too salty?"

"No, I don't think so." I'm careful not to burn my tongue. Julia's a great cook and she doesn't need any advice from me.

"Speaking of salty... did you and Graham have a fight last night or something?"

I'm relieved that Julia's busy with dinner and can't see the flash of panic I feel contort my face. "Not really," I answer her, careful not to let my voice give anything away. "Why do you ask?" I try to sound innocent but I'm pretty sure I'm failing miserably.

"Well, you seemed okay last night, but today you're both acting weird."

"Weird? We're not acting weird." Yeah, that sounds totally believable. *Way to get defensive, Cassie.* I fill my wine glass and turn just in time to get a glimpse of Graham's butt in his athletic shorts from the top of the ladder. I take a giant swig. "He keeps calling me that nickname again," I tell her as I pour her a generous serving of red. "So maybe that's the pissed off vibe you're getting."

"Seriously?" Julia turns to face me with a respectable amount of righteous indignation. I mentally give her five more points in her standing as best friend. "Do you want me to talk to him about that? In his defense, I honestly don't think he remembers why they used to call you that. Not that that's an excuse. So rude."

"You don't have to." I don't want Graham to think I've spent all night talking about him. I'd rather let him think he's been the furthest thing from my mind. Even if that's becoming one of the bigger lies I'm having to tell. I've been doing nothing today but dissecting every detail of last night which means dissecting every detail of Graham. "He'll quit eventually."

"Sure, but in the meantime you have to sit there and get annoyed. That's not going to work if you two are going to plan all this stuff with me. I can't have miserable brides-maids." Julia's teasing with the last part, but that barely registers.

"How much are you expecting us to help, really? I thought you'd hire a wedding planner or something. Isn't that what people do?" The thought of dealing with Graham on a regular basis for eternity makes my head start to ache; they haven't even set a date which means this could drag on for months.

"Well, it's the second wedding for both of us so we were hoping to keep things a little more low key. And who needs a wedding planner when you have a great group of people ready and willing to help?"

Julia says the last part with less conviction than she should and I know she's waiting for me to back her up. She wants me to tell her there's nothing I would rather do than help her plan another wedding. But let's get real here. I've done this with her before. I know how much time even the simplest wedding is going to eat up. Time I don't have and time I don't want to spend with Graham Stevens. Maybe before last night I would have been more easygoing about it, but tonight I know there's no way I'll be committing to making wedding favors and helping with the seating arrangement for their reception. No way, no how.

But none of that gets a chance to come out of my mouth because Zach and Graham move to the kitchen island, apparently finished setting up the fan in the living room. Julia turns to kiss Zach as he slides one hand over the curve of her hip and I can't keep my eyes from looking right at Graham to gauge his reaction. To his credit there's only a flicker of discomfort, which he quickly quells with a swig from his bottle of beer. But I see it and it tells me everything I need to know about Graham and how he's still pining for Julia. It might have been me in his bed last night, but it's Julia who's in his heart. For all I know he was picturing her when he was screwing me.

I choose the wrong time to take another sip of wine and find myself choking, the idea of my body with Julia's face making it hard for me to swallow. Graham's over in an instant, whacking me on the back. When the thumping turns to rubbing I wrench myself away from him.

"God, Graham! Get off me," I sputter, effectively silencing the entire room and drawing attention to Graham's hands still resting on my shoulders. He pulls back like I'm made of pure electricity and not the sexual kind. He holds his hands up near his face, surrendering.

"Whoa, whoa. I was only trying to keep you from dying. Sorry. Won't do it again."

"Let's get dinner organized," Julia interjects, the confusion on her face mirrored in Zach's expression. "You two stay in your corners." She hands me a basket of rolls—home-made, of course—and shoves me toward the dining room table. She's close behind me with the salad, hissing in my ear. "What the hell is going on with you two?"

"Nothing. We just don't always get along," I whisper back, fully aware of how well it turns out we can actually get along given the right circumstances. My shoulders still burn where Graham's hands ended up during his attempt at the Heimlich. "I don't like him getting in my space."

The words are barely out of my mouth when Graham joins us with the pasta. Of course he heard me and gives me a smirk that I'm sure Julia can see. I glare at him, only making the entire situation worse. It's like we're back in middle school with me wanting to keep my cool and Graham making it impossible. Adult Cassie has left the building.

"We have to clear the air here." Julia's all business, hands on her hips and mouth set in a serious line. "I don't have all the details, but Graham, you have to stop poking Cassie."

Now it's Graham's turn to choke. "What? I'm not... we haven't been..."

"Yes, you have. She's told me all about it so quit trying to act innocent."

Graham's mouth drops open as his blond head swivels to gape at me. "She's told you *everything*?" Horror slides across his face. We'd just sworn each other to secrecy a few hours ago and the betrayal clearly has him blindsided. Except, I haven't told Julia anything about what's happened and seeing Graham's face harden makes me vow to keep the secret if only to never have to see fury like that in those blue eyes ever again.

"I didn't... I haven't..." I look directly at Graham who clearly hates me more than ever right now.

"Don't let him weasel out of it, Cassie. She told me you keep calling her that stupid nickname. Knock it off."

Graham's shoulders visibly relax and his fingers release the death grip he has on the neck of his beer bottle. "That's what she's mad about?" he asks. "I call her that all the time."

"I know," Julia chastises. "And it has to stop. It isn't nice and you know it."

"What's not nice about it?" Graham seems genuinely perplexed. "There's nothing wrong with 'Mama.' Right, Cass?"

I keep my face neutral, putting the old mask I've always worn back on. I'm not about to give Graham permission to call me anything, not something that dredges up old memories. Especially now that he's seen me naked.

"God, Graham, do you even remember what it means? Why you and your friends started calling her that?"

Graham's face clouds. He doesn't remember. Of course he doesn't. Must be nice. For him it was some stupid thing he blurted out when he was thirteen years old, not the lasting mark of shame I carried around for years afterward. Thankfully Zach stays busy in the kitchen, keeping him from witnessing this new humiliation.

"Wasn't it like little mama? Because Cassie's so bossy? Because she acted like she was our mother?" Graham struggles for a good answer, flailing a bit. Julia keeps her angry face on, arms crossed over her chest, and lets him dig the hole deeper. "It was forever ago, I don't remember how it started," he finally confesses.

"Well, get ready to feel like an ass." I have to hand it to Julia, she's a master at handling Graham. He stands across the table from her, waiting for her to lower the boom. He doesn't even try to escape or look for a way to soften things. He just sort of opens his hands like he's waiting to catch whatever terrible thing she's getting ready to throw at him. "You and your dumb friends used to call Cassie Mama because of Mama Cass."

Graham blinks. He doesn't even seem to remember the reference.

"Is that not ringing any bells?" Julia plows on. "The fat girl in the Mamas and the Papas? The one who allegedly choked on her sandwich and died?"

My feet are rooted to the spot next to Julia. As much as I would love to flee to the kitchen, I can't seem to move. Can't take my eyes off Graham's stupid blinking face as he tries to process this information. He's still drawing a blank.

"They sang *California Dreaming*. You and your moronic friends found that record at Jamie Allen's house when we were there for her birthday party in seventh grade. You cannot expect me to believe you have zero memory of this." Julia's ripping him a new one. If only I was able to enjoy it.

"So, we called Cassie 'Mama' because..." Graham still can't connect the dots. My face starts to heat; I'm sure I'm starting to look like a giant red stop sign. But this conversation isn't going to end until Julia's gotten Graham to see just how terrible that name makes me feel.

"Because she was chubby, you idiot."

Graham's eyes widen and his mouth twists.

"It was my fat girl name until we graduated high school," I tell him, not caring that he can hear the hurt in my voice. I curse myself for not bringing my wine in here with me. Middle school Cassie could really use a drink.

Graham's still shaking his head. "We called you that because you were..." To his credit he can't seem to get that last word out.

"Fat." I finish for him. "You called me that because I was fat."

He looks like I've slapped him.

"I'm going back in the kitchen now to see if Zach's fallen in the sauce," Julia tells us. "And you," she points an accusing finger in Graham's direction, "are going to apologize and stop being such a dick. Then maybe Cassie can forgive you and we can all try to get through this evening in one piece." She leaves us alone, staring at each other over the dining room table.

"Cassie, I..."

I cut him off. "Don't."

"I didn't remember it that way. Obviously, I wouldn't have kept calling you that if I had." The fingers on his right hand flex and I'm thankful Graham's on the other side of the table. If he were to try to touch me now in some attempt to soothe me, I don't know what I'd do. As is I'm torn between pounding my fists on his chest and bursting into tears.

Neither of those reactions will make this dinner finish any faster.

"Just forget about it," I tell him, pretending I don't care. Trying to, at least until Zach rescues me with the delivery of my wine glass. Then I'm drowning my sorrows and helping Julia get us all settled for what promises to be the world's most awkward dinner party.

4

Graham

This evening will go down in history as the absolute worst dinner ever. The food's great because Julia doesn't do anything half ass when it comes to entertaining. She's got everything organized so we're like the cast from one of those cooking shows that gets to enjoy the meal the host has demonstrated. It should be easy for us all to talk, even if it means discussing Julia and Zach's wedding—a subject that still hurts a bit, if I'm being honest. But any of my feelings about Julia's new life have been pushed aside by the horrible feeling sitting in my gut now that I know how much of a jerk I've been to Cassie.

How could I have forgotten how horrible that nickname is? I've been calling her something for years that cut pretty deep. I'll cop to the fact that I used the name because it riled her up, but it never occurred to me that it drove her crazy because it was legitimately awful. I don't think of myself as the guy who goes for mean just for the hell of it but in Cassie's eyes—and maybe Julia's too—that's exactly who I am. My pasta's like sawdust in my mouth as I tell myself just to get through this dinner so I can figure out some way to make it up to Cassie. She's not looking at me, letting her green eyes slide right over me. We're seated next to each other so there's no real chance to force her to make eye contact. And what would be the point of that anyway? Short of making her cry I've done a great job of making her feel uncomfortable today. From the time we woke up until now this day has been one horrible revelation after another.

"And that's why we were thinking about Mexico." Julia finishes what was obviously a much longer thought. "What do you guys think?" She's holding Zach's hand under the table and has to let go of him to get more animated. "It could be really great, but we wanted to check with you guys first. Zach's sisters are all in, but if you two think it's a bad idea then we could reconsider."

"Mexico?" I ask like the dumb ass I am tonight. "What about Mexico?"

Julia's brow crinkles in irritation. "For the wedding. Like I just explained for ten minutes. Were you really not listening?"

I shrug. Might as well just confirm my status as the biggest jerk at this table.

"We'd go down for the week or a few days, whatever works best for everybody. And it would limit the numbers for the final headcount if we had a destination wedding. We've both been married here before so it wouldn't have any of the old mojo, you know? Fresh start and all of that. Plus, it could be a vacation, which could be fun." Julia seems to be trying to convince herself as much as she's trying to convince us. "You think it's stupid."

"No," I start, hoping Cassie will chime in. I'm sure she doesn't think the idea of vacationing in Mexico with me sounds anything like fun. "I just need to think about sched-uling. When are we talking about?"

"December, maybe? That gives us six months."

"Six months of prep?" Cassie blurts out. She's clearly not thrilled.

"No, that's the best part. If we find a place that does most of the wedding stuff as a package then there isn't much prep. They give us options and we choose. Easy peasy." I watch as Zach slides a hand onto Julia's thigh and gives it a squeeze. She beams at him and my heart constricts a little.

"So, no prep and some time on the beach when it's cold as balls here. Is that what you're telling us?" Cassie asks.

"My balls aren't cold." It's out of my mouth before I can stop it. The look on Cassie's face almost makes it worth it until I remember that I've been accidentally horrible to her since we were kids. Remembering that she's more than familiar with my balls makes her irritated eye roll even more regrettable.

Zach doesn't seem to appreciate my joke either, possibly because he knows that the temperature of my balls is some-thing his future wife is familiar with as well. I think about crawling under the table. Zach clears his throat and addresses Cassie, ignoring me and my inability to be a reasonable dinner guest. "Yep. Less prep and some beach time. Do you think you could make that work? We'd help pay for your plane ticket and hotel. We don't want it to be a burden for anyone."

"I would gladly pay for a Mexican vacation if it meant I had to spend less time with Graham for the next six months." Cassie gets right to the point.

Ouch.

"There is that advantage." Julia's not afraid to pile on either, I guess. I think about standing up for myself, but tonight's not the night for that. Julia's already rising from her chair and moving toward the kitchen, calling out over her shoulder, "Who's ready for dessert?"

"Hey, I'm sorry about tonight. I'll work on being less of an asshole from now on." My apology to Julia earns me an arm pat. It's a far cry from the kisses she used to give me, and I try to keep myself from leaning into her touch.

"I'm not really the one you should be apologizing to." She tilts her head in Cassie's direction. "You need to work things out with her or this wedding is going to be a nightmare."

This wedding is my nightmare even without this Cassie friction. But I can never tell Julia this. I'm sure Zach suspects I'm still carrying around feelings for his fiancée that I should have gotten over long ago, but if Julia agrees she's not saying anything. We had our chance and I blew it so now I have to live with the consequences. Which makes the Cassie thing so much more important to fix. I can't shake the feeling that while I've been thinking I'm basically a good guy, that's never been the general consensus.

"I'll fix it." I pull her in for a quick hug. She smells like I always remember, and I close my eyes for the briefest second before making myself let her go. "I need to see if I can get an Uber out here."

"I thought your car was at my parents' house. You'll never get an Uber in the suburbs on a Sunday."

"Your dad picked me up after his golf game. I can figure it out." I'm already swiping at my phone. "It won't be a problem."

"Why don't you just ride with Cassie?" Julia suggests like

it's the most innocent thing in the world. "She goes right past your place." She yells to Cassie in the kitchen, "Cass, Graham needs a ride home!"

When Cassie looks up from the sink, I see the animosity clearly on her face.

"You can drop him off, right?" Julia yells, not even giving Cassie the chance to protest. We're fighting, sure, but it doesn't make sense for Cassie to tell her no. Not that this will stop Cassie if she decides not to cooperate. Even worse, I have flashes of Cassie dumping me on the side of the interstate once we leave here. Or of her driving me down some secluded country road and leaving me there to teach me a well-deserved lesson about keeping my big mouth shut.

"I can figure it out. I don't need a ride."

"You do need a ride and I'm not going to let you sleep here. Just go with her and it will give you a chance to talk without an audience. She has to listen in the car." Julia seems to have forgotten who we're talking about. Cassie never has to listen, not if she doesn't want to hear what you're saying, and she's done listening to me today.

Cassie stares me down, the space from the kitchen to the living room crackling with anger. Her eyes locked with mine are all the warning I should need but when she gives in, I don't fight it. She shrugs. "Fine. Be ready to go in five." And she's back rinsing dishes and ignoring me.

When I finally slide into the passenger seat of Cassie's car, the last thing I want to do is beg for her forgiveness, so we sit in silence for the first ten minutes. She's waiting me out, not even trying to make small talk. I can hear her breathing over the hum of the engine as we play a game of chicken to see who'll blink first.

I lose, of course, because I'm the one who should be talking here. I clear my throat and examine Cassie's profile.

"I'm sorry," I start but then fizzle out. I know what I should be saying here, but there's only so many ways to say you're sorry and I've got plenty to apologize for tonight.

"It's fine," Cassie lies. "Can we please not talk?"

"You and I both know nothing is fine right now, Cassie."

Silence. Not even so much as a sideways glance. She keeps her eyes on the road and her hands on the wheel. There's no way I can talk to her like this, not when she's planning on ignoring me in the name of safe driving.

"I swear I didn't remember all that about the nickname. I would never have called you that if I had remembered how it started. I don't even remember you being that fat."

That does it. Cassie's head swivels, her lips already snarling. "You don't even remember me being *that fat*? That's supposed to make it better? Of course you don't remember. You don't remember what I looked like; you don't remember how I got that nickname. You don't remember because it wasn't a big deal to *you*, but it was a big deal to *me*. Just shut up, Graham. You can't make this better right now."

"Cassie, just..." I can't talk to her while she's driving, not if she's going to get upset. "Can you pull over? Just stop the car for a second, okay?"

I'm shocked when she eases the car over to the side of the road and puts it into park. She doesn't turn to face me, doesn't take her hands off the steering wheel, but she's listening. Unfortunately, I don't have anything worth saying.

"Can you look at me, please?" I know she doesn't want to, but she turns her stony face away from the windshield. "I would never have kept calling you that if I had any idea that it was hurting you. I'm not mean, Cassie. I like to rile you up, sure, but I'm not mean-spirited. You have to know that."

"How would I know that, Graham? From my perspective

you've always been like this. You've always called me a name I hated. You don't take no for an answer and I don't mean that as a compliment. You've always been that guy. You're great to Julia, but not to me. So, sure, I know you *can* be a good guy, but you do things that aren't always considerate. You're overbearing and controlling. Basically, you're a dick. That's what I know."

I stare at Cassie, unsure of what to say. "I'm not a bad guy, Cassie." I say it as much to myself as to her.

"Graham." She turns her body in her seat, twisting in the seatbelt. "Last night you fucked me and then this morning you called me my fat girl nickname. You saw me naked and right after you reminded me of all the stupid, hurtful things people ever said to me about my body. So, no, you don't get to defend yourself right now."

"But I didn't know what I was saying! Jesus, Cassie. Forget about the sex for two seconds—which was fan-fuck-ing-tastic, by the way, since I didn't get a chance to tell you before you ran out this morning." Cassie raises an eyebrow, clearly not impressed with my apology so far. "But you have to know that your body is amazing. Guys look at you all the time. Even today when I was waiting for you in the coffee shop dudes were checking you out on the street." Cassie's eyes narrow. Reminding her about this morning is not one of my smartest moves. "Look, this is coming out all wrong." I slam my head back into the headrest with a groan and squeeze my eyes shut. "I'm trying to say I'm sorry. I'm horri-fied at my own behavior right now. But for the record, I think you're gorgeous and I'll never call you that name again. Ever."

"Okay." Cassie lets the word linger between us. She's wary, waiting for me to say something to make her feel bad again because that's apparently what I do.

"Okay?" It comes out more hopeful than I'd anticipated. God, I sound like I've just asked her to the prom or something.

"You think I'm gorgeous?" Cassie says it like she doesn't believe it, eyes still narrowed.

"Yes. Damn, Cassie, like you've never looked in a mirror." I open my eyes and look into hers. "And, while I think we both regret last night, I don't regret seeing you naked. At all."

Her eyebrow shoots up again as she lets out a little puff of air. "You'll never call me 'Mama' again? You promise?"

"I promise."

"And we're still never telling anyone about last night, right?"

"Right."

"It's all in the vault."

"Yep. In the vault." I offer her my hand to shake on it and Cassie slides her palm against mine. I close my hand over hers but neither of us makes the move to shake and instead we end up awkwardly holding hands across the center console. Her hand is small and soft and I forget to let her go. We stay like that for longer than necessary before Cassie pulls her hand away, flexing her fingers and moving to put the car back in drive.

As she eases us back onto the road, I let myself exhale.

"Too bad you'll never get to see me naked again," Cassie tosses over her shoulder at me, her head turned to check for oncoming traffic.

I laugh. Flirty Cassie is back.

"I've got my memories." I tap the side of my head like an idiot. "It's all up here."

Cassie scoffs, but she's laughing too, turning the radio on. Maybe I've dodged a bullet here.

"And since we're apologizing, I should tell you I'm sorry

about getting so aggressive on the way home last night. That wasn't reasonable. I should never have grabbed you like that."

"Apology accepted. Obviously I didn't have much of an issue with it in the end." Images of Cassie climbing into my lap and sliding her hand over my stomach have me shifting in my seat.

"Well, that isn't my usual method of convincing someone to take me home. I promise I'll find another victim next time."

This should make me feel relieved. I should be laughing along with her, glad to have gotten this worked out. So why am I mentally flipping through every moment of last night like I'm watching old game tape? Why am I thinking about asking Cassie to pull over again so I can lean in and kiss her? Why does the thought of her with someone else suddenly make me want to put my fist through the window?

5

Cassie

The flowers are there at the nurses' station when I come in for my shift Monday night. A huge vase full of summertime—sunflowers, roses, lilies, and some kind of purple flower I can't identify. Someone must have really messed up to be sending these to the hospital.

"Who got flowers?" I ask as I breeze around the corner of the desk. I touch the edge of the vase longingly. I'm not a girly girl exactly, but even I appreciate flowers every now and then. Being a strictly no relationship girl means getting a bouquet hardly ever happens. And flowers at work? Never. My own occasional purchases of cellophane wrapped bunches from Whole Foods have to be enough. "Who's in the doghouse?"

"We were all about to ask you that same question." Delia swivels in her chair. "Getting something like that," she gestures to the floral explosion, "means you're on charts all night. We all agreed."

"What? Those can't be for me," I protest. "Who would send me flowers?"

"Maybe that guy from 328 last week," Stephanie suggests. "The one who kept asking you for sponge baths?"

I roll my eyes. Delia and Stephanie both giggle and high five. They've been waiting for a chance to remind me about that pervert.

"I don't think I was the only one he was trying to get to rub him with a sponge." I point a finger at Stephanie. She's barely out of nursing school and gets her fair share of inappropriate comments from unruly patients. You'd be surprised what people ask nurses to do when they're supposedly recovering from surgery.

"I think he had this hospital confused with that strip club down the street," Delia says, shaking her head. Her braids sway as she laughs. "He kept complaining that we weren't 'full service,' whatever that means. He'll probably ding us on our evaluation."

"What's he going to complain about?" I ask. "No one would get really, really close to my penis?"

Stephanie laughs. "He won't phrase it that way, I'm sure. He'll think of a better way to say, 'I really wanted a hand job and no one would give me one.'"

Delia pulls her bifocals from inside her scrubs where they hang on a long chain. I'm always teasing her about her glasses, but in the years we've worked together she's never lost them during a shift. She sees me eyeing the crazy chain around her neck and scowls at me, pulling the card from the plastic spear in the flower arrangement. "Are you Miss Cassidy Blake?"

I reach for the card but I'm not quick enough. Delia holds it just out of my reach, her glasses perched on the end of her nose. "Wait, wait. We need to know what happened this weekend that would convince someone to send you flowers. You were off Saturday and Sunday so we'll give you a minute to think through the possibilities."

"How should I know?" I ask. "Give me the card."

Delia hands it over, but gives me no privacy when I go to open it. I'm hoping it isn't from a patient. I'll never hear the end of it if it is. I pull the envelope open and slide out the tiny cardboard square inside. I'm confronted with a message in all block letters:

APOLOGY FLOWERS
— G

A ping from the call system diverts attention away from me for a second. "Which room is that?" Stephanie leans over to look at the computer screen. "I can take care of it." Her blonde ponytail swings behind her as she moves down the hall. "I expect to hear all about these mystery flowers when I get back!" she calls to me as I worry my bottom lip between my teeth.

"Why are you making that face?" Delia asks.

"What face?"

"The one you make when you smell something terrible. That guy from 328 didn't really send you flowers, did he?" Delia pulls the card from my fingers. Her brow knits as she reads what Graham has written. "What kind of a card is this? Doesn't he, and I assume it's a he, know that the card is supposed to have an actual apology written on it?" Delia shakes her head. "Who is this fool?"

"He's just a friend. He apologized in person. I don't know why he sent flowers."

"Oh, he's a *friend*, is he?" Delia asks. "Is he your usual kind of friend or is he a friend like from the normal definition?"

I purse my lips. A few days ago I would have hesitated to call Graham any kind of friend at all. Now I'm struggling for the right words to explain our relationship.

"I think that long pause is all the answer I need," Delia tells me. She's got that look on her face that lets me know I'm about to get a lecture. "Why can't you just find some nice boy to date? Why do you always have to choose these knuckleheads?"

"I didn't choose this knucklehead, exactly. He's always been around. And I don't date so I can avoid most of the knuckleheads, you know that."

Delia is unconvinced. "At least this one sent flowers even if he got it wrong. Do I even want to know what he did?"

"No, you don't." The story doesn't make either one of us look like anything less than crazy. And I've put all the real details in the vault anyway. I can't be telling it all over work. Eventually Delia would put two and two together and she'd be sure to have a problem with me sleeping with Graham. Even if it was just a one-time thing. Which it was, making these flowers even more confusing.

"So, what are you going to do now?" Delia's back to shuffling papers on the desk.

"Get the meds ready. Isn't it almost time for us to hand out some meds?" I shove the card in the pocket of my scrub pants.

"You know that's not what I'm talking about. Let me guess, you plan on ignoring him."

"You know me too well, D, too well." Because what's the other option here?

"You could text him to tell him you got the flowers," she

suggests. I'm pretty sure Delia's a mind reader. "That would be the polite thing to do." She pulls her glasses off her face and shoves them back down the front of her scrub top. "Not that you care about being polite."

"I'll think about it." I touch a soft petal on one of the roses closest to me.

"I'm just saying, he may be an idiot, but this is the first idiot to send you flowers. That should count for something."

"Maybe."

Or maybe that's just another reason to steer clear.

6

Graham

I wait all day to hear from Cassie. I'm supposed to be spending time thinking about my options, planning the next step of my life without football. I've got things in the works because I always knew football wasn't forever, but now that it's really over this part is less satisfying than I thought it would be. I remind myself I had a good run. I'm in my thirties for God's sake. Not many other guys can say they had that long of a career. But when I look across the surface of my desk, I can't find anything to get excited about. Other guys do car dealerships or restaurants but none of that's for me. I've done a good job of saving and investing, but I'm still going to need something to fill my time. Even if I had all the money in the world, sitting here looking out the window can only take up so much of my day. I had always envisioned myself at this stage with a wife and a family. A Super Bowl win. Instead I'm looking at a desk covered in papers that I have no interest in reading.

What I am interested in is Cassie. I know she got the flowers because I spent an hour this morning making sure the flower shop delivered them. I had wanted her to see them when she walked into work, before she started her shift. I imagined her face lighting up when she saw the flowers although it did cross my mind she would lose that smile once she opened the card. The card I obsessed over for way too long before writing down the stupidest thing that popped into my head. Apology flowers? So smooth. But I couldn't exactly say what I was feeling, could I?

Dear Cassie,

I'm glad we worked things out because I can't stop thinking about you naked.

— Graham

That would never fly. Maybe if the situation were different. I can see Cassie appreciating that sentiment from someone else. The key here being that person not be me— not a dick who called her a hurtful name for years, not the ex-boyfriend of her best friend, not the guy who's done just about everything wrong so far. Still, I sent the flowers because I wanted an excuse to talk to her. And then I waited.

I don't usually have to wait around, so when twenty-four hours pass without a peep from Cassie, I start to get a little annoyed. Sure we'd decided to keep the sex part a secret and we agreed it couldn't happen again but that doesn't mean we've gone radio silent, does it? I sent her flowers and in my experience, girls love flowers. In the past, flowers at work would get an excited phone call, at least a gushy text. In the past, flowers would have gotten me a blow job. But this is Cassie we're talking about so apparently flowers gets a person nothing.

I convince myself maybe Cassie doesn't have my number, but I know that's not true. And she could make up some excuse to get it from Julia if she wanted to get in touch with me. They'd probably have to talk about our ride home the other night though and Julia would get to hear all about what a dick I've been. But she's probably known for a while. It isn't a stretch to imagine Cassie telling her this, reminding her that I've always been a jerk.

I chase that depressing idea away by thinking about Cassie's tits. I remember the way they filled my hands and the breathy sounds she made when I had my mouth on them. It's a terrible but effective diversion as it not only gets me hard as a rock, but also reminds me that Saturday night was the first and last time I will see those particular breasts in person. So now not only is Cassie not calling, but I've got her on a pornographic loop running through my head. She's gone from being a blip on my radar to being the only thing I can think about.

Fuck it.

I reach for my phone and scroll through my contacts until I find Cassie's number. Like an ass I've put "Mama" in parentheses next to her name. I delete that like she's standing beside me. Can't have her seeing that. My index finger hovers over the screen before I let the part of me that should know better touch the green button. I put it on speaker and listen as it rings and rings. I hadn't planned on leaving a message and now my brain runs through possible options in order to sound less like I've been hanging around my house moping and more like I accidentally dialed her number. Which would fit well with her overall impression of me as a jerk and probably set me back to square one. Assuming I've even been making progress here. But we're supposed to be friends, right? And friends can call each other. Although, reminiscing about her boobs is probably not a friendly thing to do.

Mercifully Cassie answers on what feels like the millionth ring.

"Hello?" She sounds groggy, her voice rough and deep.

"Hey. It's me" And when she doesn't say anything I follow up with the equally interesting, "Um, Graham."

"I know who it is. You're programmed into my phone."

"With my name or as something else?"

"With your name. What else would I put you in as?"

I have plenty of suggestions, but I don't want to give Cassie any ideas. "I don't know. Never mind."

And then we sit there, both breathing into the phone. I can hear her moving around and something like sheets rustling. It's the middle of the day, but it sounds like she's in bed. I can almost picture it in my head even though I've never been inside Cassie's apartment. I imagine her auburn hair fanned out over a white pillowcase, the creamy skin on her neck exposed, the sheet covering her breasts.

"Graham?"

"Yeah."

"You called me."

"Oh, yeah. I wanted to see if you got something at work."

"You woke me up for that?" Cassie asks, irritated.

"Were you sleeping?"

"Yeah, I just worked a twelve-hour shift and I've got to be back at the hospital tonight." I hear her stretching, imagine the sheet falling lower. This is doing nothing to get rid of my earlier issue. If this is how worked up I am just using my imagination, I'm going to need to think of some good excuses not to see Cassie in person ever again.

"Are you in bed?" I ask because I'm a glutton for punishment.

"That's the best place to sleep." She says it like she's talking to a five-year-old.

"Are you wearing pajamas?" I cringe as soon as the question's out of my mouth. It isn't any of my business what she wears to sleep in. Recently repaired friendship line officially crossed.

"Seriously? Did you just ask what I'm wearing? Just because you sent me flowers doesn't mean I'm going to spend what should be my six hours of sleep having phone sex with you." She's laughing and I'm not sure if I should be offended or relieved. Cassie's not mad at the suggestion of phone sex but she's also not willing to participate. My dick twitches in my pants. *Sorry, buddy*.

"You did get the flowers then?"

"Yes, they're very pretty. Everyone at the nurses' station loved them." I don't care about the other nurses, but I keep my mouth shut. "But you didn't need to do that. We're good. No need to send me anything."

"I know. I just..." *Wanted to have an excuse to talk to you.* "Wanted to be sure you knew how sorry I was."

"You get friendship points for that, I guess."

"How many points? Is there a scale or something?"

"Is there a scale? Very cute. Sure. There's a scale but it's super top secret." I can hear the smile in her voice. "Food would have gotten you more points, probably, but the flowers were appreciated."

"So, next time I insult you over the course of several years I should send food." I'm smiling back. I'm on the phone with Cassie Blake and we're both smiling. Hell is definitely freezing over.

"Yes, preferably something chocolate. Now if you'll excuse me, I really need a few more hours of sleep so I don't accidentally kill someone."

"Too tired to tell me what you're wearing? We're done talking now?"

Again Cassie laughs. It's some sort of miracle. I keep expecting her to threaten me, waiting for her normal growl to put me back in my place. "Oh, we're done," she tells me. "It would take far more than flowers to get that information. Bye, Graham."

"Bye, Cassie."

I spend the next two hours scouring the Internet for every chocolate thing under the sun that can be delivered.

Cassie

I should never have been nice to him.

I should have known that being civil to Graham would end up backfiring, but he caught me off guard with the phone call. Waking me up to check on the flower delivery is the kind of thing that normally makes me furious. Especially when it just shows Graham to be the way he always has been—less concerned with other people than he is with himself. But instead of picking a fight I ended up flirting with him. That was a terrible idea and now I'm paying for it every time I come into work and there's another delivery there for me.

First it was cupcakes. Chocolate cupcakes with swirls of chocolate icing on top.

Next came the muffins, followed by a delivery of the biggest box of assorted chocolates I've ever seen.

Today there's one of those fresh fruit bouquets, the apple slices and strawberries winking from under chocolate coating.

The other nurses love this, of course, because it means

snacks for everyone in the break room. I hate it because it means more prying questions from my coworkers. Questions I have no intention of answering. Graham has to know he's riding the line here. He's choosing to send things to the hospital instead of to my house. Which means this apology thing is going on in public. So much for putting things in the vault.

And I'm sure he wants me to call to tell him how great all of his gifts are. At least that's what Delia keeps telling me. But I keep ignoring her helpful suggestions, letting her think I'm just being a bitch when in fact I'm protecting myself. No more slightly sexy phone conversations. No more flirting. No more accidents.

I need to get Graham out of my system and the best way to do that is to replace all these naked images of him with naked images of some other guy. Interchangeable men. Just the way I've always done it. No muss, no fuss. Of course I've got Graham on the brain—I haven't been out since we hooked up. Which is why when Stephanie mentions that she and some of her girlfriends are going out dancing I jump at the chance to tag along. Being out with Steph and her cute twenty-something friends is a guaranteed way to attract some male attention. Attention that I desperately need to get back on track. I've spent years not giving Graham a second thought. It shouldn't be hard to get him out of my head.

The club's packed by the time we get there. Stephanie's friends are all outfitted in an array of tight-fitting dresses and short skirts. I feel practically provincial in the outfit I've put together. But my low-cut V-neck top and leather pants are usually enough to do the trick. I'm in all black. Who needs more color when you're working red hair and lips? No need for overkill. Something I should explain to Stephanie's friends. More than one of them looks like they've forgotten to wear pants. Desperate, but effective if the stares we're getting from the packs of men we pass on our way in is any indication.

"Drinks?" I yell toward Stephanie, but there's no way she can hear me over the pounding bass in here. When she mouths what I assume is "What?" back at me, I herd her and her friends toward the bar. You'd be surprised how quickly a space opens up at a crowded bar for a group of half-naked women, especially attractive ones. And you'd be surprised how quickly someone offers to pay for our first round of drinks. Or maybe you wouldn't. Either way I end up leaning against the cool metal of the bar top with a vodka tonic in my hand in record time.

I know not everyone thinks picking up a man at a bar is a great idea, but I'm not most people. You can't get no strings attached by sleeping with the guys on your company's adult kickball team. Not that I'd ever be on an adult kickball team, but you get the picture. I don't want commitment—I barely want conversation—so a place like this is perfect. I survey the crowd under the pulsing lights. There are a few guys who look promising. One candidate makes eye contact from across the room, but I don't let my eyes linger; I never go with the first interested man I see. I keep scanning, shamelessly raking my gaze over bodies like I'm shopping for a car. Which one of these boys would I like to take for a test drive? Hmmm, so many choices.

Stephanie and her friends have moved to the dance floor where they're busy making themselves look even more like porn stars. I think about joining them, but I'm thoroughly enjoying myself and all these sexual possibilities. I down the rest of my drink and turn to order another when the bartender slides a fresh one in front of me.

"Here you go. From that guy down there at the end of the bar." He angles his head toward the left with a jerk.

Another win for me. At this rate I won't have to pay for a drink all night. I turn to see who this mystery benefactor might be, hoping for drop dead gorgeous and built like a tank, but keeping my expectations low. There's a group of gigantic guys at the end of the bar. All thick shoulders and broad chests, big hands wrapped around their pint glasses. Any of those boys would be worth considering, but none of them seem to be looking my way. If one of them bought me this drink then he's being awfully sneaky about it. No eye contact from the first one, a dark-haired behemoth who keeps shooting glances at the dance floor. Nothing from contestant number two either, another bruiser with short dreadlocks who's doubled over laughing at whatever the third dude is telling him. Number three has his back to me, the muscles in his shoulders pulling the fabric of his shirt tight. He runs his hand through his blond hair and gives the back of his neck a squeeze, his bicep flexing with the movement. Number three looks like he has potential.

But number three also starts to look more than a little familiar.

When he finally turns toward me, lifting one eyebrow as he zeroes in on my face, I have to stifle an exasperated groan and try not to roll my eyes. Because, of course, it's Graham's annoying but undeniably handsome face staring back at me.

Thanks, Universe.

He motions for me to come and join him but I'll be damned if I'm coming when he calls me. Or coming for him ever again. I keep this in mind as he makes an exaggerated pout from his side of the bar. Then he's elbowing his buddies and gesturing toward me, making heads swivel and giant legs move until they're all standing in front of me. The crowd parts so there's no jostling, just the smooth arrival of their butts into three suddenly vacant seats next to me. I am cursed. Suddenly this drink doesn't feel so free anymore.

Graham leans in and brushes a kiss on my cheek, breathing a *hi* into the shell of my ear. I shiver. He pulls back but keeps one hand on the small of my back. He's too close but there's no real way to get free of him smashed against the bar, surrounded by his burly friends.

"Cassie, this is Andre and this is Calvin. Guys, this is Cassie." They both extend huge hands which I shake reflexively. We're murmuring our hellos when a fourth, much smaller man joins us.

"Dude." He gives Graham a shove right in the chest. "You all moved without telling me where you were going. I came back from the bathroom and nobody's there. Plenty of hot ladies on the way there and back, by the way." He doesn't seem to notice me and Graham doesn't move to shove him back so I relax.

"We moved to talk to Cassie," Graham explains and new guy turns to look at me. He's not unattractive, but the way he slides his eyes over me and leaves them resting on my chest has me crossing my arms in front of me.

"Oh, helloooo," new guy croons, getting entirely too close for a handshake. Graham stiffens and his friends both grimace. "I'm Dave Preston. I manage these guys." He aims a thumb at Graham and his group. "What was your name again, baby, Callie?"

"Cassie," Graham corrects. "And stop. Just no."

"No?" Dave asks, confused.

"Cassie's off limits. She's my..." He drags out the word for so long I think he's about to say "mine" and for some reason my stomach does a happy little flip flop. *What the hell, Cassie?* "She's my friend," he clarifies. "We go way back."

"Okay," Dave says, still holding my hand. "So?"

"So stop touching her. She's not for you." Which, by omission, sounds like I'm for Graham. Like he's going all caveman and about to pummel this idiot who thought he could drag me to *his* cave instead. Eyebrows shoot up all around.

"Okay, okay, fine." Dave releases me. "You've already peed on her. I get it."

I gag and roll my eyes. Of course this jackass is friends with Graham. I pull my hand away from his and get ready to rip into him. Only Graham beats me to it, putting me behind him and leaning forward in a way that keeps me from doing my worst but doesn't seem to ensure Dave's safety. Angry Graham is not someone you'd like to meet on a regular basis and Dave seems to know this.

The set of Graham's shoulders makes Dave shrink back and I use this moment to escape. "I'm going to dance! Nice to meet you!" I yell over my shoulder as I sprint to where Stephanie and her friends are grinding up against a group of guys who don't look old enough to have gotten into this bar. I avoid the potential jailbait and dance by myself. There are plenty of guys more than willing to bop along with me and I dance with a few of them. But I never stay with one for very long; I twirl away. If Graham wasn't here watching from the bar, I'd be more aggressive. I did come here looking for a hook up. But I can feel him staring at me and every time I look his way he's looking right back.

Until he's gone.

I notice immediately and the frantic feeling that overcomes me catches me by surprise. Would he just leave? Without telling me? Without saying anything at all?

Someone bumps into me from behind as I swivel around looking for Graham. I turn to apologize and end up with my face pressed tight against a rock-hard chest. I tilt my head up and find myself looking directly into Graham's blue eyes. He smirks.

"I thought you'd left," I tell him, my voice giving away too much of the panic I was feeling earlier.

"I'm not leaving you here," he yells over the music. "This place is a meat market. What're you doing here anyway?"

I manage a shrug and a guilty look that has Graham scowling.

"Aw, Cassie. Seriously?" He takes one look at the other guys on the dance floor and shakes his head. "That's it. We're leaving."

"I'm not leaving," I protest. "I'm having a good time. I want to dance."

Graham shakes his head again. "You're done dancing with the douchebags in here." He surveys the crowd again. "No more dancing for you."

"Please?" Why am I begging Graham to let me stay? I'm a grown woman and he's not the boss of me. Although from the way everyone else on the dance floor is giving us a wide berth he must look like he is.

"Nope."

"Okay, I won't dance with any more of these 'douchebags.'" I make liberal use of the finger quotes. "But then *you* have to dance with me." I don't know why I suggest this but by the time my brain catches up with my mouth it's too late. Graham stands in front of me and for the first time tonight he looks unsure. I give him a hard poke in between his pectoral muscles, resisting the urge to flatten my palm out and rub it over him.

"I don't know about that," he stalls. "I'm not a great

dancer." This might be the truth but we both know his reluctance isn't entirely about his two left feet.

"I'm sure you're fine. Don't you guys do victory dances on the field and stuff?" It's meant as a dig, but Graham can't hear me. The music's getting louder and I have to put my mouth against his ear to be heard.

"What?" he yells and I know there's only one way to keep him from hauling me over his shoulder and ending my evening.

I just go back to dancing. Graham stands there, seemingly unable to figure out what to do next. I dance around him, taunting, hoping he'll give in and start to move. His friends are doubled over at the bar watching us and when he sees them whipping out their phones and starting to record his humiliation, I get ready for him to stomp off. But he doesn't. Instead he goes for it and I'm tipping my head back and laughing at the way he flails himself around.

He's right; he isn't a great dancer. But what he lacks in talent he makes up for in effort. And I'm used to making up for less than talented partners so he ends up looking fine. I'm the one really doing all the work, which would be a great sexual joke except I'm refusing to think about Graham and sex. And I already know that he's much better at fucking than dancing. Which I try to put out of my head.

Unfortunately, Graham is exceptionally good at doing one thing: grinding. Which is making it harder and harder to keep from thinking about him naked. Because once we end up rubbing all over each other my brain takes a vacation from pretty much anything but the feeling of his body up against mine.

Under the pulsing lights I start to forget about all the reasons fooling around with Graham is a bad idea. His hands feel like they belong on my hips, my arms seem to have found a home wrapped around his neck, and when he leans his face in close to mine I instinctively tilt my chin up and part my lips as if kissing him is the most normal thing in the world. But the second our lips touch I come back to reality. Graham isn't for me. He can't be and so I pull back. He furrows his brow, and he looks like a confused toddler as I shake my head and work my way out of his embrace.

"Bathroom," I manage to get out before I turn and run in what I'm hoping is the direction of the ladies' room. I have to get away from Graham before I make another decision I'll regret in the morning. I round the corner and move down the hall. A hand grabs my elbow. I turn to find myself staring up at a heavily breathing Graham under the harsh florescent lights.

"What the hell was that?" he asks, face angrier than I'd like.

"You kissed me!" I'm accusing him, hoping he'll see the issue here and back down.

Instead his nostrils flare and he moves in closer. "You kissed me back." His hand comes to rest on the exposed skin of my upper arm. "Don't pretend you didn't." He leans in, letting his lips graze my ear. "And you liked it."

I did like it.

"We said it was a one-time thing. We decided. Which means no kissing, obviously." I move to put some space between us but Graham's having none of it. He keeps moving forward until I'm pressed against the wall. I can feel him breathing as he brackets my body with his arms, pinning me in.

"I know what we said," he tells me. "But that doesn't change how you make me feel."

"How I make you feel?" I whisper, knowing I'm playing with fire. "How do I make you feel?"

Graham doesn't answer, he merely pushes closer to me and grinds his hips against mine. I can feel his erection between us, his breath against my neck. I put my hand on his chest, planning to push him off me, but when I feel the way his heart is beating against my palm I end up leaving my hand there, letting the warmth of his chest and the thumping of his heart hypnotize me. He drags his nose along my neck, nipping the edge of my jaw as he goes. By the time his mouth makes it to mine any resolve I might have had is gone.

I lean into Graham's kiss, letting him explore my mouth. He's gentle and unhurried like we have all the time in the world. Like we aren't in some sketchy hallway in the depths of this bar. Like we can be together without any consequences. He nips at my bottom lip and wraps his arms around me, pulling me toward him. When I slide my hand from his chest to the back of his neck, he responds with a growl, deepening the kiss and pulling me in even tighter. Heat licks through my body, every nerve humming.

The sound of a door unlocking and swinging open has us breaking apart like two teenagers caught by the porch light. The poor woman lets out a surprised yelp followed by mumbled apologies as she scurries away. Graham moves to go right back to making out, apparently not giving a shit about the drawbacks of this location.

"No, wait." This time I refuse to let him distract me. "We can't do this."

Graham lets out a groan of frustration, pulling his hands through his hair. "I know," he says but doesn't sound convinced. He looks at me and groans again. "The thing is, Cassie," he starts, obviously conflicted. "The thing is, I know we shouldn't, but I can't stop thinking about you. About last time." He seems almost embarrassed about it like he's confessing something dark and terrible.

"Me, neither," I whisper, knowing this is the wrong answer here. I should tell him I'm not feeling anything, let him think it's all one-sided. Then he'll leave me alone and we can go back to being sworn enemies like we agreed. But he's standing here looking like he could eat me up and instead of running away from the big bad wolf I find myself edging in closer. "One more time won't hurt, will it?"

8

Graham

It takes me two seconds to realize I've been given the green light. Cassie's standing there licking her lips and waiting on me to make a move and I'm still dumbfounded that she might be okay with this. "What did you say?" I lower my lips dangerously close to her ear.

Cassie doesn't pull away, if anything she gets impossibly closer. "You heard me." She runs one hand over my stomach down to the waistband of my pants. She leaves it there, tracing her fingers along the edge of my belt.

"You're on board for this?" I drag my mouth along the column of her neck, desperate to get my hands on more of her. If she says no, if she changes her mind, I'll back off even if every cell in my body is telling me to do the opposite. I know what we've already decided and I can't have the ambiguity from last time.

"For sex?" Cassie asks, still sliding her hands around in the red zone. "Yes."

I don't hesitate. I press her back to the wall and crush my lips to hers. I find the edge of her shirt and propel my hand over the expanse of smooth skin underneath. I palm her breast, my thumb zoning in on her nipple. Cassie groans into my mouth and one long leg wraps itself around my waist. I haul her against me, enjoying the friction against my cock but I know if I don't get her out of this hallway and back to my bedroom I'm likely to come in my pants. I release her breast and Cassie protests, whining. Repositioning my hand over her ass I contemplate carrying her out of the bar. Even though I know that'll be entirely too much of a scene I can't think of any faster way to get her to the car.

"Let's go," I mumble, my face still pressed tight against Cassie's.

"Go?" she asks, the confusion almost covering up the lust in her eyes.

"Unless you want me to fuck you here." I'm joking, but Cassie doesn't blink. I pull my head back and watch as she scans the weird little hallway.

"Well, not *here*," she clarifies before sliding down my body like a firehouse pole. "But maybe in there." She takes my hand and yanks me toward the unoccupied bathroom door.

"In the bathroom?" She can't be serious. She'd rather have sex in the bathroom of a bar than let me take her back to my place again. I shake my head. "No way. This is too public, Cassie."

"We've been in this hallway forever and no one else has come down here." She's right about that, but still, when she'd said yes I'd been picturing her spread out across my bed. I'd been imagining plenty of time to do the things I wanted to her.

"We can't go back to your house or to mine. That'd be too..." Cassie leaves me to fill in the blanks. Too planned. Too private. Too personal. As much as my dick is begging me to take her up on her offer, my brain can't seem to accept it. Just sex? I'm pretty sure I can handle that even if it means ignoring all the reasons I should be keeping my hands to myself. We've already slept together and I can't seem to shake the need to do it again. But here? Like this? Maybe not.

Cassie senses my hesitation and slides back up against me, her hand palming me through the fabric of my pants. I congratulate myself on the decision not to wear jeans tonight. I can feel the warmth of Cassie's hand as she gives me a squeeze and all the blood rushes from my brain. "You're so hard," she whispers and I somehow become impossibly harder, my cock threatening to punch through my zipper. "I don't want to wait. I need you inside me now. Please?" I know I'm being played here. I know that Cassie's relying on the fact that I'm so worked up I won't be able to come up with a better plan, that I'll give in and do what she wants. So it's no surprise when my brain officially surrenders, letting Cassie lead me down the hall and into the bathroom where she locks the door behind us with a click.

It's a single stall—toilet and sink—and surprisingly clean. Why it's tucked away like this I have no idea, but I'm hopeful that means no one is going to come knocking on the door. Once we're inside Cassie's all business, back to wrapping her arms around my neck and rubbing against me.

"I wish I'd worn a skirt. That'd make this so much easier," she tells me which lets me know this isn't the first time Cassie's done this. I wince at the thought of some other guy pounding her up against some other bathroom wall.

But if she'd worn a skirt I'd probably already be inside her. At least this way I get to spend a few minutes peeling her out of some of her clothes. Because there's the drawback I've just realized about this bathroom idea: I can't really get

Cassie naked. Which is maybe why she suggested it. A quickie in the bathroom scratches the itch, but means no breakfast, no sleepover, no second helpings. It means no strings and I've already agreed to it.

Cassie's working on the buckle of my belt when I cover her hand with mine. She's used to being the alpha and it shows. But even if I've agreed to this location that doesn't mean she's running the show. Not by a long shot.

I walk her back until her thighs hit the sink. She lets me lead her, running her hands to the back of my neck. Cassie's not short, but I still have to lean over to find her mouth even in the heels she's wearing. She goes for my belt again and I move just out of her reach. The noise she makes is one of disappointment and I have to give her a scolding *tsk tsk*. I know she's thinking this should be fast, but even if I'm restricted to this spot, I'm not about to waste what could be my last time with Cassie on a wham, bam, thank you ma'am.

"So impatient," I chide as I kiss my way down the front of her. I slide my hands back under her shirt and give her tits the attention they deserve. At least I give them the attention I can give them here with Cassie still completely covered up. Her nipples strain through the fabric of her bra, the material so sheer that I can feel every inch of her through the lace. It kills me not to be able to yank her black top over her head, ditch the bra, and pull one of those hard little nubs into my mouth. She's groaning as I run my hands over her, but this is nothing compared with what I'd do if we were somewhere more private.

But I can improvise.

I run my hands along the edges of her leather-clad hips. I am enjoying these pants but I'll enjoy taking them off of her even more. I pepper kisses all along Cassie's chest and stomach until I'm almost kneeling in front of her. She looks down at me and our eyes lock. I wait two breaths before I make a move to reach for the button and pop it open. She's panting as I ease the zipper down and hook my thumbs in the waistband. I'm torturing us both, but I make myself take my time revealing Cassie's creamy thighs inch by delicious inch.

I take a second to appreciate the lacy black thong. It's the only thing separating me from my final destination. I lean in close and feel Cassie shudder when I exhale. She does it again when I press closer and take the edge of her panties in my teeth. I pull, letting my nose trail along her slit. I finish the job with my hands and run my palms back up the front of her thighs to spread her wide. I can still hear the music from the club thumping through the walls, but that does nothing to muffle Cassie's moan when I slide my tongue along her opening. Her knees buckle a bit before she steadies herself against the sink, throwing her head back as I devour her.

Cassie writhes against my face, making these little whimpering noises that have my whole body going tight. I work her with my tongue, holding her still with my fingers splayed across her thighs. Not that she has anywhere to go with her ass firmly against the sink. I smile against her and ease first one finger in and then two, curling them just enough to hit a spot that makes her shudder. "Come on, Cassie," I urge her as I continue my assault. She answers me with the sexiest little gasp right before I feel the muscles of her pussy start to clamp down on my fingers. She pulls at the short hair on the back of my neck as she rides out her orgasm.

But I'm nowhere near done with her.

I pull my mouth away. Her cry of disappointment is replaced with a grunt of understanding as I spin her around to face the mirror. I fumble with my belt buckle one handed, but manage to get myself organized without breaking contact. I run my hand down her back to her hip, wishing we were skin to skin. The cold rush of air when I pull my other hand back to slap on a condom has me working hard to get back to Cassie and give myself some relief. I lean over her, my chest flat against her back, and position myself at her opening. "Hold on," I warn her before I thrust forward.

Once I'm inside her, it takes everything I've got not to just start hammering like crazy. I take a few deep breaths, inhaling the scent of Cassie's hair and giving her time to adjust. She grinds against me and my eyes nearly roll back in my head she feels so good. "God, Cassie," I groan into her ear. "I love fucking you."

Cassie turns her head and captures my mouth with hers. "Then fuck me."

"Yes, ma'am." I start moving. I pump in and out, Cassie meeting me thrust for thrust. She grips the edge of the sink with white knuckles as I slam into her, groaning louder than I intend to but unable to make myself stop. The sound of our bodies slapping together echoes off the white walls. Anyone who comes even close to this bathroom is going to know exactly what we're doing and neither of us seems to care. I move to cup Cassie's breasts again and she arches into me, giving me better access. Cursing the layers still between us, I pull the cups of her lacy bra down so I can run my callused fingers over her. Cassie gives me an appreciative *hmmm* and squeezes her eyes shut. I look over her shoulder and watch myself fuck her, enjoying the way her mouth falls open and her head lolls to the side. Reaching forward to find her clit, I rub in circles as I slide in and out of her and watch as her face scrunches up. I can feel how close she is, making it harder and harder for me to keep myself from coming.

"Open your eyes," I tell her, my voice surprisingly gruff. Her eyes snap open and meet mine in the mirror. "I want you looking at me when you come." She holds my gaze, her breathing shallow and uneven, and I watch her features change as I feel her body give in to mine. She slams back against me and lets out a groan that I accidentally answer with my own. And then we're both coming, eyes locked together, bodies humming. "Like a fucking firecracker," I mumble into her hair as I try to keep her close to me for a few seconds longer. Because Cassie is like a firecracker: beautiful and unexpected but sure to burn my hands if I hold her too long.

9

Graham

"Thanks for cockblocking me the other night."

I snap back from my daydream and try to focus. "What? When did I cock block you?"

"At the bar. Don't act like you don't remember. Even Calvin and Andre thought I had a shot with that redhead. What's her name again? Karen or something? Your friend." The way Dave emphasizes friend makes the hair on the back of my neck stand up. I know none of the guys saw anything that would make them think Cassie and I are anything more than friends. If you don't count our pornographic dancing, that is. Or the kiss I gave her on the very public dance floor. It doesn't help that instead of listening to what Dave was saying I was actually running through all the sordid details from my trip to the ladies' room with Cassie. I'm lucky the stack of papers Dave's given me is covering my crotch.

"She's out of your league, bro," I tell him, trying to act like it doesn't bother me to talk about Cassie with some other guy, especially a jerk like my agent. Dave Preston may be good at what he does, but he's not anyone I want near Cassie in any capacity. "Calvin and Andre were blowing smoke up your ass." Those guys will say anything to try to get Dave to try his luck at picking someone up. Plenty of times his big shot bullshit works on women, but when it doesn't, he can really go down in flames. It's become one of our favorite things to do when we all go out. But having to watch him try that routine out on Cassie? I can't even bring myself to think about it.

"Well, she didn't seem too happy about you groping her either, so I guess she's even out of your league, *bro*. I was almost hoping to see a photo of you getting rejected on social media. Guess no one had their phones out, lucky for you." I let that slide with a shrug. No use giving Dave any ideas about what may or may not have happened after that. Once we put ourselves back together and agreed to put yet another "mistake" in the vault, I had come back into the bar like nothing had happened. I watched Cassie like a hawk, of course, giving my meanest stare to any guy who came near her. Either it was effective or Cassie had already gotten what she came for because she went home solo. And I know this because even though Cassie'd kill me if she found out, I followed her home. I told myself I'd done it because I was worried about her safety. It had nothing to do with the weird feeling developing in my chest, the same feeling that's coming back again as Dave waxes poetic about Cassie's ass.

"Can we get back to business?" I ask, desperate to steer this meeting back on track. I'm here to talk about my options, not punch my agent in the mouth because he can't stop talking about the girl I can't stop thinking about. "Have you got something for me or not?" I shouldn't snap at Dave, he's just the messenger. It isn't his fault that since my football career is effectively over there aren't a ton of offers rolling in. It's time for my second act and I need Dave to help me figure out what that might be. Biting his head off is counterproductive.

I stare at the life-sized photo of me that hangs behind Dave's desk. It's me in beast mode, arms spread wide after a tackle, head thrown back. Even though my helmet's on, the number on the jersey is clearly mine—until they eventually give that number to some new guy. The rest of the office is covered in framed magazine covers and ad copy. It's the only thing to look at against the stark white walls and black furniture. Dave thinks this minimalistic vibe forces everyone to see the fruits of his labor. He's probably right, but now all it's doing is making me wonder how long I have before my photo moves from the prime position. How long before someone else becomes his star client and takes my place over the desk?

"Did you see that *Bleacher Report* article on Jacobs?" Dave asks, technically moving back to business but not giving me the information I came here for. "He's looking good. An up-and-comer. Not as photogenic as you, maybe, but the pictures still looked good."

"Yeah, I saw it. He looked good." I shift in my seat, making the leather of the couch creak under me. "If he can keep working like he has been he should have a break out season." I don't tell Dave that when I saw the article it took everything in me not to throw my laptop through the window. Not that I begrudge a new guy getting the chance to make his way in the league. That's not it at all. When I saw the article I wasn't seeing anything about football. With its glowing description of Jacobs' life, all I could see was the part about his family. His college sweetheart wife and their infant son mocked me in vibrant color. The fact that after football for him there'll be family only reinforced the fact that for me now there's nothing.

"Let's hope so." Dave sits back down at the chair behind his desk. "It'd be nice to have another Graham Stevens around here."

I try to smile at what I think was intended as a compliment but my face refuses to cooperate. Dave clears his throat and barrels on. "Since we're sure now that you won't be back on the field as a player, we need to map out a strategy here." I nod and wait to hear Dave's plan, hopeful he's got a good one. "There's probably going to be a phasing out of some of the apparel endorsements we've got going right now. If you aren't on the field those companies are going to start to get less interested. You could go to lesser known products, pull a Brett Favre with the toothpaste and stuff."

I know this already but still hate to be reminded of it. "Okay, so fewer endorsements. Got it. What's next, then?"

"Well, there's some interest in seeing what you can do as an announcer. You have the right look for it and when you open your mouth you don't sound like an idiot." Dave smirks. "Most of the time at least. I've got you a screen test that could line you up for a slot for one of the games over Thanksgiving. We won't know until closer to the time which one the network wants you for. Or we could try to get you settled on a college game. Either one would be a good start to see how you feel about it. If the network likes what they see there'd be a good possibility of more."

"So, it'd be like an audition?"

"Of sorts, I guess. Something that you and the network would be trying out. They love your face already and so do the fans, obviously. That's why the team's been keeping you on the sidelines this season instead of putting you out to pasture right away. They've been hinting that there might be something in the front office, if you're interested."

I frown. I've hated being in limbo with the team for the past year. They've had me working with the defense, coaching my teammates in a capacity I'd never felt comfortable with. But there hasn't been much else to focus on if I wasn't able to play. And to hear Dave tell it, they've kept me visible not because they thought I'd ever come back, but because fans like seeing my face. I try to shake it off and move forward, but I never imagined myself wearing a suit and talking about football. I've only ever thought about being on the field. I make the plays; I don't comment on them.

"Think of it like a long interview after the game. You like doing those, right?"

"I don't know if 'like' is the right word for that."

"But you don't hate it. And you're good at it. Reporters have always eaten you up. Try to think of this as an opportunity. If you hate it then we try something else. There are still companies wanting to use you for all sorts of ads and promotions and we need to get those organized soon. You need to be thinking long term here, Graham. The announcer gig would be a step toward that. Plenty of other guys would jump at this."

I give in. "I'll try it. Send me the details for the other things and I'll see what I can stomach."

"I know it isn't what we'd planned, G, but we can make things work. You've got a career; it just has to be different now. You can still be in football if that's what you want." Dave gives me his best pitying look. "On the up side, you've gotten out before too much of your brain got scrambled, hopefully. And you're still knee deep in pussy so there's that." So much for the pep talk.

"And on that note, I'm out of here." I rise from the sofa and let Dave come over to walk me out. He claps me on the back but has trouble reaching higher than my shoulder blades.

"I'm on it, G. No worries."

But I'm not convinced. The anxiety I'd been feeling coming into this meeting is still churning in my belly, threatening to make my breakfast a repeat visitor. I need a good workout to get rid of some of this negative energy but heading to the weight room with the team isn't a possibility, at least not one that will do anything to relieve this stress. So I do the one thing guaranteed to fix my problem in the short term—I text Cassie.

Me: U home or at work?

C: Home. Why?

Me: Want to go lift?

C: Weights?

Me: You lifting anything else?

C: 8 oz curls?

Me: I need a motivating workout partner. Meet me at the gym?

C: To work out? Together? I feel like that's a bad idea.

She's right. It is a terrible idea, but it's the only thing I can think of that will make me feel even marginally better. Instead of continuing our text battle I go for the big guns. Cassie answers on the second ring.

"Hello?" she asks, pretending she doesn't know it's me. "No matter what you're selling, I'm not buying."

"Not even the chance to spend an hour with me? You're totally interested in buying that." I hope that's clever enough to keep her on the line until I can charm her into meeting me.

"I've been getting that for free. Why would I start paying?" Cassie isn't hanging up.

"Hmmm. Good point. I guess I could give you another free sample before I start charging." I immediately cringe. Too flirty. Especially if I'm not trying to get in her pants again. Which I'm totally not trying to do. Though, I admit if Cassie was offering, I'd have a hard time saying no.

"As tempting as that sounds, you and I both know there's no way I'm meeting you at the gym. And there's no way I'd ever pay you." Cassie pauses a little too long. "To hang out. I'd never pay you to hang out." She's flustered. I can almost hear the blush through the static of our connection.

"I'm not kidding about working out. I really need to sweat out some of the bullshit from the meeting I just had."

"You had a bad meeting? About what?" Cassie's voice actually softens a little. I take advantage of her momentary weakness to beg a little.

"A terrible meeting," I confess knowing full well I'll never tell her what it was about. "With my douchey agent. Do you feel sorry enough for me now to meet up? No shenanigans. I promise. Nothing vault worthy."

"I don't know..." Cassie hesitates.

"Have you lifted today?" I ask because this call is all about exercise. It isn't in any way about needing Cassie to soothe my irritated nerves with her pretty face and her sassy mouth. That's what I'm telling myself, anyway.

"No."

"Great. I'll meet you at your gym in ten minutes."

"Wait, hold up. Don't you have teammates to work out with?" Cassie asks and I can almost hear her slap her forehead. Of course I don't have teammates. Not anymore. "Sorry."

"No worries." I swallow the lump of regret that's threatening to form in my throat. "Ten minutes?"

"Fine," Cassie sighs into the phone. "But we're working out. Nothing extracurricular. I'm serious."

"I can keep my hands to myself if you can," I tell her, sliding behind the wheel of my car and putting the key in the ignition. "I know it'll be difficult for you..."

"I'll be difficult for *me*?" Cassie sputters. "You're such an ass."

"What was that about my ass? That's the kind of thing I'm talking about. Off limits, Cass. Off limits."

She nearly growls into the phone. "I'll see you in ten minutes, dickhead." And then hangs up on me.

Immediately my shoulders loosen up. I know seeing Cassie isn't a long-term fix, but even just the twinge of excitement I'm feeling is worth the risk. With nothing else to look forward to, the promise of Cassie in her workout tights gives me a glimmer of something positive in an otherwise shitty day. I ease my car into traffic, humming to myself in a way that should have me questioning just what I'm expecting from Cassie today. I can keep my hands to myself. Probably.

10

Cassie

"Do you like Chinese food?"

"Do I like Chinese food? Why do I get the feeling this is about to turn into some offensive joke or something?" I work to pull the corner of the fitted sheet tight on the edge of the bed. "Don't you ever just say 'hello'?" I never should have answered the phone, but that little tingle that keeps reappearing when I see Graham's name flicker on the screen convinced me not to let it go to voicemail. I've been chalking it up to animosity, ignoring any other pesky feelings that might creep in.

"I wouldn't tell an offensive joke, Firecracker. I'm upset you'd even think that." Graham's mock indignation does nothing to convince me that this call is anything but trouble.

"You can't keep calling me Firecracker." I'm already blushing.

"No? I need a new nickname for you since the old one is out. No one has to know where it came from."

"It's a sex nickname. You can't call me that in front of

other people." I sigh and position the flat sheet, tucking the corners.

"People will think it's because of the red hair, Cassie. It's not like I'm going to tell anyone it's because you explode like a firecracker whenever I put my dick in you."

"God, Graham!" The heat moves higher on my cheekbones. I'm lucky no one else is here to see me turn into a flaming hot tomato.

"Okay, it happens when I use my mouth, too. And my hands. Maybe just when I look at you." He's teasing, but other parts of my body start to feel uncomfortably warm. "You can give me a sex nickname. To make it even."

"I'm not giving you a sex nickname. Especially since we're not having sex again." I don't sound very convinced. So far, Graham and I are exceptionally bad at not having sex with each other. It's like after that first time we broke the seal and now we can't stop. Every time we both agree it can't happen again and that we'll never tell a soul and then we end up together and we forget all those promises. There was the bar. The car after the gym. And some not quite sex in the alleyway outside Mamacita's when we "accidentally" ran into each other.

"I can give you some suggestions, if you want, but we're getting off track. You never answered my original question about Chinese food."

"You're seriously asking if I like Chinese food? You called to ask me that?" I finish making the bed and walk back out to the living room. I've spent all day cleaning after neglecting my apartment for far too long. I've got another shift bright and early tomorrow morning but I couldn't let the laundry fester for another day. I flop down on the sofa and unscrew the cap on my bottle of water. "Are you taking a poll or something?"

Graham laughs in his deep throaty way and I can almost picture his chest moving up and down. Thinking about Graham's chest brings about an unfortunate wave of tingles that I suppress with a swallow of water.

"I'm not taking a poll. Look out your window."

I turn to find Graham standing down on the lawn holding a giant paper bag. He manages a wave with the fingers holding his phone. He's wearing one of those tight athletic T-shirts and I can almost see his abs from here. I consider pulling the curtains shut, but he knows I'm home. There's no hiding from him now.

"You cannot come up," I tell him, trying hard to stand my ground even as my feet itch to run and open the door.

"Not even if I have dinner?"

My stomach growls. "You cannot come into my apartment."

"Do you want me to leave?" His face clouds. "I'm going to take the food with me."

I don't want him to leave. I want to be able to invite him up and have dinner like two normal people. But I know if Graham's here we won't be just having dinner. We've already proven we can't be trusted and alone in my apartment will provide the kind of opportunity I've been trying to avoid.

"I have an early shift in the morning." I let the cautious-ness I feel seep into my voice. "And you do realize that a booty call requires an actual call. A call you make before you come over, not one you make from the front door."

"This isn't a booty call," Graham tells me, still juggling the bag and the phone outside my window. "This is dinner. I get bored eating alone." He pauses. "Do you want this to be a booty call?" He's as unsure as I am.

"No. Never mind. Come up. I'll let you in."

"Great!" Graham nearly sprints to the stairs and I hear him barrel up them. Hopefully my neighbors won't decide they need to see what the commotion is. I don't need witnesses to my lack of self-control. He's at the door before I can scoot across the living room. "Come on, food's getting cold!"

I unbolt the door and turn the knob. Graham's eager face greets me once the door swings open. "What if it turns out I don't like Chinese food?"

His face falls a little.

"I can go and get something else," he suggests. "We can order in or I can make something." He's not going to be deterred, I guess.

"No, I'm just messing with you. I like Chinese. What'd you get?" I take the bag from him and turn toward the kitchen. Graham follows behind, looking the place over.

"I've never been inside your apartment." He swivels a bit, taking in the framed photos on the walls and nearly tripping over the coffee table. "It's nice. It smells like you." Graham pulls a big hand behind his neck and squeezes. "Sorry."

"You're apologizing because you said my apartment smells nice?" I raise an eyebrow. "I mean, I'm assuming that's what you meant."

"It smells great. I never actually thought you'd let me up here."

"Ah."

"So, I didn't actually think this part through." He seems like a giant in my apartment. A nervous, bumbling giant. After all his bravado over the phone, Graham's not sure where to put his hands. He settles them on his hips and stands like I imagine he does on the sidelines. I've never actually watched any of his games. He could have been running around naked for all I know. Except I probably would have ended up watching that.

"Well, let's unpack some of this stuff. I'll get plates." I point him in the direction of the kitchen table and he goes willingly, somehow fitting his enormous frame into one of my kitchen chairs. When I set a plate down in front of him he looks up, startling me. His blue eyes stare into my green ones with something that looks like relief.

"Thanks for not sending me home," he says as he reaches for the bag and starts pawing through it. "I was going crazy sitting there by myself."

"And the first person you decided to torture is me? I would have thought you'd hit up those guys from the bar. Don't those guys eat?"

"Oh, they eat, but during the preseason they aren't around to have Chinese food with me. And they're not really supposed to be eating like this anyway. Too much salt." Graham takes a pair of chopsticks and breaks them apart, rubs them together. When he hands them to me he doesn't hold my gaze for long. He reaches for another pair of chopsticks and goes through the motions for himself.

"But you're okay with Chinese? Not afraid of ruining your health?" My joke falls flat. Graham sticks out his bottom lip a bit before giving me a shrug.

"Not so much anymore."

I know this isn't exactly true. Graham still treats his body like he's using it to make a living. He's still at the gym, still walking around with so little body fat you could bounce a quarter off his ass. But now that he's not part of a team I can see how he'd be lonely.

"You missing it?" I let my voice soften. He obviously does, but I'm not going to push him. It's a weakness he might confess to Julia or confide in her father about, not necessarily something he'd tell me. It would expose a bit of him I might use against him.

Graham surprises me with a sigh and a *yeah* that hangs in the air long enough to embarrass him. He clears his throat and straightens up. "But I'm fine. Football couldn't last forever." He reaches for one of the takeout containers and pulls the flaps open. "And now I can show up unannounced at your house."

"That's true," I tell him as we open the other containers and start filling our plates. "But don't pretend we're both not going to run two extra miles tomorrow to work this dinner off."

Graham smiles.

"And after we eat, we can do something fun." I watch Graham's expression change from solemn to molten in a split second.

"Like what?" I can feel him sliding his chair closer to mine.

"Wait and see."

After dinner I make Graham watch television. He sits on my couch, taking up entirely too much room, arms folded over his chest.

"This isn't what I thought you were talking about," he tells me accusingly. "Not at all."

"What? You can't appreciate a good *MacGyver* episode?" I ask innocently. "I have all seven seasons on DVD, but they may be on Netflix now. Do you want me to check?"

"Only if it inspires a little Netflix and chill, which I don't think it's gonna." Graham's sullen but there's no way I'm going to let him convince me to have sex with him in my apartment. Every time we've been together there have been time constraints, location issues, restricted nudity. Okay, maybe not the first time, but every time after that. In some way I've convinced myself that this makes those times not count. Bringing Graham to my bed would most certainly count, especially after he paid for dinner. I put the DVD in the machine and press play. Graham shifts in his seat, angry muscles bunching.

"You said this wasn't a booty call," I remind him. "Just two friends having dinner."

"And I was fine with that until you promised something else." Pouty Graham turns out to be both hilarious and annoying. He's like a toddler in time out.

"I told you we'd do something fun. Watching *MacGyver* is fun."

"What you *alluded to* before was not watching *MacGyver*."

I settle myself on the chair across from the TV. "What exactly did you think I was *alluding to*?"

Graham scowls and slumps lower on the sofa. "Fine. Maybe I was reading too much into things. We'll watch your show, but I just want to let you know, for the record, that I'm staying here because I'm polite. Not because I'm interested in watching some old sitcom with you."

"Because you're polite?" I almost snort repeating what he's told me. "Let me just say, for the record, that no one has ever found you polite. And *MacGyver* is an action show, not a sitcom."

"If you say so." Graham gives me a grunt. "But you don't have to watch it from way over there."

"Yes I do." I pull a pillow in front of me for good measure. "Now be quiet or you're going to miss all the dialogue."

Graham snorts, but stops talking. It takes all of ten minutes for him to become engrossed in the show, occasionally yelling at the TV and giving me a play-by-play of how implausible he finds not only the storylines but the stunts.

"What's with that barrel roll there at the end? They just decided to have some guy roll across there thirty seconds after the shooting stopped? This show is ridiculous."

"You've actually never seen this?" I'm incredulous. "I thought all boys watched *MacGyver.*"

"You've obviously been hanging out with the wrong kind of boys," Graham tells me with just a hint of righteous indignation. "I mean, the idea of making a bunch of inventions or whatever out of a piece of chewing gum and a shoelace is kind of cool, but come on."

"It's a classic," I argue, sitting up straighter and preparing to launch the pillow at Graham's head. "And they've even come out with a new version so obviously I'm not the only one who likes it."

"A new version of this?" Graham seems unconvinced. "Who would watch that? And there's no way you can call this a classic."

Of course I take the bait. *MacGyver* not a classic? Who is he kidding? "Okay then, Mr. Television Expert, what are you going to say is a classic?"

"I'm less into TV than movies." Graham shifts to face me. "And you'd have to give me a genre."

"A genre?" This is getting ridiculous. I cross my arms over my chest.

"Yeah, a genre. Like, ask me about a classic musical and I'll give you an example." He's serious. There's not even a hint of sarcasm on his handsome face. Not even the slightest shadow of a smile on his lips.

"Alright, then let's just start with that one, shall we? Classic musical. Hit me."

"Too easy. I don't even have to think about that one. *Singin' in the Rain*, obviously." I wait for him to burst out laughing, but it never happens.

Instead, Graham just stretches out his long legs and crosses his ankles, motions for me to continue. "Go again. Next genre."

"Um, okay, horror? That's a genre, right?" I'm feeling like I'm on shaky ground here. Is Graham some kind of film aficionado?

"Here everybody else would say *Psycho* and I agree that's a great movie. I mean, you can't go wrong with Hitchcock. But have you ever seen *Repulsion*? That's Polanski and it is freaky as fuck." Graham waits for me to answer but I'm having trouble getting my mouth to work. Who is this person?

"What?" he asks me, completely unaware of the seismic shift going on in my brain. "If you haven't seen that we should watch it now. Maybe we can find it online somewhere. I'll hold your hand through the scary parts." He gives me a raised eyebrow, but I'm not even bothered by his suggestion of physical contact.

"Are you actually into movies? Old ones?"

"Sure. I took a class in college and that kind of sparked my interest, I guess." He looks confused. "Is that weird or something?"

"Not weird, exactly. Just unexpected. I thought you'd be spending your time throwing tractor tires around, not watching black and white movies."

Graham is starting to look uncomfortable. "I am doing the tractor tire thing, but when you travel the way I have been, you need something to occupy your time. I can't read on a bus so I started watching movies. Now when the team's flying between games I just... Well, when I *was* flying with the team..." He stops and gives me a half-hearted shrug. "I like movies. I do things other than football."

"I know." I can't keep the defensiveness out of my voice. I've actually never considered what Graham does outside of football. Never actually really considered Graham at all. He's always been on the edge of my world, but I've managed not to give him much thought other than when he annoyed me. And now when I think of him it certainly isn't for his brain; it isn't for what he thinks or how he feels. Hot shame rises in my belly but I'm quick to tamp it down. "Give me another one."

"Another movie? Um, okay. *Citizen Kane* is probably one of my favorites. That's film noir but some people classify that as a tragedy because it has the elements, you know? And I like the usual stuff. *Casablanca*. That's a romance but I still like that one." He tilts his head and shifts on the couch again.

"*Casablanca*'s a romance? But they don't even end up together."

"Well, sure, but that whole story is about the relationship between the two characters. And he gives her up in the end so she can be safe. That's why everybody loves that movie. You think the characters are one way, but then they make different choices. And the ending."

"What about the ending?" For some reason I want Graham to keep talking. I have absolutely no interest in classic movies, but I want to keep hearing the timbre of his voice and watch his mouth move.

"You don't remember the ending?" He's shocked, furrowing his brows over those cornflower blue eyes. "Come over here." Graham pats the space next to him as he fishes his phone out of his pocket. And even though I know the dangers of putting my body next to his, I stand and join him on the couch. He's busy jamming his fingers on the screen, face knotted in concentration. "I'm sure there's a clip of it on YouTube." He's so engrossed in finding the information that he barely notices our bodies joined from the hip down.

But I notice. Against my will my entire body lights up. It's a virtual *yes, please* to feeling the heat of his leg against mine, the spicy way he smells, and the rock-hard planes of his body. He's got a little stubble on his face and I immediately think of how it would feel under my palms, between my legs. I lean in closer until our faces are almost touching. I need to see the phone screen, obviously, but it gives me an excuse to let my chest slide against his arm. Graham doesn't seem to register the contact, still searching for the scene he wants to show me.

"Here! This one." He's triumphant as he turns to look at me, his face inches from mine. He startles a bit at the closeness and then lowers his voice. "We can watch it, if you want to."

I don't want to. What I want in this moment is to close the extra two inches between us and suck his lower lip between mine, to slide my hand up his thigh and feel the muscles of his leg strain against the fabric of his athletic pants. These are all terrible ideas that will lead to much worse ones down the line. I know this and I do it anyway, enjoying the surprised look on Graham's face before he realizes what's happening.

"Cassidy?"

"Hmm?" I mumble as I plaster my mouth along Graham's neck, tasting the warm skin there with my tongue.

"Do you want to show me your bedroom?"

Yes, yes I do.

Graham

"I think Cassie might be seeing someone."

I choke, sputtering iced tea down my chin and onto the front of my shirt. "What?" I strangle out as Julia hands me a wad of paper napkins.

"I think Cassie's seeing someone. She won't tell me anything, but she's been out with this guy more than once."

"Like, on dates?" I ask, trying to look uninterested. If Cassie's going out on dates—repeaters—with some guy, I want to know about it.

"Not on dates. Well, maybe on dates, I don't know. Like I said she's all hush hush about it." Julia reaches out to steal a fry off my plate. "Probably she's just sleeping with him. I can't imagine he's convinced her to actually go to dinner or something. Either way it's been more than once."

"More than once?" Cassie's been with me more than once, but that still leaves plenty of time for this mystery person. And we never set any ground rules. We're not exclusive—we're accidental—so I can't really get upset if she's seeing other people. I can feel the sandwich I've just eaten turn to stone in my stomach. "How do you know that?"

"She accidentally told me." Julia goes back to chewing. "But when I pressed her for more details she got all defensive. That's a sure sign."

"Sign of what?"

"That she likes him. You know how she is. She's usually hit it and quit it. No repeat performances. But this guy's gotten a repeat, maybe more than one." Julia leans in conspiratorially. "And she even knows what he does for a living."

"Why's that weird? Is he a circus clown or something? A stripper?" I pretend to laugh.

"No, she just usually doesn't find out the details, that's all." Julia's back to her sandwich, taking another bite and chewing.

"So? What's the guy do for a living?" I wait while she chews for what seems like an eternity. How much chewing does one bite take? And why am I so impatient to find out more about this guy? *Because he's your competition, dumb ass*, I remind myself. And because he's a repeater which Julia is making sound more and more like a unicorn.

"She was vague. She thinks he's an analyst or something. I don't know."

"An analyst. Like a stock market guy?" I picture some nerdy guy with glasses making out with Cassie although I'm pretty sure if he's with her it would be more of a Clark Kent situation. Fucking Superman underneath his button down. I pick at the lettuce on my plate. "That's what she told you?"

"She didn't really tell me anything. She got all evasive and pretended she had to be somewhere. She hasn't said anything to you? You haven't seen some guy hanging around?"

"Me?" I almost squeak before coughing to cover it up. "Why would she say anything to me?" As far as Julia knows, Cassie and I are still sworn enemies who only put up with each other for her sake. She has no idea Cassie's now the reigning queen of my dirty fantasies.

"I thought you guys were hanging out some," Julia offers. "You seem friendlier."

"Oh." I try to play it off. "Um, I guess we've been hanging out occasionally."

"But you haven't noticed anyone in particular? She's still just got her usual hook up stuff going on?"

Hearing Julia talk about Cassie hooking up leaves me with a sour stomach. I push my plate away and take a long sip of my drink. "I haven't noticed anyone."

"She hasn't said anything?"

"Like what?"

"She hasn't mentioned anyone? Maybe that she's thinking about bringing a plus one to the wedding?"

"Nope." *Over my dead body.*

"Well, I'm going to get to the bottom of it," Julia says with way too much enthusiasm.

"You do that, Velma," I respond. "You should really call Shaggy and the gang to help you out."

"Let me know if you stumble upon any clues." It's all game to Julia. At least she didn't try to make me Fred in this scenario.

"I'll be sure to let you know if she confesses to having a secret boyfriend. Don't know when I'll see her though." I pretend to be moving on to the next topic even as I pull out my phone. "Should we get the check? I need to get going."

"Sure. I've got a million photos to edit."

She's waving down the waitress as I text Cassie to see if I can see her tonight. It's time to up the ante.

"Work stuff?" Julia asks and I nod, hitting send.

"Always something." Something like Cassie driving me crazy.

12

Cassie

"I thought having a destination wedding meant we didn't have to help you choose stuff?"

Julia's giving me what could only be explained as the stink eye. "What are you complaining about? This is the first thing I've asked for opinions on and it's alcohol."

She does have a point.

"I'm asking you to help us choose the champagne! I thought it would be fun." Julia pouts. Luckily, Zach swoops in to save the day and plants a loud smacking kiss on her. That's one way to keep her from talking, I guess. And she's right—champagne tasting would normally sound like fun. Who wouldn't want to hang out with their bestie and down a few bottles of bubbly in the name of wedding research?

A bridesmaid who happens to be secretly sleeping with one of the other bridesmaids, that's who.

Or another member of the wedding party, I guess. Whatever the hell we're calling Graham these days. Any way you slice it that person is me. The thought of having to pretend Graham and I hate each other for an entire evening is causing me levels of dread I usually find myself experiencing for a trip to the dentist. Because while Graham and I might not be best buddies, I'm finding it harder and harder to resist him. And not just in the bedroom. It may have started out only being physical attraction, but now? Now I find myself laughing at his jokes and wishing he was around. Missing him when he isn't. Dangerous territory to be sure, made even more dangerous by an evening full of drinks and conversation.

I catch sight of him out of the corner of my eye and have to work to contain the shiver that threatens to take over my body. Graham's laughing at something Julia's dad has said, head thrown back and chest heaving. The muscles in his arms flex when he brings his hand to his face. Whatever Steve's telling Graham must be hilarious because he's got him howling. I resist the urge to walk over to them and slide my arms around Graham's waist, to touch him in a way that would let everyone know what's going on. *No, Cassie. Keep your hands to yourself.* As long as I keep a safe distance from him things should be okay. Unfortunately, right now a million miles away would feel too close. Across Julia's living room is most certainly not enough space to keep my body from responding to the magnet that is Graham Stevens.

And apparently I'm not the only one drawn to Graham's boisterous laughter. Both of Zach's sisters magically appear on either side of him before I have a chance to move. Julia's father's retelling his joke and they're laughing along with Graham. One of them brushes her hand along Graham's bicep and I swallow a growl. There is no world in which Graham Stevens is mine, but my brain can't seem to convince my body. *Hands off, bitch* is the only thing I'll be capable of saying if those fingers don't make a hasty retreat.

Julia saves me from my thought of an epic throw down

by shoving two bottles of champagne in my hands. "Here, can you take these over to the table?" she asks me, completely unaware of my angst. The labels are covered up with large white stickers and all identifying markers have been removed.

"What the hell?" I gesture to the defaced bottles. "You took off the labels?"

"You can't have a blind taste test if people know what they're drinking," Julia tells me, exasperated. "Can you just put those on the table? I'll bring out the comment cards when we bring out the glasses."

How Julia has time to put together an event that requires removing the labels from thirty bottles of champagne I'll never know. I can barely keep clean sheets on my bed.

The main reason for my dirty sheets slides up next to me as I'm putting the bottles out. Graham leans over to look at the labels, letting his entire torso brush up against mine. My nipples tighten. I'm sure everyone can now see them through my shirt.

"How's my little firecracker?" He keeps his body pressed against mine for longer than necessary. "Thinking about what we talked about?"

Sadly, our conversation is all I've been thinking about. But Graham isn't going to be excited to hear what I have to say no matter how excited my body is to see him.

"The answer's still no." I don't turn to look at him. I don't want to see disappointment on his face. Truth be told I don't want to risk seeing relief either.

"You aren't even going to think about it?" He pulls one of the bottles forward and pretends to scrutinize it. "You aren't even giving the idea a chance."

"I don't do that. You know this. We've talked about it."

"But you've never had *me* ask, right? That's a whole

different situation." Graham brushes his hand over mine, reaching for the other bottle. I involuntarily let the fingers on my hand flex. He threads his fingers through mine for a split second and then lets me go. "Don't say no just yet. Give it a little more time." And then he walks away, giving me a view of his perfect ass.

But there's no way I can say yes to what Graham's offering. We both know it even if he thinks he can convince me otherwise. The answer is always going to be no for more reasons than I'd like to even bother to count. He wants something I don't give to anyone. Something I especially can't give to him.

Graham wants to take me on a date.

13

Graham

I don't know why asking Cassie to leave the house with me has her jumping out of her skin. Sure, I asked her when she was naked, but I'm serious about not hiding out. And, okay, it wasn't fair to ask her two seconds after I made her come all over my face, but it's not like there's a perfect time to ask your fuck buddy to try something a little more conventional, right? I like her. The sex is amazing. Why wouldn't we want to see if our relationship could be more than that?

One look around this room has me remembering all the reasons Cassie wants to keep us a secret. As we all negotiate our seats in Julia's living room, I can see Cassie working to put as much distance between us as possible. She told me she doesn't date. Nothing personal. And then she kicked me out of her apartment because no sleepovers. Fuck that. I muscle my way across the room and take the seat next to her on the couch.

The look Cassie gives me should have me scurrying away but I stand my ground. I plant my butt firmly next to hers and give her a smirk. The only way to make me move is to cause a scene and I know she'd rather die than call attention to us right now. I give her thigh a pat and she shoots daggers at me with those green eyes. If she thinks she can scare me off she's seriously mistaken.

"Everyone take a sip of the first one and put your notes down on the comment card," Julia calls out to us as she and Zach move through the room handing out champagne flutes. This really is a production. I feel a twinge of guilt at not helping with the planning. Is that something Cassie and I were supposed to be doing? Maybe instead of screwing like horny teenagers we should have been checking in with Julia. The fact that Zach's sisters have obviously been helping only makes me feel guiltier. A brush of Cassie's arm against mine as she reaches for her glass makes all thoughts of wedding planning whoosh out of my head. Guilt? What guilt?

She takes a swig of her champagne and starts to furiously scribble on the card in front of her. I lean forward and put my card on the coffee table next to hers, letting my shoulder bump up against her. Again Cassie gives me a dirty look which I meet with a smile. I take a drink of the bubbly liquid in my glass. "Too sweet," I announce.

"I thought you liked sweet," Cassie says without looking up from her writing.

"Sometimes I like sweet. But not always," I tell the back of her head, since she refuses to make eye contact.

"I wouldn't have guessed that. Based on other things I've seen you choose."

"So just because I liked something in the past means I have to like that thing forever?" I'm sure anyone overhearing this conversation thinks we're crazy.

"That seems to be how you normally work," Cassie responds and I can't help but notice her looking at Julia.

"Well, let me clear things up for you. Maybe my tastes are changing. In the past I've liked sweet, but I'm realizing now I have a soft spot for things that are a little more tart. A little more prickly."

"Can you describe champagne as 'prickly'?" one of Zach's sisters asks. "Maybe we should talk about the terms we want to use so that everyone's on the same page."

Cassie laughs at this, giving me a chance to see her pretty face. "If Graham wants to describe his champagne as 'prickly' I think we should let him."

"It will make for interesting reading once we collect the cards, I guess." This from Zach as he hands us our second sample. "Just make sure we can tell what that means. If prickly is good."

"Prickly is very good. The best," I clarify. Cassie rolls her eyes. "I'd choose prickly any day."

Cassie is drunk.

Somewhere along the line she went from just tasting the samples to throwing back entire glasses of champagne. Now I wouldn't be surprised to find her swilling out of one of the bottles. I watch her careen around the room as Julia tries to rein her in. Julia's been trying to convince Cassie to stay in the guest room but, as expected, drunk belligerent Cassie is insisting on going home.

"I can take her," I offer, pretending I'm not eager to be alone with Cassie.

"No way!" Cassie protests, slurring a bit. "I'm not going anywhere with Graham. We all know where that will lead."

Julia looks confused but I just shrug. "I think we can chalk that one up to the champagne," I say and brush the comment off.

"If you could take her I would really appreciate it." Julia's holding Cassie up with one arm. "I can't get her to stay here and I definitely don't want her driving."

"No problem." I slide my arm around Cassie's waist. "I'll get her home."

"And you can't tease her about this later," Julia warns me. "She'll never forgive me if you do. Just get her home. No incriminating photos or anything stupid like that."

I pretend to act shocked. "Like I'd do something to annoy Cassie." I'm totally keeping up the ruse that she and I can barely stand each other. I should be nominated for an Oscar. This is an award-winning performance.

"Graham." Julia's voice holds an unnecessary warning.

"Okay. Got it." I lean forward and give Julia a peck on the cheek. "Thanks for putting this together. It was fun. I promise Cassie and I will up our game for the next few things. We'll be more help."

Julia gives me that look that tells me she'll believe it when she sees it but she's distracted by Cassie making a move toward my mouth with hers. "Maybe you should bring a bucket or something. She's really drunk. You don't want her puking on the drive."

"We're fine. I'll text you to let you know she's home safe." And with that I haul Cassie's ass out of there and strap her in the front seat of my car.

We're less than five minutes down the road before she starts messing with my belt. Cassie's drunk enough that she's having trouble but she still manages to be distracting. "Cut it out." I bat her hands away. "I'm trying to drive here."

"You worry about the driving and I'll worry about this."

Cassie goes for my crotch again, leaning her head over into my seat and I almost swerve into oncoming traffic.

"Jesus, Cassie!" This drive home is going to prove more challenging than I originally thought. Drunk Cassie is handsy and determined to get into my pants.

"Are you seriously complaining about me trying to put your dick in my mouth?" Cassie asks, her gaze unsteady when I glance over at her.

"Normally I would be more than happy to let you do whatever you want to my dick, but tonight you're a little too drunk for me to enjoy it, baby." I try to give her a push back to the passenger side, but Cassie resists.

"It looks like you're enjoying it," she slurs as she moves her hand back to my lap. Sure enough I'm standing at attention, the front of my pants straining against my erection. My cock doesn't always communicate effectively with my brain.

"That always happens when you touch me, Cassie. It probably always will." I take her errant hand in mine and place it on the center console. I keep my fingers entwined with hers as we drive.

"No, it won't always happen." Cassie makes a sad face. "Boys always leave. You'll get tired of me eventually. That's the only thing my mama's ever been right about."

"What are you talking about?" I laugh. "You're worried about me getting tired of you?" But Cassie's snoring in the seat next to me, her mouth hanging open and her eyes closed. I pick up her hand and give it a kiss. She should be worried that I'll never get tired of her, not the other way around. I am definitely more invested in tart rather than sweet right now.

She's still passed out when I put the car in park. I come around to the passenger side and unbuckle her seatbelt. She stirs a little when I slide her out into my arms but then she settles with her head on my chest. I take a deep breath of her and bury my face in her curls. She'd never let me snuggle up to her like this if she were awake. Like I said, prickly.

Her apartment's dark once I get the front door open. I nearly trip over a pair of hospital scrubs and Cassie's running shoes as I make my way down the hallway to her bedroom. She must have rushed home from work to get ready to go to Julia's. I grin at the thought of Cassie stripping down as she runs through the apartment. I lay her on her bed and work to ease her boots off. It takes me a minute to realize the buckles are fake and they have zippers on the side. Girls' shoes and all that.

I hesitate when it comes to getting Cassie undressed. I've seen her naked more than a few times now but tonight she's not begging me to help her wiggle out of her jeans. I take a deep breath and try to be as clinical as possible: shirt over her head, pants eased over her hips. I know she hates sleeping in her bra from conversations. She's never let me spend the night to see firsthand how she should be dressed for bed. But getting her down to only her panties seems like taking this tuck in a little too far. I leave the bra on, grab the T-shirt I've strategically left under the bed, and put that on her, wrestling her arms through the sleeves.

I'm pulling the covers up to Cassie's chin when she groans.

"You okay, Firecracker?" I whisper.

Cassie answers me with a muffled *mrumph*. She dips her head a little and takes a sniff of the material on her shoulder. "This smells like you."

"Yeah." Busted. "Is that okay?"

"Sure. I guess." Cassie doesn't sound excited.

"I'm going to hang out on the couch for a while." There's

no way Cassie will let me sleep in here with her and I don't want to leave her by herself. And I need to text Julia or else I'll catch hell for not taking care of Cassie like I promised.

"No. You should just come here and do what you want to do." Cassie's working to pull the shirt back up over her head but only gets it stuck under her chin. This doesn't seem to bother her as she reaches around to unhook her bra and wiggle it off. Her tits spill out, a sliver of moonlight from the window falling across her chest.

"Wait just a second," I blurt out. "I just got that shirt on you." I can't help but stare at her breasts even though I remind myself that I shouldn't. I put one knee on the bed and wrestle her arms back in. "That's better." I smooth the fabric back down, careful not to really touch her.

But Cassie has other plans. She takes advantage of my proximity to give my hand a hard tug. I fall forward and land on top of her. "No, that's better," she says. "Take your pants off." She's reaching for buttons and sticking her hand up my shirt.

"Not tonight." I roll off of her and try to escape her roving hands. "You should sleep it off. You've had too much champagne."

Cassie pouts. "See," she says with a sigh. "Already bored."

"Cassie, I'm not bored." I don't know why I'm explaining this. "Would I be trying to take this thing to the next level if I was bored? Come on, you're drunk."

"You don't want to go out with me," Cassie tells me. "No one dates the fat girl. Fat girls are for fucking and now you won't even do that." Her eyes look watery. Shit.

"What the hell are you talking about?"

"I don't have to tell you. You know." Cassie points an accusing finger at me. "You don't want to date Mama Cass.

You want that skinny girl. The blonde one. Everybody wants the skinny blonde one. But you like brunettes, too. Skinny though, no fatties for you."

I sit frozen next to her. Cassie's so angry I'm afraid to touch her. She's shaking and snarling until her shoulders suddenly slump and all that venom turns to sadness. "But you'll still fuck the fat girl. Everybody will. You should just do that and leave."

I swallow hard. Cassie curls away from me and lets her head flop back on the pillow. I feel worse than if I'd actually gone ahead and had sex with her. Her breathing evens out and I slide my body next to hers, spooning her before I can stop myself. I move a rogue curl from her face and watch her forehead wrinkle. She'd kill me if she knew I was doing this —looking at her like this—but I'm pretty confident she won't remember any of this in the morning. Not the car ride home, not trying to get me naked, not telling me all about her Achilles heel. All the times I've ever said something hateful or ugly to her float through my head. I could banish the guilt with the excuse that I was immature but I can't help seeing my part in where Cassie is now. She's still carrying all that around with her, protecting herself from having anyone hurt her again. I'm sure I'm not the only asshole who's done things to wound her but I'm the only one who's here now. I'm the only one who can try to make amends. Cassie stiffens against me and I hold my breath. I'm not ready to leave her bed yet, not ready to leave her at all. I fall asleep with my heart in her hands and my head in the crook of her neck.

14

Cassie

I wake up in the morning next to an unmistakably Graham-shaped indentation in my bed. He's nowhere to be found, but if my rumpled sheets and the lingering smell of him on my pillow is any indication, he was definitely here. I roll my head to check the time and find he's left something on my bedside table. My eyes focus on the note he's left: *Eat me. Drink me.* Very *Alice in Wonderland* but I let it slide, thankful for the large glass of water and the two ibuprofen tablets. I do as I've been told and then let my head fall back on my pillow. Ouch. I gather up the one Graham's apparently been sleeping on and snuggle it against my chest. As long as no one's here to see it I can spend two clandestine minutes breathing him in.

Right on cue my phone vibrates from somewhere on the floor. I throw the pillow aside guiltily and fish for it. Of course it's Graham and I begin to wonder if this is one of those still-in-the-house situations. I consider checking under the bed but swipe to answer the call instead.

"Hello?" God, my head. Definitely needed the ibuprofen.

"Hey, sleepyhead. I didn't wake you up, did I?" There's genuine concern in Graham's voice. I immediately go on red alert.

"No, I was already up," I confess although I consider lying to make him feel a little guilty. "It isn't that late."

"It's almost noon." Shit. He's right. "I wouldn't have pegged you as the kind to stay in bed all day. Not that I'd know, since I never get to wake up over there."

Liar. "Is that so?"

"Yep. Forced out every single time. And after I'm *extremely* nice to you."

"And were you *extremely* nice to me last night?"

"What? No." Any playfulness is gone from Graham's voice. "You were drunk. All I did was put you in bed."

Whoa. "Calm down. I wasn't accusing you of anything." Holy overreaction. "I was talking about how it looked like you slept in my bed last night. With me."

"Oh." He's relieved. "I swear I stayed fully clothed."

"I'm sure you did." I'd planned to make a big deal of it. Graham did break one of my cardinal rules, after all. But he seems so upset at even the thought that I might think he manhandled me without my consent that I don't have the heart to tease him.

"I didn't want to leave you alone. I just stayed until I was sure you were okay." There's that concern again. Why's he being so nice? So *gentle*? I rack my brain for clues from last night but come up empty. What happened that has him acting like I'm breakable or something?

"Thanks, I guess?" I'm not sure what else to say. "Did I make an ass of myself last night?" I must have for Graham to be avoiding all these opportunities to make fun of my behavior. He had to put me in bed for God's sake. A fact that makes me only slightly self-conscious until I realize I'm wearing what appears to be one of Graham's T-shirts and only my panties.

"No, you were fine. Drunk but fine. Don't worry. Our secret's still in the vault. You weren't particularly chatty at the party."

I ignore the implication that I was chatty after we left. Hopefully I was too out of it to try to have a conversation with Graham, especially since I'm sniffing his pillow this morning. "And how did I end up in one of your shirts?"

"Well, like I said, I don't know what sleepy time's like over there so I had to use my best judgment. And that shirt is super comfortable so I put that on you. For the record you took off your own bra. I was a model citizen."

A little flit of disappointment pricks my belly. "Noted. You were basically my night nurse."

"Exactly. But now I'm calling to see if you might want me to bring you lunch. I can also do dinner if you don't have to work. We could go out."

I have to commend Graham on his stubbornness. He really doesn't give up. "We've talked about that," I tell him, the slightest hint of warning in my voice. "I don't date."

"Right, I've been thinking about that and I think I have a solution. Why don't we just not call it a date and see how it feels to be out in public together?"

"We do that all the time, Graham," I remind him. "But what you want isn't that. You want to act like we're together. And we're not doing more than friends. If you act in public like we act in private there's no way people won't know what's really going on."

"Would that be so bad? So what if people know about us?"

My head continues to throb. Why can't Graham see that this will end badly? What we're doing already is bound to blow up in our faces. And when it comes to an end, which it always does, he and I probably won't be able to stand each other. That's all without the interference of our friends and family. Shit show doesn't even begin to describe how things are going to look. And if we let people know we're seeing each other? I'd have to not only explain all our sneaking around to Julia, I'd have to admit to having started this in the first place. Julia wants Graham to find his soul mate, not to spend his time screwing around with someone like me who has no intention of letting things get serious.

"Can we not do this now?" I whine. "My head is killing me and I need to get up."

"Fine. We won't hash this out now, but we are going to keep talking about this. Lunch? Can we talk about that? Do you want me to bring something over?" He sounds irritated.

"No, you don't have to do that. And I've got work tonight so no dinner." My gut is telling me to avoid Graham today.

"I know I don't have to. I want to. I want to see you, Cassie."

"But today's not great," I lie. Today's as good as any other day. But today I'm wearing his T-shirt and feeling way too good about it.

"Alright." He lets out a sigh of frustration and I can picture him running his hand through his hair. "I have to go out of town for a few days. Work stuff. I'll call you when I get back, okay?"

Another twinge of disappointment. "Sure. Call when you get back." I bite back a request to have him call me from wherever he's going. *That's too much like a girlfriend, Cassie. Danger zone.*

"And Cassie?"

"Yeah."

"No matter what you call this. No matter how hard you fight it. It isn't nothing. I'll talk to you in a few days."

Graham doesn't even wait for me to protest; he just hangs up on me. I consider calling him right back to argue but that's a certain way to have him win this disagreement. And I don't want to argue, especially when I know he's right.

15
————

Graham

The view from my hotel room does nothing to improve my mood. It should—I'm in one of the plushest suites of the nicest hotel in town. I've told Dave this is a complete waste of money but he claims the company is insisting on it. Maybe that's the truth, but it strikes me as unnecessary to have them trying to impress me. I've already signed the contract and agreed to the ad campaign. I'm going to be eating pizza on the beach, shirtless for some reason. No need for them to act like it's anything else.

As I wait for Dave to get his ass over here I have nothing to think about but Cassie. I don't like how I left things with her, but I can't fix it until I'm back in town and we can talk face-to-face. Hanging up on her was a calculated move, one that obviously backfired. I had expected her to call me back and yell a little to give me a chance to make a few more of my points. Instead she waited me out, ignoring me until I got on the plane and flew to Miami. She hasn't even asked where I was going or what I was doing. Am I overestimating her interest in this? In me? Now all I can do is stew over the possibility that she's out with her girlfriends or—let's get real, my actual concern—that she's hooking up with someone else. My pride keeps me from calling to confirm anything, but my brain can't seem to stop turning over every unhappy possibility.

"Dude, please tell me you aren't going to make that face all day?" Dave chastises me after using the key card I didn't know he had. "No one's going to want to buy anything you're selling with your face looking like that."

I scowl. "Who gave you a key to my room?"

"The front desk. When I checked you in. I always ask for two keys. I'll give you the extra one for my room if it makes you feel better. It isn't as nice as this, but you can help yourself to the mini bar."

I'm not even sure why Dave insisted on coming with me for this shoot. He hasn't done that in years. I don't need babysitting the way his younger clients do and I can easily handle this on my own. A car picks me up, I do the work, and then the car drops me off again. No need for additional adult supervision.

"You ready to go? The car's probably downstairs."

I nod and grab my bag. "How long do you think this will take?" I ask, not really caring about the answer.

"A couple of hours, tops. I told them not to oil you up too much. I know you hate that. And it'll make us take longer to get out of the hotel tonight. I've got quite a few places we should check out." Dave's excitement about tonight's possible activities makes me nervous.

"I'm not going out tonight." I usher him out the door and into the hall.

"Sure you are. You aren't going to pass up the chance to party in Miami now that you aren't having to worry about team schedules and your workouts as much, are you? We don't have to do anything crazy." Dave and I have a very different definition of crazy and I have no intention of going anywhere with him tonight. Suddenly his desire to come on this trip is becoming clearer.

"I'm not interested in partying, Dave. I want to finish this job and get back home."

"You won't even come out to be my wing man? That hurts, Graham. And I'm sure we could find somebody for you. From the looks of it you could really use a little stress relief."

I roll my eyes. "I'm fine. Just not interested."

"Is this about that redhead? Are you still on about that? What's her name again? Carrie or something?"

Just the thought of Cassie's name in Dave's mouth has my fists clinching. "That's not any of your business."

"Nice try. You know that technically it is. If you've got a new girlfriend it would be nice for me to know so I don't book you for some celebrity bachelor auction and make your friend all upset. Don't be all territorial about her; I'm not going to try to steal her away." Dave laughs like that's one of his better jokes. I keep my face stony as I move to punch the elevator button.

"She's not my girlfriend," I tell him as the doors open.

"That's good," Dave responds as he slides in and pushes the button for the lobby. "Because if this is what you're like getting laid on the regular then I'd be concerned with her technique."

I try and fail to contain my snarl. "Again. Off limits."

"Ah, so there is sex then. But no relationship. That's the way to go, really. I would have suggested something like that myself but I know how you are. It is good to have something to keep your mind off the injury though and all the rest. It's good to have a distraction."

I bristle. Cassie's more than a preoccupation, but Dave drones on as we watch the display count down the passing floors. I keep my eyes on the numbers, breathing in and out. "And she'd be a good distraction. I bet she's a handful. She'd take your mind off all this other real stuff."

I shut my eyes and try to keep a little Zen. It's that or punch Dave in the face and since he's managing my career that would probably be a stupid decision. Telling him he's wrong and explaining the situation would only make things worse. Because my feelings for Cassie are real, not a diversion.

"But now it makes sense why you haven't gotten serious about any of the information I keep sending over. You can't keep avoiding it forever. We've got to make some decisions. You're lucky that between me and your financial advisor we've put together a solid plan, but you have to be the one making the ultimate decision. I know you hate thinking about investing and all that shit, but we need to get some things in motion before the world forgets who you are. The endorsements you have will continue for a while and we can add some more. A Super Bowl win would have helped that, but you made two appearances and you've got a great record personally and professionally. Let's capitalize on that. Take two more weeks to work this girl out of your system and then let's get serious."

I blink. Work Cassie out of my system and then get serious? Dave has no idea what he's talking about. Sure, I've been avoiding him and I've sure as hell been avoiding things like this photo shoot. And as for the future? I haven't made any real business decisions in a while. The main thing I've decided is that I want to get Cassie to think about our relationship. I've been putting most of my energy there.

Which is exactly what Dave's accusing me of right now. I

feel a bit of panic as the elevator doors open back up. What if Dave's right? He's terrible at pretty much everything but putting deals together; he's the absolute last person I'd ask for advice about a woman. The business part though... What if I am using my feelings for Cassie to keep me from thinking about other things?

I bat that suggestion away. That's what's supposed to happen when you think you might be moving from infatuation to something real. Doubt begins to cloud my thinking. Cassie's seen me as a selfish jerk for years when I've only ever thought I was determined. Pushing to get my way was a positive not a negative because it proved I was tenacious. So now I'm pushing Cassie instead of pushing people around on the field. Is my interest in Cassie only my way of keeping myself occupied? What if she's right not to trust me to be steady and stable? Because if I'm using her to escape my problems, I'm just creating ones for her. Problems I now know will hurt more than she'd ever admit.

16

Cassie

Graham doesn't call. I half expect him to; I will him to, but the universe doesn't seem to send out that message. He hung up on me and then went out of town, but the part of me that wants this unrealistic relationship to continue still wants the phone to ring. Every time it does I leap out of my skin, hoping against hope that it will be that stupid man. This does not bode well for me getting out of this without a few bruises and bumps.

I end up at Julia's eventually, licking wounds she doesn't even know I have as we look over the menu options for her (second) fairytale wedding. Beef or chicken? Who the hell cares? Not me, the world's worst maid of honor.

"We're doing more of a Mexican theme for the rehearsal dinner," Julia tells me as she thumbs through a giant stack of food descriptions and prices. "Since everyone will be there already on Friday night, we're inviting everyone to that, too. Last time it was just family and the wedding party for me and I think the same for Zach's other rehearsal dinner. Does it sound weird to talk about it like that?"

When I don't answer Julia clears her throat. "Well, I guess that answers my question."

"What?" I stutter. I'm not even sure what the question actually was. Terrible choice for maid of honor confirmed.

"Well, if you aren't even going to answer then I can probably guess that it sounds weird to be talking about my first wedding and comparing it to this one. And if that's weird then I should watch what I say about Zach's first wedding, right? Comparing it, I mean." She waits expectantly.

"No, I wasn't trying to tell you anything about that." I really wasn't, but I can't tell her I wasn't paying attention because I was hoping Graham would be here. That he'd at least call. I'm not sure he's even home and the one way I have of finding out without Julia's help requires me to make the first move. And I am absolutely not doing that. "Why isn't Graham here helping with this?" There. Now if Julia knows where he is and what he's doing she's sure to spill it.

"Graham? I thought you'd be glad to do this without him."

"I am glad." Luckily Julia's bent back over the menus and doesn't have to see my guilty, lying face. "I was just wondering how he managed to get out of this particular obligation. He's as good at picking out food as I am. Maybe better." I reach for one of the pieces of paper so I have something to look at. Something to occupy my hands instead of my phone.

"He does like to eat," Julia concedes. "But he's out of town for some photo shoot."

I choke a little. "A photo shoot?" My face flies up from the sheaf of paper. That's what he meant by "work"?

"Yeah, some endorsement deal. Pizza or something. Don't tease him about it. He gets really grumpy about having to do them but he needs to, especially now."

"Why especially now?" I know nothing about Graham's endorsements. Nothing about how he makes money. I've never even seen him play football much less talked with him about it or anything else having to do with his career. But Julia still seems to be in the know. My heart clenches a little. Stupid heart.

"You know, because he isn't playing anymore." Julia says it matter of factly, like I should know exactly what that means.

"So?" I shouldn't care but I can't help but be curious. If Julia finds that odd she doesn't let on. She seems more concerned with getting the menu I'm clenching out of my hands.

"Well, if he's done playing he has to figure out what to do next. And he has to try to capitalize on the endorsements and things he can get now while he's still able to, you know..."

I don't know. "Still able to? What does that mean?"

"While he's still recognizable and people haven't forgotten him. He's only got a window of opportunity for that now. Eventually people won't be willing to pay him to sell their products because he won't be able to convince people to buy stuff. If he's not tearing it up on the field, they'll get someone else to shill sneakers and beef jerky."

"Beef jerky?"

"Yeah, don't bring that one up. Graham loves beef jerky, but the ads for that are a little bit ridiculous."

How have I missed all of this? Oh yeah, I've spent the last few years doing my best to spend as little time as possible with anything Graham-related. Even if that's changed, the odds of us running into some beef jerky advertisement are pretty slim if I keep him trapped in my bedroom and refuse to be seen in public together. "So, if he isn't playing football and his endorsements are going to dry up what's Graham going to do?"

"That's what he's supposed to be figuring out. He's got options, but he's never had any real job other than football so he's not sure what he wants. And he's distracted apparently. There's some girl."

"A girl?" I try to sound uninterested but I'm sure if Julia looked, she'd see the steam rising off of me. Some girl? Probably a woman who's thrilled to spend time with him in public. One who will happily let him post her face on social media and not try to hide him inside her house whenever he wants to see her.

"That's what Graham's agent says. When he gets frustrated with Graham, he calls my dad. He's not supposed to, but I think he knows Dad can talk sense into that thick skull better than anyone. Graham would be furious if he found out. Look at the price for this lobster! Who'd pay that?" Julia shoves a menu under my nose, but I'm not ready to get back to wedding planning.

"Wait, so Graham has a girlfriend and that's keeping him from what? From finding a job?"

Julia sighs. "Not exactly. He's supposed to be looking at investments and business opportunities, but he's been putting it off. This chicken looks good. What do you think about this?"

I don't even pretend to look at the description of whatever mystery concoction Julia's considering. "But he has a girlfriend?"

"I don't think he has a girlfriend exactly." Julia grimaces. "I didn't ask for details and my dad didn't volunteer any. When Graham's ready to tell me, he'll tell me. Why all this interest?"

"I'm not interested," I lie. "I guess I just don't know much about this side of him. It's like secret life of Graham." I keep the actual secrets to myself.

"It's only a secret to you, Cassie. Everyone else knows all about this. Well, not the possible girlfriend part, but the rest is common knowledge." Julia gives me an irritated look. "If you tried having a regular conversation with him you'd know these things. I think if you gave him a chance you'd actually like him. Underneath all that macho bullshit of his is a reasonable guy."

I give Julia a *harrumph.* No sense in letting on that I know that already. "Is he worried about money? If he isn't playing then he won't have a paycheck." I'm not concerned with how much money Graham has, but I've watched enough TV to know that professional athletes make bad financial decisions. The thought of Graham feeling stressed about his next move has me surprisingly upset.

"I think he's fine for money. He had pretty big contracts and he always knew he'd have to do something after football. I just think it was over sooner than he expected." A flash of concern passes over Julia's face but she shakes it off. "He's good with budgeting and my dad made sure he hooked up with a financial planner. I think now the worry is less about the money and more about what Graham's going to do to fill his time. My dad didn't seem too worried about the girlfriend, but I'm nervous he's diverting his attention. This wedding stuff probably isn't helping."

I fidget in my seat. Would asking more questions look like concern for Julia or Graham? I can't help but feel the guilt radiating off her shoulders. An adrift Graham isn't completely Julia's fault. She's moved on—twice—while he chose to hang around waiting on her. A bubble of fear rises in my chest. Maybe he still is.

"But your dad doesn't think the new girl is a serious

thing?" I can't help myself. If Steve knows anything about my competition I'll need to get as much information out of his daughter as possible. Poor Julia's not even aware of my super sleuthing, possibly because I'm not really all that super at it.

"No, he seemed surprisingly chill about it. I think we all want Graham to find someone. I really want him to be happy, to have a family of his own. He's never had great luck with the women he dates. I think they're attracted to him for the wrong reasons."

For the perks of dating an athlete? For his money? For his body? For nothing but sex? I lump myself into Julia's broad category of women not worthy of Graham Stevens.

"But Dad seemed almost relieved after he got off the phone with Dave. Dave's Graham's agent," Julia tells me unnecessarily. I've met Dave in all his womanizing glory. Again I put the facts I'm omitting into the category of *not a lie.* "So I just have to trust that he thinks this woman isn't a terrible match for Graham."

"But you didn't ask about her?" I'm like a dog with a bone. "What does she look like? Did you get a name so we can Google her?" If it's not me we're talking about, I need to know who she is. But we can't be talking about me, can we? And what if we are?

"Why would I want to Google her?" Julia asks. "Anyway, I'm sure Dave vets all the girls Graham dates."

"Seriously? His agent *vets* them?" Another reason to keep my relationship with Graham to myself. "Isn't that a little intrusive?"

"Not when there are people who would want to take advantage of him. Dave's just protecting his investment, really. It's in his best interest for Graham to be happy, but it's more important to him for Graham to keep making money.

Paying some huge divorce settlement or paternity suit means more hassle for Dave." Julia doesn't seem to think too highly of Graham's agent. Not that I can blame her.

"Then how does he keep his private life, you know, private?" Any jealousy I've been feeling towards Graham's mystery girl is slowly being replaced by pity. And the tiniest glimmer of fear. Who'd want to have their life scrutinized like that?

"Graham?" Julia looks at me with amusement. "Graham doesn't have a private life. He's a former professional athlete. People want to know everything about him. It all comes out eventually."

Gulp.

17

Graham

You promised you'd call.

It seems like a legitimate reason to pull up Cassie's number on my phone and dial it without all this hesitation. That's what I keep telling myself as I hold the phone in my hand and stare at her contact information. Once again the screen goes dark and I have to hit the home button and put in my password for the millionth time. Still, I don't actually make a move to put the call through. I told her I'd call when I got back, but now I'm doubting my decision to come on so strong. To push her so hard to give me more before she's ready. To keep chasing her because I don't like hearing no.

My inability to dial her number only makes it more ridiculous that I'm parked in front of her apartment. I can actually see Cassie's shadow behind the blinds in her living room. I had almost hoped she'd be at work but I have no idea which days she's at the hospital this week thanks to my stubborn refusal to call her from Miami. That certainly worked out great. I guess absence really does make the heart grow fonder because all I could think about the whole time

I was away was Cassie and this situation we're in. But maybe it hasn't exactly been my heart that's been doing the thinking here. I thought about that more than I'd like, too. Then, I got off the plane exhausted and instead of driving straight home my brain went on autopilot and I find myself here, stalking Cassie from the parking lot.

Her shadow moves through the living room again and I know I'm going to have to make a decision. I can't reasonably sit out here all night. I let my head rest on the steering wheel. In a perfect world, I wouldn't be overthinking this. In a perfect world I'd be upstairs already, tangled up with Cassie. Right now nothing about this feels perfect.

I groan and accidentally whack my head on the horn. The noise isn't loud but it's enough to have Cassie moving to the window, pulling up the blinds, and looking down at the dim parking lot. She scans the spaces and her eyes come to rest on the hood of my car. When my phone starts to vibrate in my hand I have no doubt who's on the other end.

"Hello?"

"What are you doing?"

"Nothing." I debate playing it off even more than this, but there's no denying. Cassie sees me hunkered down here. "What are *you* doing?"

"Talking to a crazy person, apparently. How long have you been sitting out there?" Cassie stands at the window, her cell phone pressed to her ear. Even from down here I can see the amusement on her face.

"Not that long. I wasn't sure you were home," I lie.

"Do you want to come up?" She asks it like it isn't a big thing and even though I've been inside her apartment a handful of times now I'm not sure tonight that would be a good idea.

"I don't think I should."

"Um, okay." Cassie waits for me to tell her why; I keep my mouth shut. "Then I guess I'm going to hang up now and let you get back to watching the squirrels or whatever." She pulls the phone from her face and dramatically presses the end call button. My ear fills with silence. Cassie stays in front of the window, hands on her hips.

What the hell am I doing? Sitting here straddling the fence while Cassie pouts close enough for me to see the outline of her bra through the window? I pick up my phone and call her back.

"Hello?" she answers like I'm just calling her out of the blue.

"Hey, sorry about that."

"No problem." She actually doesn't sound too bothered.

"Can you come down here?" I don't trust myself to get out of the car.

"I guess," Cassie says. "Give me a minute."

I watch her move away from the window. Picture her walking through the apartment, grabbing her keys and turning the knob on the front door. Watch as she comes through the building's entrance. Before I know it she's rapping a knuckle on the driver's side window. I roll it down, already embarrassed that I've called her out here.

"What's up?" Cassie asks like it's the most normal thing in the world for us to be hanging out in this parking lot. "How was your trip?" I look up at her—tight yoga pants and tank top, hair pulled up in a ponytail, freckles sprinkled over the bridge of her nose—and immediately relax.

"Can you get in?"

She moves to the other side of the car without hesitation. "You aren't planning on kidnapping me or anything are you? Because I have to work in the morning," she deadpans as she slides into the passenger seat and closes the door.

I shake my head even though the idea of speeding off with Cassie to some place where no one knows us does hold more than a little appeal. "I keep turning and twisting things over and I need you to help me figure out what to do."

"What to do?" Cassie looks concerned. "About what?"

"About this." I gesture between us. "About how to handle this. Cassie, I want to do right by you but I can't figure out how to do that if things stay the way they are."

"Oh." It's a whisper between us.

"There's something here, right? I'm not the only one feeling it, am I?" I know I sound crazy, begging her to validate my feelings. It's like we're in some after school special and I'm the stereotypical girl wishing her crush would open up, needing to have a glimmer of hope.

Cassie lets out a sigh. "You know I'm not good at this, Graham. I keep telling you that. You don't want to do this with me. I've got issues, obviously, and I can't give you what you want." She pulls on her fingers, twisting them in her lap.

"Sure you can. I want a chance. Just the possibility. If you don't feel anything—if there's nothing here—then say the word. But I can't keep sitting in limbo. I'm not built that way. When I say I want to do this, I mean it. I want more than sex, Cassie. I think you might too."

Cassie's hands move to her face, massage her temples. "Why can't you just be like other guys?"

"And do what? Only have sex with you?"

"Yes."

I think of someone else with Cassie, just using her for her body like some blow-up doll. My fists clench and I have to make myself breathe. "You've been hanging out with the wrong guys."

"Maybe now you're hanging out with the wrong girl." Cassie's suggestion makes me bristle.

"You don't really think that, do you?" She can't. Unless I'm completely wrong about what's been going on here.

Cassie lets out a breath. "No. I wish I did."

"You don't have to sound so disappointed." Her lack of enthusiasm is a punch in the gut.

"You know this won't end well. It can't," Cassie tells me but she seems resigned to let things ride. She isn't denying anything, isn't breaking things off. That little glimmer of hope becomes more like a ray. "The truth is you're already getting more than I've ever given anyone else. I just need you to stop pushing so hard. I'm not ready to quit this, but..."

"But you aren't ready to tell anyone," I finish her thought. Now I'm the one who's disappointed.

"Can you handle that?"

"Can I handle keeping this a secret? Maybe. But for how long, Cassie? I can't do this forever."

She reaches across and takes my hand, the contact both maddening and steadying. I'm desperate to be with her, but not having it on my terms is driving me crazy. "I'm not asking you for forever. I'm just asking you to be a little more patient."

This is where I should walk away. Should get myself back to making decisions about my future and not worrying about something that's obviously temporary. A distraction. Anyone else would see Cassie's reluctance as a red flag and run as fast as they could away from this. That's what she expects me to do only I'm not like every other man she's been with. And so I give in. Lean toward her and let my lips slide over hers. She gasps but then settles into the kiss, pressing close.

"Is that a yes, then?" she asks, the tiniest hint of unsureness in her voice.

I kiss her again. "That's a yes for now, I guess."

"Good." She's surprisingly relieved. Because I've stopped pushing or because I'm not running? With Cassie it's impossible to tell. Either way she's getting what she wants—at least until I can convince her that she wants something else. "*Now* do you want to come up? I have food in the fridge for once. I can make dinner and we can watch a movie."

"That sounds like a date." I can't help myself. "And I'm not watching *When Harry Met Sally* again."

"No promises." Cassie shrugs. "Are you in or not?"

Oh, I'm in.

18

Cassie

"And then she had the nerve to act like she hadn't asked me to cut it short like that! Can you believe that? Like I'd just take the scissors to a customer's hair without them asking me to. That woman is crazy. She threatened to find someone else to do her hair and I was like, 'Well be my guest, lady.' I don't need clients like that. I have enough stress in my life."

I'm not sure exactly what stress my mother's referring to, but I'm sure she's likely to tell me in the next three minutes. One thing you can always count on with Val is her need to give you all the gory details whether you want them or not. Want to know how I wrecked her body by having the gall to be born? She'll tell you all about it. Questions about the wrinkles I've given her by being such a wild child? No need to even ask—Val will volunteer it. And the way my father ruined her life when he walked out? That one you don't even need to wait for. That litany of complaints is on her greatest hits list. If you live within one hundred miles of here and haven't heard about how Henry

Blake made my mother's life miserable, you should consider yourself lucky.

"I mean, between trying to make a living and worrying about what you're up to."

Here we go.

"I worry, you know. Especially since you're still livin' by yourself. If you hadn't dropped out of school I might worry less, but I guess we can't change those bad decisions, can we?"

I guess not, but we can certainly discuss them. Over and over and over again.

"It's not like I didn't go back, Mom." I try not to get sucked back into this old argument again.

"Well sure, but now your degree isn't from a good school and I never got back the tuition I had to pay upfront before you decided partying was your major." She puts her hands on her hips and I brace myself for more criticism.

"That was more than ten years ago. I've apologized and apologized. I've offered to pay you back. I could give you the money if you wanted it."

"No, that's not the point." Of course it isn't. The point is that she has something to beat me over the head with. "The point is that you were more than a little selfish and it wouldn't kill you to be a little less selfish now."

Ah, so here it comes. The reason Val's summoned me to her house. It isn't for some mother daughter bonding over lunch as promised. Such a shocker. There's something she wants and she thinks I can help her get it. That was the reason for the saccharine phone call about how we never spend any time together. Of course we don't. Ever since I was old enough to figure out how to extricate myself from Val's toxic unhappiness I've spent as much time away from her as possible. In middle school I joined every after school club that would take me. In high school I ran to Julia's house with her stable, if overbearing, parents. And in college? Well, the first time, I ran into whatever set of arms would open up for me, preferably one with a bottle of whiskey. That's how I ended up failing out and flushing Val's much mentioned tuition money down the proverbial toilet.

When I finally got my shit together and went back to school, I had wised up a bit. I paid my own way, did the work, and came away with an associate's degree that was enough to get me started. A nursing job and more education meant not having to hear my shortcomings every day. Now I can limit that lecture to a few times a year. So do I owe my mother? Not as much as she thinks.

"And what is this thing you want me to do in the name of unselfishness?" I ask. "Are we at least going to eat while you plead your case here?"

"Eat?" my mother asks like it's the first she's heard of it. "You can help yourself to whatever's in the fridge, I guess. I thought you'd take me somewhere. Who wants to eat here?"

"So, just to be clear, you invited me to come over for lunch expecting me to take you to a restaurant?" I would say I'm surprised but nothing surprises me anymore. Not where my mother's concerned.

"Sure. What's wrong with that? I expected you to *volunteer* to take me somewhere, but obviously you need to be reminded that your mama would enjoy being catered to a bit every now and then."

Obviously. "I'm not taking you out to lunch today, Mom. I wouldn't have driven all the way over here if we could have just met somewhere. We'll have to make do with whatever you've got here."

"What, do you have plans or something?" Val asks in

that voice that lets me know she's fishing for information. "What's so important you can't make time for your mother?"

I do have plans. Hot, sweaty plans with my top secret not-boyfriend. Plans I will never tell my mother, not even if she enlisted every soldier from Guantanamo to torture it out of me. "No. No plans. I just need to get home in time to get ready for work."

"Sure you do," Val tells me with a sneer. "I didn't know you were doing daytime whoring now. I thought you were limiting yourself to evening hours. If you end up pregnant, I'm not raising a baby. I've told you that. I've had my fill of diapers, late nights, and no appreciation. Your father made sure of that."

Her words hit a little too close to home, but I keep from confessing the extent of my "whoring" and start digging in the fridge. "Thanks for that bit of heartfelt advice." The thought of Val with a grandchild makes me shudder.

"Don't think I didn't notice you changin' the subject." Val leans back in her chair. It's the same rickety one she sat in the entire time I was growing up. She pushes the thing back on two legs and hangs her skinny arms off the back. The only thing missing now is her once constant cigarette. She quit smoking a few years ago once she realized sucking on those things really was giving her some pretty prominent wrinkles. They may have kept her thin, but it's harder to pick up a new boyfriend every three months with a pucker like that, apparently.

"I didn't change the subject. You did," I remind her. "Do you at least have bread or something? If this turkey isn't too old we can make sandwiches."

"Forget about the sandwiches. Tell me about this wedding. Mexico, right?'

I get a worrisome feeling in my belly. I haven't told Val

anything about Julia's wedding and there are a million reasons to keep her in the dark. Aside from the plethora of chances she'd have to remind me of my old maid status and other failures to snag a man, there's the possibility of her being rude in some way to Julia or her family. Now, with the addition of Graham, I have no intention of chatting about anything wedding-related.

"Where did you hear about the wedding?" I keep my face in the fridge, repeatedly rearranging the three vegetables in the crisper. Val isn't big on green stuff.

"I ran into Francine at Kroger's. She told me all about it. Seems like a fun vacation."

"It isn't really a vacation. We're going to be busy." I can already tell where this is going. I'm sure Julia's mother was just making small talk, but I wish I'd thought to tell her to keep any details from Val. She's forgotten the cardinal rule: Keep Val Blake as uninformed as possible or deal with the consequences.

Val sets her mouth in a hard line. "You aren't going to have any time for the beach or sightseeing? Nothing like that?"

"Nope."

"Um hum." She doesn't believe me. "You bringin' a plus one?"

I lift my head out of the refrigerator to give her a look. "Of course not."

"Don't want to commit yourself to one man for more than a day? I get it."

I glare at her. "That would be a pretty expensive date, don't you think? Taking some guy to Mexico?"

"Aren't Fran and Steve picking up the tab?"

"For everyone's travel expenses? No." I marvel at Val's understanding of the world.

"They expect everyone to pay their own way? That's tacky." Val seems more than a little smug in her pronouncement.

"That's how destination weddings work, Mama. You can't expect the bride's family to pay for everything. And I think Julia and Zach are paying for this themselves. They offered to help me out with expenses but I can swing it on my own." I say that last bit with more pride than necessary —but my mother doesn't notice. Me being able to pay my own way might impress a less narcissistic parent, but it doesn't even make Val think twice.

"Well, tell them you need their help and then bring me as your plus one," Val suggests, still balanced on the back two legs of her chair. "It could be a mother daughter trip."

A mother daughter trip? Is she insane? When I was a kid the idea of my mother and I taking a trip together would have made my year, my life, maybe. I would have loved for her to invite me to do just about anything. Instead, when Val had the chance to get out of town she went with a man. None of them would appreciate her dragging a "brat" along. I was left at home with a box of cereal and strict instructions not to burn the house down. Val was always either desperately looking for a new man or chasing after one she'd lost—things I promised myself I'd never do.

"I'm not bringing you to Mexico," I state flatly.

My mother's face begins to twist. "*I'm not bringing you to Mexico,*" she mimics back at me. "After all I've done for you, you won't even bring me on a free trip."

"It isn't free! And I've told you, I'm going to be busy with wedding stuff."

"Well, I'm sure I could find a way to entertain myself," Val informs me. "If you were busy and all. And aren't there other girls in the wedding who could do stuff while you and I go out? I already bought a new bikini."

I'm absolutely sure I would rather poke my eyes out with a stick than accompany my mother out in her new bikini. "Not really. Julia's only got me and Graham." I leave out the part about Zach having sisters. Too late I realize that I should have left out the part about Graham instead.

"Julia's got Graham, does she? She's marrying someone else and she's still got that boy running around. You have to admit she's good. Probably never going to set that one free."

I poke my head back behind the open fridge door and let the cold air take some of the heat from my face. I'm basically air conditioning the entire kitchen at this point, but I can't risk letting my mother see any trace of how her words have affected me. If she gets even an inkling of something, she won't let it go and I'll be in for more torture.

"Don't you have a boyfriend who could take you on a trip?" I ask to divert attention back to Val.

"Ricky?" she asks. So that's the new one's name. "He don't like the beach and anyway he'd probably want to go someplace like Panama City or something. Nothing exotic like Mexico."

"He sounds like a winner," I interject before I can stop myself.

"Well, at least I've got someone hanging around for more than five minutes. I don't see you with some fabulous man hangin' off your arm. And Ricky's cute. Steady job. Keeps his truck clean."

"He's a catch then. I stand corrected." Although, if the past is any indicator Ricky will turn out to be somewhat toothless and that truck will belong to his mother. "Are we making sandwiches or what?"

"You can make a sandwich for yourself if you're hungry.

I'm trying to make sure I fit into that new swimsuit. You should maybe start worrying about that as well." Val reaches over to pinch at my thighs. "And you think about what I said about Mexico. It'd be a nice thing to do for your mama."

"Yes, ma'am," I say and that placates her a bit.

"At least you remember your manners. I made sure I taught you those."

Certainly wouldn't want to forget my manners, even if I would like to forget everything else she taught me.

Graham

"I'm looking for Cassidy Blake. She's a nurse here?"

The woman behind the desk gives me the once over before answering. "She's a nurse here."

"Is she here today? I wanted to say hello. I was in the building." I try to add one of my award-winning smiles to thaw the ice, but this woman is somehow immune to my charm.

"You were in the building?"

"Yeah, on the fifth floor." I'm reluctant to give out too much information. Even if I'm no longer with the team I still ask them to schedule me for hospital visits. I always loved doing the outreach stuff. Not so much the corporate events, but the things with kids? For those I'm all in. Today I've been with a few other players visiting kids recovering from cancer treatment, signing things and taking photos. But it isn't my place to talk about that with this nurse and if she doesn't recognize me then it makes even less sense to say anything. I don't do it to be able to brag about it.

"I see," she says. She's older and looks like she isn't in the habit of taking shit from anybody. She and Cassie must be an extremely angry team.

"So, Cassie," I remind her. "Is she here today?" I know she's at work because she told me this morning when I left her apartment that she was going to be here. We're in the sleep over stage now thank God, but she's still holding firm on the no actual dates thing. I'm trying to move slowly. Trying not to scare her. Showing up at work was an impulsive decision I'm starting to regret.

"Do you see her here?" The nurse gestures around with her arm.

"Well, no. But you're the only nurse I see and while I'm sure you could run this floor all by yourself, I don't think that's hospital regulation."

She smiles a little at my compliment, but doesn't make any move to help me out. If she knows where Cassie is, she isn't telling.

"This is the right floor, isn't it? This is where I usually send things."

"You send things?" Her eyebrows shoot up.

"Sometimes. When she's mad at me." I lean against the counter. She's interested. "Which is frequently."

The woman laughs. "I can see that." She pulls her glasses off her face and tucks them down the front of her scrubs. "You send the cupcakes?" she asks, pretending to rifle through some files in front of her.

"Yeah. Cassie share those?"

"You think she had a choice?" she asks and I laugh. "You should send more of those," she tells me, giving the counter a tap.

"Yes, ma'am. I'm sure I'll need to apologize to her sooner rather than later."

She gives me a *cluck cluck*. "Don't let her scare you off. She's not as tough as she acts."

"Don't worry. I can handle tough."

"I imagine you can. If I see her, I'll tell her you stopped by..." she tapers off, waiting for me to introduce myself.

I extend my hand. "Graham." I leave off my last name, not that this woman will recognize me. And even if she did, she doesn't seem like the type to care.

"Well, nice to finally meet you, Graham. I'm Delia. I'll be sure to mention our conversation to Cassie if she turns up tonight." She's grinning from ear to ear.

"I'd appreciate it. Nice meeting you as well. I won't keep you; I'm sure you have things to get back to." I make my way back down the hall so Cassie can come out from wherever she's hiding and get back to work.

But before I can get through the double doors I hear Delia's loud cackle. "Good lord, Cassie! That's who you're running from?" I don't bother turning around. I just keep walking, the smile on my face bright enough to light the whole hallway.

I make a mental note to send Delia those cupcakes. At least a dozen.

Cassie

"You can't keep changing the rules."

"Changing the rules?" Graham rolls his eyes. "I'm just following the rules we agreed to when we started."

I narrow my eyes at him. I know a lie when I hear one and no amount of Graham Stevens charm is going to change that. "We both agreed that if you land on any of the blue properties it would be additional clothing. I own Boardwalk and I've already got a hotel on it so there's no way you can only take off one sock."

"Hmmm," he stalls, acting like he's mulling it over. "But I'm down to almost nothing over here, Firecracker."

"That's the point of strip Monopoly, genius." I cross my arms over my chest. I've already lost my scrub top but I'm still wearing my bra—a purple lacy number that I would never have worn to work if I hadn't planned on coming straight to Graham's house after. And you can bet that the panties under these scrub pants match although it is taking forever for this big reveal. Strip Monopoly has taken longer than anticipated to get to the stripping part. "Two articles of clothing, please, and make it snappy."

Graham peels off his left sock and spins it over his head. When he lets it go, it thumps directly into my lap. He really doesn't have many choices left. He started out wearing fewer items of clothing but I'm not cutting him any slack. He's terrible at Monopoly and I'm taking full advantage.

"Next time we play I'm making sure we start out evenly matched," Graham says.

"Good luck with that," I snort. "There's no way you'd even beat me at this game."

"Sure I would. I even have extra incentive because I'm dying to see what's going on under those pants." He tugs off his remaining sock, leaving him only in his boxer briefs. "Happy now?"

"Extremely." I try to ignore the way he stretches out his legs, almost touching me with his toes. If I'm going to beat the world's most competitive man, I cannot get distracted. We're sitting on his bed having one of the best Saturday evenings I've ever had and that's saying a lot. We've been spending plenty of nights together, all of them fabulous in a way that makes my stomach nervous.

I pick up the dice and blow on them for luck, noticing the way Graham's pupils dilate as he watches me. I try to concentrate on the game board, block out the hungry way he's looking at me and the close proximity of all those muscles. I move the top hat a few spaces forward.

"I didn't think it would be this fun to crush you in Monopoly but it is strangely satisfying." Besting Graham at anything is worth waiting a little longer to get my hands on him.

"That's probably because you didn't think you'd be able to get me naked this fast."

"There are faster ways to get you naked." I look up from the board. "I will admit strip Monopoly was not something I thought was a thing, but since it's the only board game you have..."

"We could watch another movie." Graham gives me a smile and that hopeful face I find hard to resist. "Or we could do something else."

I try not to let my eyes slide over his naked chest or the obvious bulge in his boxers. But the way he says it is so dirty sounding I have trouble keeping my head down. "You only want to quit because you're so obviously losing." I busy my hands rearranging my stacks of play money.

"What?" He makes a show of acting wounded. "Are you calling me a quitter? Me? Graham Stevens, master of the comeback?" He clutches his chest.

"Settle down over there. Maybe you're not as committed to board games as you are to football." I give him a dismissive wave. "Do you want to order dinner in?" I ignore the smile that spreads over Graham's face.

"You can stay for dinner?" The excitement in his voice is hard to miss.

"Yes, actually." My work schedule means I can't always stay no matter how much I might want to. And lately I've been really, really wanting to. More than I should if I'm trying to keep my distance and convince Graham that this will never work. "My next shift isn't until Monday. I can beat you at this game all weekend."

The way Graham's face lights up hits me directly in the chest. I will never get tired of the unabashed excitement that takes over his features when I've made him happy. He's got no poker face and I've never been more grateful for that as the idea of an entire weekend here with him starts a few flutters in my belly. There are way better uses for this bed and I'm ready to get to them as soon as I finish schooling him in this game.

"Okay. I want to buy this railroad. And I want to put another hotel over there. Can you give me one?" I hold my hand out, waiting for the plastic piece.

But Graham doesn't even bother pretending to give me another hotel, instead he reaches forward, takes my hand, and pulls me into his lap. The game board goes flying, plastic pieces sliding under the bed and skittering all over the bedroom floor. I yelp but don't bother pulling back. Graham ends up flat on his back with me sprawled out on top of him, my breasts smashed up against his chest. My face is inches from his and I stare into his eyes, barely able to breathe. For a few beats neither of us blinks.

"That was cheating," I whisper.

"It was," he whispers back. "But it was worth it. Game's over."

Later that night, as we watch *When Harry Met Sally* for the fifth time, I slide my bare feet under Graham's thighs. He startles but lets my feet stay there, tucked underneath him.

"You cold? Want a blanket?"

"No." What I want is to touch him but I don't want to have to say that.

He grunts and gives me a quick glance. "Here. Put those in my lap." He wrestles my feet out from under him and puts them on his massive thighs. One big hand closes around my left foot, the thumb pressing along the arch.

I can't stifle the groan that makes its way out of my mouth.

Graham chuckles but doesn't stop pressing along the

bottom of my foot, his other hand starting to massage the foot as well. "That okay?" he asks, the light from the big screen TV flickering on his face in the dark.

"That is more than okay. That is criminally good. Please, don't stop doing whatever it is you're doing." My head involuntarily rolls back onto the couch cushion.

Graham shifts on the couch, turning toward me. "You're on your feet all day. It's important to take care of them. Is that too much pressure?"

"No, just right, but you can't see the TV facing like that," I tell him, although I'm hoping he doesn't stop moving his hands.

"How many times have we seen this movie? I don't think I need to give it my undivided attention." He keeps his eyes focused on me, his thumbs running along the bottom of my foot in a way that has my eyes rolling back in my head. When he reaches for the right foot, I pull it out of his grasp.

"You don't have to do that."

"I can't do just one foot, Cassie. You have two." He motions for me to give it back.

"But…"

I try to keep my foot out of his grasp but with his long arms he easily reaches it.

"But nothing. Let me take care of you for a minute. Seriously, woman, don't test me." He tilts his head to the side, daring me to say something.

"Well, you *are* good at it."

"Add it to the list." And that cocky smile's back, taunting me. I'd scowl, but once those hands start working on my foot again, I don't have the ability to do anything but try to keep my purring to a minimum. "I like it when you let me be nice to you."

I don't have to look at Graham to know the expression

on his face. Normally, I'd make a joke or roll my eyes. I'd protect myself better. I'd do my best to put an end to this thing that's happening as he stares at me and I stare back.

But tonight, I don't. Tonight I let Graham be nice to me. And I let myself enjoy it.

Cassie

Thanksgiving isn't one of my favorite holidays. Not that I'm against gratitude or anything, but having a holiday that involves copious amounts of food and a focus on eating until you're stuffed makes the fat girl in me uncomfortable. I've got portion control all handled now, but that won't stop my mother from giving me a look when she sees how much I've put on my plate. Luckily, this year she can't say anything out loud without looking like an ass. We're at Fran and Steve's house and my mother would never risk acting like a bitch in front of Fran. She'll save it for the car ride back to her condo where she can berate me for twenty solid minutes before I drop her off. And while I will most certainly be grateful to be rid of her for a while, that sweet relief is a long way away.

Currently, Val's positioned on Fran's couch, yammering away about some issue at the hair salon. She's always trying to make things sound dramatic and important in front of Julia's parents. They make her nervous and she'll overcompensate with a few too many glasses of wine in order to "loosen up." Fran and Steve have seen this all before and so their invitation to family Thanksgiving was a surprise for sure. I tried to decline as nicely as I could, pretending to have a shift at work that I couldn't get out of, but Val was insistent that we would make it to dinner. Normally I try to work at the hospital in order to avoid even the possibility of Thanksgiving with my mother. Val doesn't cook, so there's never any hard feelings about me picking up holiday shifts. Growing up, Thanksgiving was more of a hassle for her than a celebration. We've fallen into the blissful routine of doing nothing at all as a family and I'm not about to complain. But Val was sure as hell going to make it to Fran's house for turkey and she wasn't going to let me use work as an excuse to keep her from it. I wasn't going to ruin things for her, something she spent an hour telling me all about.

I have spent years ruining her life, apparently.

To make matters worse, I had forgotten how much of a football holiday Thanksgiving is and how close Julia's family has become with Graham's. When my mother and I wobble through the front door—Val had done a little pre-party drinking—the first thing I see is the face of the mother of the man I'm currently secretly sleeping with. I have to work hard to keep my jaw off the floor as I watch Fran and Jackie work in tandem like a well-oiled Thanksgiving machine. They celebrate the holiday together every year and it's easy to see how seamlessly a Julia/Graham connection would have fit in. But instead Julia's here with Zach and his ring's on her finger. Zach's parents are here as well. His sisters help to set the table and entertain Julia's children. It's obvious now why Val and I were extended an invitation—we're the buffer. Without us it's a three-ring circus of Graham, Julia, and Zach's families. I help myself to a glass of wine as soon as I can make my way to the kitchen and fill it all the way to the rim.

The only thing keeping me from slitting my wrists at this dinner is the certainty that Graham isn't here. Having to watch him witness Julia and Zach discuss for the millionth time how the wedding details are coming together and hear about how excited they are to finally make things official would be painful for us all. I've already seen his mother wince a few times when the lovebirds have gotten a little too affectionate. They are fairly disgusting. They're not shy about reminding us all that they're madly in love. Get a room. There's a bit of hand patting from Fran. Apparently Graham's mystery girlfriend hasn't been discussed with Jackie. Or with me either. I squash that thought down just like I've been doing since Julia told me about her. Lucky for Graham he's got a solid work excuse that's keeping him far, far away.

I couldn't actually tell you where Graham is, but Julia's father seems to have all the details. Graham's managed to snag a gig working one of the million college games on television today. It's a big network opportunity and Julia's father is as proud as if Graham was his own son which, in a way he almost is. Steve keeps checking the television, making sure we're on the right channel, shushing Noah and Charlie when they talk over the announcers.

"Okay, everybody, quit talking now!" Steve bellows as he works to get the volume just right on the big screen TV in the living room. "They're going to start. If you keep talking, we'll miss the beginning!"

"Are we going to watch the whole game?" I'm met with annoyed glares from half the room. "I mean, Graham's probably going to be on like five minutes total."

"He'll be talking off and on," Steve assures me. "We'll

want to see it all. And this should be a good game anyway. Just sit there and let your dinner digest."

"Can't we at least have pie or something?" I'm going to need something to do with my hands.

"No!" Both Charlie and Noah shout it in unison. Julia's kids have gotten awfully vocal.

"We have to wait for Graham to tell us," Charlie clarifies.

"Graham isn't even here," I remind him. "That's why we have to watch this stupid game."

"He might not be able to do that this year, bud," Steve tells him and ruffles his hair. "We have to wait and see."

"But he might be able to, right? He will if he can. It's tradition." Charlie seems convinced. The fact that Graham's miles and miles away in some TV studio apparently does nothing to convince him that we shouldn't wait on pie.

"If he can, he will. He doesn't ever let you guys down." Steve gives the boys a nod and that seems to settle it for them. I'm still in the dark.

"We have to wait on dessert?"

"Yes!" the boys yell at me again and I'm forced to amuse myself with my empty wine glass.

When Graham's face finally appears on the screen the whole room erupts into cheers. There he is, in living color, wearing the tie I can never tell anyone I helped pick out. I chose the blue one he has on because it brings out his eyes. I know nothing about television, but had a vague idea that he should pop a bit. I secretly pat myself on the back for my fabulous choice as his face fills the frame, eyes exceptionally prominent.

Steve shushes us all again, moving close to the TV to be able to hear better. Graham and two other guys in suits sit discussing the game that's about to start. Graham towers over the other two, even sitting down. "Are those other guys football players?" I ask and get the shush again. Graham's face appears again, this time close up, and it's like he's been projected onto the living room wall.

"He's, like, three hundred pounds of teeth!" I think I whisper it to myself, but obviously not because Steve swivels, mouth flying open.

"He's not three hundred pounds! He's probably closer to two ninety." Graham's mother nods in agreement.

"I didn't mean it literally," I grumble and make a note to keep quiet from now on.

That isn't too difficult as the game gets started and the coverage moves from the studio to the action on the field. It's college football, but Graham has some connection to the teams, or the conference, or something. They keep switching to someone on the sideline and it's hard for me to tell who's talking when the camera pans to the two teams running back and forth. Julia's family intermittently cheers and groans like they have some vested interest in the outcome of this game. Zach's parents are surprisingly interested as well and his sisters bounce around on the couch like they're at a Beyoncé concert. My mother keeps to herself, nursing a glass of wine and rolling her eyes.

By half time I am thoroughly confused. Luckily, half time is another chance for Graham and his buddies to wax poetic about the game so far. At least, that's what I think they're doing. It all sounds like blah, blah, blah to me, even though Steve keeps commenting about how great Graham's doing. He's making "great points" and "really adding to the conversation." I'm just interested in watching Graham's face and the way he fills out the suit he's wearing. My chest swells a little with pride. Even if I have to keep it to myself it feels good to know that Graham wants me. I imagine every other woman in America watching this game is enjoying looking at the man I can take home any night I like. I couldn't tell you two things about football, but I can attest to the fact that Graham looks handsome. A fact my mother makes plain to the entire room when she looks over at Julia and opens her big mouth.

"I still can't believe you kicked that out of bed," she announces before getting up to refill her wine glass. "That is one fine man."

The entire room is shocked into silence. I close my eyes and pray to whomever might be listening for lightning to strike the house. Not a huge bolt. Just a little one would work. Another unanswered prayer, apparently, as the noise from the television drones on and everyone works to get their chins off the floor.

I try to redirect with a question for Steve in the hopes that everyone will forget Val's unfortunate but not entirely unpredictable outburst. "So... what's the deal with all the moving around?"

Steve looks at me like I have two heads. "The moving around?" he asks. "Like the running?"

"No, like all the guys going on the field and coming off and then going back on again. That." I have no idea what I'm asking but it has everyone looking at me instead of waiting for my mother to come back from the kitchen and dazzle us with her deep thoughts.

"It depends on what's happening in the game. You know this. There's offense and defense and special teams..." Steve stops when he sees the confused look on my face. "You don't actually know this?"

I shrug and Steve's brow furrows.

"How can you not know this when you and Graham... Does he not..." Steve flounders while everyone else watches.

"When Graham and I what?" Stupid question but too

late to take it back now. I watch an internal war wage itself all over Steve's face only to have him turn back to the television.

"It's probably better that way," he says more to himself than to me. "Better not to have to talk about football."

I get an uneasy feeling in the pit of my stomach, but asking for clarification seems like a dumb move. The split second of panic I feel starts to dissipate as soon as the game resumes and all eyes shift back to the TV. There are more guys running into each other and the constant flipping from the sideline to the field and back again.

Steve comes over and positions himself on the couch next to me. I've spent hours and hours here in this house with Julia's parents but his close proximity right now makes me suspicious. There's plenty of space next to Julia's mother or near his grandkids so why is Steve sitting next to me watching me pretend to watch the game?

"You really don't know anything about football, do you?" he asks and doesn't seem surprised when I shake my head. "Do you know anything about the scoring? The teams? Do you even know what position he used to play?" I shake my head again and Steve takes in a deep breath, letting it out slowly. "Alright, let's have a little lesson here." And he proceeds to baby step me through the stupidity that is football.

By the end of the third quarter I wouldn't say I'm in any way an expert, but I'm beginning to see why people might like to watch the game. The kids on the field are athletic and every now and then something exciting happens. Usually I have no idea which team is on offense and which one is on defense, but at least now I know those two things exist. That's progress, I guess. Steve's even given me the Cliff Notes version of Graham's career which is supposedly pretty impressive to people who know football. I try to act like I understand all the awards and stats that come out of his mouth. And now I know that Graham used to be something called a defensive end. I can already see that Google and I are about to become good friends.

"Why am I getting this crash course in all things football?" I finally get the courage up to ask.

Steve plays it off like it's nothing. "Everyone should know a little about football," he tells me but has trouble meeting my eyes.

"Uh huh. That's it?" I know there's more to this than him wanting me to understand the game. This conversation has been too Graham-focused for me not to suspect he knows something. I can't believe Graham would have told Julia's dad about us but all signs are pointing in that direction.

"I just thought you might like knowing what you're watching. That's all."

I'm about to just come right out and ask what he knows when the action on the television distracts us. One of the players is down on the field, his leg bent at an odd angle. All of the air gets sucked out of the room as we watch the camera pan from the kid's face, to his leg, and back to his face again. He's writhing around as the team doctors surround him and the other players on both teams kneel down.

"That looks pretty bad," I whisper. No one bothers to respond. We can all see that the injury is serious. When the coverage moves back to the studio Graham's face is ashen. They're carting the hurt player off the field, putting him in this golf cart thing and driving him back to the locker rooms as Graham's colleagues ask him questions about his own injury. Not knowing enough about what's happened to discuss the specifics of this college player's possible recovery, they're filling the time making Graham talk about his. He manages to keep talking, but doesn't seem happy to be the one sharing.

"Was Graham's injury like that?" I gesture to the television, hoping Steve will reassure me that whatever happened to Graham was absolutely nothing like that. Instead I'm treated to a painful grimace.

"Do yourself a favor. Don't Google it."

When the game finally ends and we get the last few minutes of Graham in the studio, I'm ready for this whole evening to be over. I can feel the pinch between my shoulder blades from balancing all the crazy in this room. Steve's still by my side, hanging on Graham's every word. He really does want him to do well. I should be happy—Graham's killing it by all accounts and he's got a room full of people here who love him and want him to succeed—but I'm ready to go back to having him all to myself. I want our little bubble back.

They're signing off from the studio and we listen to the other suits wish their families a happy Thanksgiving. They're happy to have spent this time with us, but apologize for being away from their wives and kids, parents and grandparents on this family holiday. Graham's going last and both Charlie and Noah are nearly peeing their pants with excitement.

"Say it, say it!" they both chant, little fists clenched.

I watch as Graham's face fills the screen again. "Since I'm always away for Thanksgiving, I've got this down pat. Happy turkey day to my family: my mom, Jackie; to Steve and Fran and Julia; and to my boys Noah and Charlie... now you can have pie." The other announcers laugh and Graham gives the camera a wink.

Charlie and Noah hoot and holler and run to the

kitchen with Fran, Jackie, and Julia trailing behind them. Steve slumps into the couch next to me, obviously relieved that Graham's big debut is over. I scan the other faces in the room and see some of the same shock I'm feeling.

He called them his family, called Julia's kids his boys.

Zach's sisters whisper on the couch, their heads bent together, and I can only imagine what they're saying. We're like intruders here, joining a family that was already more than complete without us.

"Like I said," my mother stage whispers to me from across the room. "Never going to let that one go." Then she settles herself down, smug and satisfied, into her chair.

22

Graham

One definite advantage to having Cassie agree to move forward even just a little bit with this attempt at a relationship is the increased access to her naked body. At least, that's supposed to be one advantage. Today I've spent all afternoon trying to coax her into the shower with me after our workout. The giant walk-in shower I have in my master bathroom should be enough to entice her to slide out of her sweaty workout gear. I try to convince her of the benefits of multiple jets and the steam function, but Cassie just sort of growls at me. She's been pissed off ever since I came home from my Thanksgiving TV audition. I have no idea why. Julia's father told me that dinner had gone well. Cassie's mom was only mildly inappropriate, and watching me on television wasn't too horrible. He even taught Cassie some football stuff so she'd be able to better follow what was going on. Still, she's been ice cold to me the past few days. Not counting the angry sex. When Cassie gets mad she likes to fuck it out of her system. It's hard to complain about that.

I half expect the house to be empty when I open the

door to the shower stall to reach for my towel. Instead Cassie's there, leaning against the tiled wall.

"What's that?" she asks me and I swear she's looking at my cock. I start to get hopeful that she's changed her mind about letting me help her get all the dirt off. Too late I realize her gaze has shifted a little to the left.

"That's a penis, Cassie. Want to come over here and get a better look?" I try to play it off like I don't know what she's really looking at, like I have no idea why her eyes are narrowing and her lip's curling up into a snarl. She's seen me naked before but she's managed to miss the one thing that usually sends most of the women I date packing in the end.

"I'm not looking at that, genius." Cassie moves forward, her face getting dangerously close to my crotch. "I'm looking at *this*." She points an accusing finger at my hip before I can get my towel wrapped safely around my waist.

I skitter to the left to avoid having Cassie get a better look, but there's no saving me now. Now that she's seen the little reminder of my dumbest mistake, she won't be able to unsee it. She'll want to do what every woman wants to do; she'll want to give me the third degree.

"Is that a tattoo?" Cassie asks even though I know she knows exactly what she's looking at.

I shrug and pull the towel off my hips, acting like I'm not concerned. I rub the fabric over my head and collect the drops of water that still cling to my chest. I keep my movements deliberate and measured to hide the way my heart is thumping, trying to claw its way out of my body through my throat. I avoid looking at Cassie in an effort to delay the inevitable—we're about to have the fight she's been spoiling for since I came home.

"It *is* a tattoo," Cassie confirms and then waits. What she expects me to do is anyone's guess. Am I supposed to explain myself? Deny it? I just shrug again and wrap the towel back around my waist. It hides the offending mark, but won't do anything to protect me from whatever Cassie decides to do next.

"When I read about that online I didn't believe it." Cassie looks genuinely perplexed. "I mean, I've never seen it, but I guess I just wasn't paying that much attention."

I don't remind her that most of our early hook ups weren't the kind where we look lovingly into each other's eyes. Hell, we barely even took our pants off. How would she have ever noticed my tattoo, especially now when it's faded? What used to be a bright reminder of the one that got away is now hardly noticeable. It could almost pass as a birthmark. Fourteen years will do that to a little cheap ink. I barely remember getting the thing although I can clearly remember why I thought it was a good idea. It was something permanent, something that would prove to Julia I was serious about getting back together. I was serious enough to put that declaration on my body forever. How could she ignore that kind of devotion?

Easily, apparently, and as I face a snarling Cassie I wonder for the millionth time why I haven't had the damn thing removed. Who spends their entire adult life with their high school sweetheart's initial inked onto their hip? A first class idiot, that's who. In other words—me.

"You were looking online? At stuff about me?" My mouth goes dry. This cannot be a good thing.

"Don't try to turn this around. I was looking at your stats and stuff when I fell down a rabbit hole of gossip." Cassie crosses her arms over her chest. She's angry, but there's a sadness in her eyes that makes me wary. She's ready to argue and who knows what she's seen on the Internet. I'm sure some of the crazy things she's read are true, but the other stuff...

"Gossip?" I try to tread lightly.

"Unless it's not just gossip." Cassie's voice quivers a little.

"You'd have to tell me what you read for me to be able to answer that."

"I'm not sure I want to know."

"Fair enough. Do you want to hash this out here in the bathroom or can you give me a second to get dressed?" I'd really rather not have my heart handed to me on a plate while I stand here in only a towel, but I'll let Cassie run the show. If she wants me to answer questions right here, right now then that's what we're going to do.

"You can get dressed, I guess. I'll wait for you in the kitchen." The heat's gone out of her voice and I suddenly regret letting her walk away from me. I hurriedly pull on a T-shirt and shorts and all but sprint to the kitchen table. Cassie's got her laptop open, her eyes scanning whatever crazy page she's found. I watch her face contort as she reads something that obviously makes her unhappy.

"What?" I ask, crossing my fingers that she's stumbled across something blatantly false. I don't have too many skeletons in my closet, but if she's found one I won't lie. I want her to be able to trust me even if it costs me and this conversation is definitely going to be expensive.

"Did you date a supermodel?" The question catches me by surprise.

"No," I tell her, confident in my response. Until Cassie turns the screen toward me and I'm faced with a photo of my arm around a certain blonde. "Oh," I correct. "That's not what it looks like."

"Well, what is it then?"

"That's business."

"Dating a model is business?" There's no way Cassie will understand this. Already, she's twisting her mouth into an angry little pucker.

"My agent set that up. She was single and I was single and we both needed to look less..." This explanation sounds ridiculous even to me.

"Less single?" Cassie supplies.

"I guess. And she's not a supermodel."

"Graham, she was in the Victoria's Secret fashion show two years ago. And the year before that. She was on a billboard in Times Square."

I had forgotten about that. "But I didn't really date her."

"Did you sleep with her?"

The question hangs in the air for longer than it should. Here's where I officially step in it.

"Once."

"Once? But you weren't dating?"

Frustration has me rubbing the back of my neck, squeezing hard enough to hurt a little. "I liked her and we were already kind of pretend dating. We tried to see if it would work." This is sounding worse and worse. *Someone please hit me over the head with the shovel instead of letting me dig this hole deeper and deeper.*

"You slept with her to see if it would work out?" Cassie's nostrils flare.

"That's not what it was like! And you can't be mad at me for something that happened before we even got together. I'm not trotting out every guy you've slept with and making you explain the situation."

"And why didn't it work out, Graham? Because you still have Julia's initial on your hip?"

I take a deep breath. She's partly right. It didn't work out because supermodel or no supermodel, no one has been able to compete with Julia. Not until now.

"That was a factor," I confess. "Really it didn't work out because it wasn't right. She wasn't right for me and I wasn't right for her either."

"Because she wasn't Julia. A fucking supermodel and you still choose Julia. What am I supposed to think about that, Graham?"

"You can think whatever you want." I'm starting to raise my voice even as I fight to keep my emotions in check. Yelling isn't going to make Cassie calm down. "But all of that's got nothing to do with you and I and what we're doing right now."

"Nothing to do with now?" Cassie laughs, a bitter, angry laugh.

"That's all in the past."

"You called them your family, Graham. That was just a few days ago. Or did you forget that already?"

"What are you talking about?" I rack my brain for information and come up empty.

"At the end of the game. You said Happy Thanksgiving to Julia and her family like they were *your family*. You called Charlie and Noah *your boys* for fuck sake."

"I always say that if I have to play on Thanksgiving! I've been saying that for years. You didn't find that on my Wikipedia page, Encyclopedia Brown?" I'm shouting now and Cassie recoils a bit.

"What do you think people think when they hear that?" Cassie straightens her spine. "When you call them your family?"

"I don't give a fuck what people think. I only care what Charlie and Noah think. I'm not about to apologize for telling the whole world I love those kids. You of all people should understand that."

Cassie stills.

"I know they've got Steve and now they've got Zach and his family, but I'll be damned if those boys ever think they don't have *me* too." I stab my index finger into my chest. "If you can't accept that then I don't know what to tell you, Cassie. I've been through what they're going through and Charlie and Noah don't need temporary. They need permanent, especially now. So, no, I don't give a fuck what other people think."

Still nothing from Cassie as she watches me lose my shit.

"I like people to know how I feel about them, Cassie. I like to tell them. Hell, I like to tell the whole world. But you won't let me tell you or anyone else how I feel about you. What was I supposed to say? 'And to the girl I'm crazy about who only lets me fuck her but never lets me tell anyone, I hope you had a great turkey day?' Jesus, Cassie. I can't win."

"You're crazy about me?" Cassie says it so softly I almost don't hear her.

"Yes. Goddamn it, Cassie." I put my head in my hands. "I'm so fucking crazy about you I can hardly see straight."

"Are you seeing anyone else?"

Seriously? What the hell is going on here? "Did you see that online, too?" I ask her. "That I've got some girlfriend?"

"Your agent told Steve you're seeing someone."

"My agent?" I'm going to fucking kill Dave. "He told Steve what, exactly?"

"He told Steve that you're seeing someone and Steve mentioned it to Julia." Cassie has the good sense to look a little sheepish about the game of telephone she's describing.

"When was this?" I ask.

"A few weeks ago," Cassie tells me.

"And you're just asking me about it now? Cassie, if you have questions you have to ask them. No wonder you're pissed." I try not to smile, but the idea of Cassie being upset I might be seeing someone else has me feeling a little smug.

"I'm glad you find that funny," she snaps.

"I find it funny that you think I'd have time for another girl. When would I fit her in? While you're at work? She'd have to have a pretty flexible schedule."

"I don't need you tell me how flexible she is," Cassie spits out and I can't keep the laugh I'm holding in from barreling out.

"Cassie, you know there's only you. The only woman I've told Dave about is you."

She furrows her brow. "Me? Why would you tell your agent about me?"

"Because he met you and then he kept asking about you." Cassie's wary look has me backtracking. "I mean, I didn't give him details. He just figured it out."

"And he told Steve?" Cassie's more upset now than she was when she thought I'd been screwing a supermodel.

"Maybe. Look, don't worry about it. I'll figure it out and I'll tell Dave to shut up."

"But if Julia's dad knows..." The look of horror on Cassie's face has me reaching out to her and pulling her onto my lap.

"He's not going to tell anyone. He hasn't even said anything to me about it. If Steve knows, then he knows. Would that be so terrible?" I know Cassie's going to think so, but it highlights the difficulty of keeping our secret. People are bound to find out and it would be better if they found out from us. Now Steve's impromptu football lesson with Cassie makes way more sense. And she had to suspect they were talking about her all along.

"And who are you to be busting my balls when Julia's told me about you going out with some analyst or something?" I had planned to never bring that ass up with Cassie ever, but while we're clearing the air...

"I don't date. You know that." Cassie looks at me like I'm the dumbest man on the planet.

"Then who's your repeater? Julia says it's more than once." Hopefully he's a figment of Julia's imagination.

"A repeater? Is that what she said?" Cassie twists in my lap to face me.

"Yeah. And she tried to get me to tell her what I knew about him so spill it." Then I can track him down and throw him off a bridge or something.

"I was talking about you. I just made that other stuff up to throw Julia off. You're the repeater, dumb ass."

Damn right I am. "You haven't been seeing someone else?"

"No," Cassie moans.

"You don't have to sound so upset about it." I nip her shoulder.

"It's just, I never intended for things to get like this."

"Like what?"

Cassie swivels until she's straddling me. "Like this." She puts her head on my chest and my arms reflexively close around her. "I'm accidentally monogamous."

I fight the urge to pump my fist in the air. "So, we're accidentally exclusive?"

"If you aren't seeing anyone else, then yeah." Cassie sounds like she's reporting the world's worst news. And when she tilts her head back to look up at me I almost expect there to be tears.

"You were really jealous." I'm having a hard time keeping the excitement out of my voice. Cassie might be feeling like she's at a funeral, but for me this moment is Christmas and my birthday all rolled into one.

"I told you I've never done this before." Her head comes back down on my chest with a thump. "I have no idea what I'm doing."

"But you just can't resist me."

"Something like that." She lets out a frustrated puff of air that I feel through the cotton of my shirt.

"Cassie, I—"

"No." She cuts me off with her hand over my mouth, shaking her head. "Don't do that. Don't say anything else."

I slide my hands to cup Cassie's face, press my lips to her cheeks, her forehead. This is where I should tell her how happy I am that she's mine, use my words. But I know Cassie doesn't want to hear those things. Not yet. So I try to show her with my body, by the way I touch her, the way I kiss her. I imagine that she's telling me how she feels when she wraps her arms around me and pulls me tighter, when she fits her body against mine.

"I'm still all sweaty," Cassie breathes against my neck.

"I can fix that." I lift her up and carry her back to my bathroom for a do over.

"Hey. Can't sleep?" Cassie's voice pulls me out of the fog.

"No. What time is it?"

"Almost three. You should come back to bed. Unless you sleep better alone." There's that doubt again.

"I sleep best when you're in my bed," I tell her and then run a hand over my face. Morning will be here before I know it and tomorrow I'll feel like shit. Not that I have anywhere to be for anyone to notice, which is why I'm sitting in my boxers in my office chair instead of enjoying the fact that Cassie's here. I look at her long legs sticking out from the bottom of one of my T-shirts and curse myself for not being able to turn off the voices in my head long enough to stay curled up with her.

"Then you must sleep like shit." She leans against the doorframe. "What're you doing in here?"

Brooding. Pouting. Shaking an angry fist at the gods of football.

"Thinking."

"About what?" Cassie pads over beside me and pulls one of the folders from the top of my desk. "Are you doing something with a car dealership?"

"Not if I can help it," I say and sigh.

"Is this all your what to do after football stuff?" She thumbs through the stack of paper on the desk.

"I guess."

"Your agent told Steve you were avoiding this. That you were using the girl you're seeing—me—not to have to think about it. True?"

"That I'm avoiding it or that I'm using you to avoid it?" I ask and watch Cassie's mouth twist. "Because, yeah, I'm avoiding this like it's my job, but you don't have any blame in that." I offer my hand to her and she takes it. Lets me pull her into my lap. I settle my hand between her thighs and she snuggles tight against my chest.

"I thought you were going to do the announcing thing."

"I am, if they decide they like me, but I need other things to keep busy and to keep money coming in. That gig won't last forever." Just like football.

"Explain the choices to me." Cassie yawns.

"It's late. We should go back to bed." I make a move to stand but Cassie won't let me.

"You know you aren't going to go to sleep. Talk to me about this. Maybe I can help you sort it out."

"That's very relationship-like," I tease.

"Is it?" She shrugs. "Then I'm better at this than I thought."

"You don't want to hear about this crap." I tilt my head to latch onto her neck. I'd much rather nibble on Cassie than go through all the boring choices sitting in front of me. She pulls away.

"Nope. Not falling for that. If you've been putting these decisions off, I'm not going to be your excuse for procrastinating. You can have that when you finish your homework. No dessert before dinner."

"Thanks, Mom." I scowl but I appreciate the way Cassie's bossing me around. And she's right—I can't ignore these decisions much longer.

"Then be a good boy and give me the short summary. Then I can try to forget that you compared me with your mother before I drag you back to the bedroom."

"My mom's awesome."

"True, but do you want to fuck her?"

I blanch. "Hard no."

"Then let's not compare me to Jackie ever again."

I laugh. "The short version of this is that I need to get myself organized for the next thirty years or so."

"That doesn't seem short."

"Exactly. So how am I supposed to decide?"

"You aren't interested in any of these offers?" Cassie flips through the stack again. "Not even this restaurant partnership? That sounds fun, maybe."

"Not really. I like to eat, but I don't want to worry about the other parts." I lean back in my chair, taking Cassie with me.

"But how involved would you have to be? I mean some of these look like you'd just be an investor."

"Some of it's passive, I guess. Once I put the money in it wouldn't require much day-to-day, but that doesn't solve the problem of what I'm going to do to burn some daylight. In case you hadn't noticed, I like routine. Without that I'm fucked."

Cassie does her best surprised face. "You like routine? You? I never would have guessed. I just thought all that getting up at six am for no reason was your way of kicking me out of bed."

"Hardly." I run my palm along her spine. "You're lucky I ever let you go anywhere. If I didn't make myself leave the house I'd try to keep you here forever, too."

Cassie twitches, but ignores me. She's still preoccupied with the files in front of her. "So other than laying around naked all day..." Cassie raises an eyebrow. "Not that there's anything wrong with that. What would you like to be doing?"

"Playing football," I answer without even thinking.

"Ah."

"You see the problem, obviously."

Cassie leans back against my chest. "You just don't have anything exciting to replace it with yet. You're in a great position. You can do some of these things." Cassie flicks the files back onto the desk. "And then you can do something you're excited about."

I'd be excited about taking you out in public. Being a dad. Still playing football. Because what have I ever really been good at other than football? I don't tell Cassie any of these things because what could she say?

"What were you doing at the hospital the other day when you came over to stalk me?" she asks.

"That was hardly stalking," I protest. "I was there and I just wanted to stop by to see my good buddy. What's stalk-erish about that?"

Cassie rolls her eyes. "Stick to the point, Stevens. Stalking aside, what were you up to?"

"Visiting sick kids."

"Even though you're not on the team anymore?" Cassie prods.

"Why would not being on the team keep me from hanging out with those kids?"

"Well, I imagine some of the guys work pretty hard to get out of that gig."

"Sure. Some guys aren't good with kids and it's a little depressing, I guess, being with those families. But I don't mind it."

"Because you're good with kids."

"I am?" I've never thought about it much before. "I like kids," I tell her simply.

"Oh, I know you like them. You go crazy over random babies and you enjoy Julia's kids. That takes infinite patience, in my opinion."

"What's wrong with babies? And Julia's kids are great. Their dad may have turned out to be a jerk, but they're great."

"Sure." Cassie looks suspiciously amused.

"What?"

"Why don't you figure out a way to do something with kids, knucklehead?"

I consider this for a second. Working with kids? Could I actually do that? "How would that work?" I ask like Cassie's got all the answers.

"However you wanted it to. You don't have to be a teacher or do it full time like Zach with all his kid classes at the gym, but you could do something that let you be with kids and tapped into all that patience and generosity you've got going on." She stays pressed up against me, rubbing her cheek along my left pectoral muscle. It would be distracting if I wasn't getting excited about this new idea. "You've got a soft spot for them so why don't you figure out a way to help some kids?"

Cassie yawns again and plants a kiss on the underside of my chin. "Now I've got to go back to bed. I think that's as much relationshipping as I can handle tonight."

I let her slide off my lap but when she tugs at my hand I stay put. "Aren't you coming? I promise not to mention the Jackie thing."

I fake a shudder. "No more Mom talk. Give me a minute. I've got a little research to do."

"Suit yourself. But you'll owe me one for all these good ideas." Not even Cassie's ass swaying down the hall makes me follow her. I've got work to do.

"Be careful what you wish for, Cassie," I yell after her. "When I give someone a raincheck, I don't forget about it."

She waves over her shoulder as she turns back into the bedroom. I open my laptop and get to work.

23

Cassie

"Explain to me again why Graham's here?"

Julia's face clouds. "He's in the wedding party."

Like that's self-explanatory.

"Sure, but isn't wedding dress shopping more of a girl thing?" I ask, shooting a glance over Julia's shoulder to where Graham sits taking up way too much space on the bridal shop's frilly couch.

"I guess, but he's the only guy in the wedding party. I couldn't exactly exclude him."

"I'm positive he wouldn't have felt bad about being left out of this." And I could have avoided having to watch him see Julia in her wedding dress. That little tattoo is still giving my self-confidence a healthy ding.

"Well, he could have pretended to be busy or something." Julia doesn't seem to see the problem here. "He'll be fine. There's champagne." She brushes off my concern by shoving a glass in my hand.

"Fine. Let's get this over with, then." I'm the best bridesmaid ever.

As the salesgirl shows Julia to a dressing room, I move to find a seat. Which turns out to be a problem. With Julia's mother here along with Zach's and both of his sisters, the only available seat is the sliver of sofa with Graham. He pats the space next to him and lifts an eyebrow. I take a deep breath and slide in next to him, careful not to let our thighs touch. Graham moves so we're connected from the hip down. My body heats.

"It's a small couch," he tells me as if that explains why we've ended up in the middle of it. He shrugs like there's nothing we can do and goes back to drinking his champagne, looking like a giant in this pink dollhouse. It's like something straight out of my bridal nightmare. Frilly everything and no shortage of sparkly.

"Should one of us go back with her? To help or something?" one of Zach's sisters asks. I still can't tell them apart. "How does this work?"

"We wait out here," Graham tells her like he's some sort of wedding dress shopping expert. "They'll bring her out once she's dressed and put her up there." He gestures to the little stage-like area in front of us.

All eyes turn to look at Graham.

"What?" he asks. "That's how they do it on that show, right?"

"What show?" I ask.

"That show about shopping for dresses. You know what I'm talking about."

"There's a show about buying wedding dresses? Who would watch that?" I'm not sure if I'm more surprised that this show exists or that Graham's been watching it.

"Oh, *Say Yes to the Dress*?" The other sister's apparently a fan.

"You've been watching a show called *Say Yes to the*

Dress?" There's no way I can let Graham off the hook for this. "On purpose?"

He's unfazed. "Sure. If I'm going to be a bridesmaid. It's research." The grin he gives me lets me know he's enjoying this way too much. I stare at those perfect teeth and seethe.

"That's so sweet," sister number one tells him and gives Graham a bright smile. "I'm sure Julia appreciates how dedicated you are."

I roll my eyes, fully aware that everyone can see my juvenile behavior. Julia's mother gives me a warning glance, but luckily we're distracted from Graham's awesomeness by the arrival of Julia in the first frilly white number. I'm thankful I'm sitting next to him. It keeps me from seeing the look on his face when he sees his dream girl all dressed up to marry someone else. As it is, I can feel him tense up—one of the drawbacks of being squeezed together on his pink monstrosity of a sofa—but it lasts for less than a second. Then he's back to being a relaxed, champagne-drinking bridesmaid.

The ladies from the shop fuss over Julia, putting her on the raised platform and spreading out the dress' train. The mothers *ooh* and *aah* seeing her in dress number one, but Julia's wearing a frown.

"It's lovely," Zach's mother tells her and all the assembled ladies agree, nodding and clucking like a bunch of chickens.

"I don't know." Julia twists to look at her back in the full-length mirror. "You don't think it's too much?"

I think this whole afternoon is too much, but I keep my opinion to myself.

And apparently the store employees think it isn't nearly enough because they move to slap a veil on Julia's head.

"For a second wedding?" Julia asks. "And this doesn't really scream 'beach,' does it?"

"It is a beautiful dress and you do look great in it," sister two says, getting up from her fluffy pink chair. "But maybe something simpler? For the beach."

Sister one agrees and then the two of them are off searching the racks with the sales ladies, looking for the perfect beach wedding dress which, if you ask me, could be purchased at any department store. But no one is asking me, obviously. The frequent yelps of excitement coming from deep in the piles of dresses have me wishing for more champagne. As if reading my mind, Graham reaches for the bottle and gives me a refill.

"Not going to help?" he asks, innocently.

"That's not really my area of expertise." I take a big swig of my bubbly.

"I'm well aware of that," he tells me, taking advantage of our close proximity to whisper in my ear. "But you have plenty of other things you do at expert level, baby."

My cheeks flush, the implication clear. And now other parts of me are getting hotter than appropriate for the bridal shop. I do my best not to meet Graham's gaze, but he's too close to fully avoid. When he pushes his hip hard against mine I almost fall off the sofa, giving him the opportunity to wrap an arm around me under the guise of steadying me. An arm that he leaves hanging off my shoulder.

"Oh my gosh, look at these!" one of the interchangeable sisters shouts as she rejoins the group. "Julia, there are so many gorgeous dresses back there."

"Now we've got plenty of choices," the other sister announces as she comes back toward us, a huge rolling rack of dresses trailing behind her. "One of these will be perfect, I know it." She runs her hand over the closest dress. "I can't wait for you to try these on!" She's almost bouncing up and down with excitement. I half expect her to rub her hands together with glee.

Julia moves toward the rack, the back of the current dress dragging along behind her. "Oh, this is more like it." She moves the dresses around, sliding the hangers on the metal bar, but stops abruptly when she reaches a particularly sparkly one in the middle. "This one isn't exactly beach, Kat."

"Oh, that one," the sister I'm guessing is Kat says in the most breathy way imaginable. "That one I just wanted you guys to see. Isn't that the most beautiful thing you've ever seen?"

More *oohs* and *aahs* from the group as Graham and I drink our champagne fused together on the couch. By now he's slid his arm down behind me and is rubbing his thumb along the small of my back. Angry looks are having no effect on his roaming hand and the only thing keeping everyone else from noticing is this supposedly fabulous dress.

"It is gorgeous, but you'd have to be a supermodel to pull off that look," not-Kat says. Which makes her Amy by process of elimination, not that I can concentrate on keeping straight which sister is which with Graham trying to shove his hand down the back of my pants.

"It would take someone gutsy to wear it, that's for sure," Julia agrees, turning to look at me. Graham's hand instantly stills. "Cassie, you should try this on."

"What? Why?" I protest, well aware that all eyes are now on me. "I'm not trying on a wedding dress."

"Come on, it'll be fun." Julia is a horrible liar.

"Oh, Cassie, this dress would be perfect for you," Amy gushes. "You have to at least come and look at it up close."

I have no interest in looking at the dress and even less

interest in trying it on, but I take the opportunity to extricate myself from Graham's grasp and propel myself toward the fluffy white concoction everyone else is drooling over. It really is beautiful, even if it's almost blinding in its razzle dazzle.

"There's an awful lot of... stuff on it, don't you think?" I ask tentatively, running my fingers over the intricate beading on the bodice.

"Well," Julia's mother interjects. "Depending on the venue you might want a little sparkle. It would depend on what kind of wedding you were having."

"I'm not the one having a wedding," I remind everyone. "I'm the one *never* having a wedding, remember?" No one seems convinced and I distinctly hear Graham stifle a laugh. He tries to hide his smile behind his champagne flute but his mouth is way too big for that to work. I consider giving him the finger but that's most certainly not acceptable bridal shop behavior. I settle on giving him a dirty look. It's nowhere near as satisfying.

"Alright, then I'm going to be forced to use my power as the bride to demand that you try on this dress," Julia proclaims, hands on her hips. "Go on, get yourself into the dressing room and squeeze your gorgeous butt into this thing."

"You can't make me try on a wedding dress," I argue. "There's nothing anywhere that says a bridesmaid has to try on wedding dresses."

"Fine. Then I'm making you try on this dress because I think it might be your *bridesmaid's* dress. I might want you to wear it at the wedding. That's reasonable, isn't it?"

We all know this is unreasonable, but there's no sense in fighting it. Until I wrap myself in this giant piece of taffeta nothing else is going to get done. "Fine." I down the rest of my champagne in one gulp. "I'm at your mercy, bridezilla."

The flurry of hands shouldn't surprise me, but before I can take another breath, I'm being muscled to the back toward the dressing rooms. My shirt gets pulled over my head, sticking under my chin. In two seconds I'm down to nothing but my underwear. Even Graham couldn't have done it any faster.

"You're going to need to lose the bra," Kat tells me, giving me the once over. "This dress is strapless."

"How much do you work out?" Amy asks me, obviously admiring my ass. "Not to sound creepy, but your body is banging."

Julia hands me a strapless bra two sizes too small. Why is everyone in here with me? Add in the two sales ladies and there's a full house to see me nearly naked. "This bra will never fit," I inform Julia as I stand there in nothing but my panties. "Is all this really necessary?"

Julia gives me a look that begs me to be a good sport as the ladies get the dress ready for me, pooling it near my feet so I can step into it. "You can try it on without a bra," one of them tells me as she urges me into the giant white cupcake. "You would buy the proper foundational garments for the actual day, of course, but just to try it on it should be fine."

I'm never buying anything called "foundational garments" especially not ones meant to go under a blindingly sparkling wedding dress. But I keep all my sass to myself and let them push and pull me into the dress. The satin slides up my body, pulling at my hips.

"This isn't going to fit," I protest but no one's really listening to me. The sales ladies tug and tuck until they're satisfied, plumping up my boobs in the front of the dress and smoothing down the fabric in the back. I'm told to suck in as they zip me and then everyone's staring. The silence is deafening. "Okay, how ridiculous do I look?" I ask and wait for the inevitable laughter.

"Oh my God," Kat and Amy say at the same time.

Julia's got her hand covering her mouth, eyes wide and misty.

"Veil?" asks one of the ladies and three traitorous heads nod in agreement. She scurries off to get one as the other woman fusses with the skirt.

"We'd take it in a little here, obviously. And work a little magic on the top here..." She takes two steps back and gives me an appreciative nod. "Do you want to go out and show everyone else or do you want to keep this dress a secret from your fiancé?"

"My what?" I sputter. "I'm not engaged. She is." I point a finger at Julia.

"Oh, well, your boyfriend then. He's going to love you in this dress."

"I don't have a boyfriend."

"That man out there isn't..." I'm glad Julia seems to be too busy hunting through the veil options with sales lady two to find this conversation interesting.

"No, no, no, no." I'm emphatic. "He's my..." Friend? Bed buddy? Secret lover?

She silences me with a wave of her hand. "Then let's get you out to the big mirror." She helps me with the back of the dress—it's heavier than I expect—and we all traipse out to the front of the store. As the other girls fawn all over me, positioning me on the platform and sticking a tiara on my head, Julia and Zach's mothers start with the expected noises. Everyone's pulling out their phones and snapping pictures.

"No blackmail photos," I beg, turning my head and accidentally catching a glimpse of myself in the mirror.

Holy shit.

The dress really is beautiful. It skims over my hips and flares out into the slightest train. It's elegant and the beading and sparkles catch the light as I twist to see myself better. I look like a grown-up. Like a bride.

When I turn, mouth open, to look at everyone else I notice Julia's mother tearing up. Francine is actually crying at the sight of me in this dress. "Oh, Cassie," she says, whispering with a reverence she usually reserves for a good monogram. "That's the dress. That is the one."

But I'm not getting married. I don't even want to! I remind myself of this as I take another look at my reflection. The trifold mirror lets me see myself from all angles and if I look over my shoulder, I can see Graham's hulking figure on the couch. He's still holding his champagne flute, but he's got it at an awkward angle, letting what's left of his drink drip out onto the floor. We lock eyes and he's all I can see. His mouth's slightly open and the goofiest grin is playing at the corners. The way he's staring at me makes it hard for me to breathe and I'm relieved that I'm the only one noticing the look on his face. Until Francine turns to look at Graham and then back to me, her lips pulling into the slightest smirk.

"When it's time, this is the dress." And she gives me a wink.

24

Cassie

I feel like my face is one fire. When I trudge up to the nurses' station Delia takes one look at me and orders me home.

"I'm fine," I tell her even as I fight the urge to press my fingers against my face to relieve some of the pressure.

"You look like hell. Don't tell me you're fine. And you should know better. You can't come in here like some petri dish. You're probably contagious." She shakes her head at me. "You should be home in bed."

I start to disagree but Delia cuts me off.

"I'm not kidding. Get out of here. We'll call someone in to cover your shift. And if you're smart, you'll stop by the ear, nose, and throat clinic downstairs. Pretty sure you're going to need some antibiotics before this is all over." Then she crosses her arms over her chest and dares me to contradict her. "Go on. Should I call that boyfriend of yours and get him to come down here? I bet he wouldn't have a problem throwing you over his shoulder and getting you back home."

I glare at her. Delia should know that threatening to call

Graham is something I'll remember later. Oh, there will be payback. Ever since he showed up here I haven't heard the end of it from her. The frequent cupcake deliveries haven't helped either. Delia loves Graham. "He's not my boyfriend and if you call him, I'll kill you. I'm serious."

"Do I look scared to you?" Delia asks, shifting her weight so one of her hips pops out at me. She looks like she's more than ready to take me in a fight. "I'm more worried about whatever disease you're carrying around than having to embarrass you in a fight. I'm getting ready to count to three..." She pulls her phone from the pocket of her scrub pants.

"You don't have his number."

"You don't know that. He could have slipped it to me when you were hiding under the desk."

"I wasn't under the desk!" I protest but Delia ignores me. I'm almost certain she doesn't have Graham's number, but she's pretty convincing. Add that to her general craftiness and she just might be telling the truth.

"One, two." She lifts her index finger and slowly moves it closer to the screen.

"Fine! I'm going but I'd just like to state, for the record, that this feels a lot like bullying."

I hear Stephanie giggle from behind me and realize that Delia and I have attracted quite a crowd. Delia gives me a smug look before wiggling her finger over her phone screen again.

I turn and stomp down the hall.

"Feel better!" Stephanie calls after me.

"And stop downstairs!" Delia yells. "You know I'm going to check!"

I'm passed out on the couch when my phone rings. Why didn't I turn the damn thing off? I curse myself for not stopping to pick up the medicine I need at the pharmacy on the way home. Maybe if I had already taken something I'd be feeling less like warmed over death right now.

"Hello?" I croak. I sound almost as bad as I feel.

"Cassie?" Graham sounds like he's sure he's dialed the wrong number.

"Hey," I manage to get out before the throbbing of my head gets the better of me.

"You sound terrible." Graham's voice is laced with concern. "Is everything okay?"

"Everything's fine. I'm just sick that's all. Delia made me come home from work." I pout.

"You must be pretty sick to miss work."

"It's a sinus infection. I had one of the ENT doctors look at me before I left the hospital." I press my face against the coolness of the nearest throw pillow. I'm pretty sure I have a fever.

"Did they give you something? A prescription? Do you need anything?" Graham's rapid-fire questions aren't helping the throbbing of my head.

"I have to go get it."

"I'll get it. Which pharmacy?" I can hear the rustling of Graham throwing on his jacket and grabbing his car keys.

"No, don't do that." I sit up. "I can get it myself."

"Cassie, you should be in bed, not running around. I can be there in ten minutes. Just tell me where to pick it up." Graham's getting irritated but there's no way I'm letting him see me like this.

"No, Graham. Thank you for the offer, but I'm used to taking care of myself. I'll be fine." Even though he's not here to see it, I stubbornly stick out my chin.

"Damn it, Cassie. I know you *can*." Graham lets out an exasperated breath. "Either you tell me which pharmacy or I just start going to all of them until I figure it out."

Who's stubborn now? We're like two Billy goats ramming into each other. It would be nice to be able to hunker down on this couch and not have to schlep to the pharmacy but giving in would mean letting Graham win. Delia's threat's still ringing in my ears. *Don't make me call your boyfriend.* Picking up my medicine and coming over to tuck me in would fall squarely in the boyfriend zone.

"Fine." I give him the address and hear his self-satisfied grunt. Not so fast, buddy. "You can pick up the medicine, but you have to leave it at the door."

"What? Why?"

"Because this isn't a booty call."

"No shit, Cassie. You're sick. I'm not expecting a blow job." I can almost hear Graham grinding his teeth. "I'll be over in a few." And then he hangs up on me.

I must drift off because the next sound I hear is the pounding of Graham's fist on my front door. I try to sit up but realize too late that moving fast doesn't agree with me. I dizzily flop back down on the sofa. "Are you trying to break the door down?" I shout, the words echoing in the space between my ears.

"Open the door, Cassie."

"Just leave it on the mat. Like we talked about." All this shouting is sure to get my neighbors out in the hall, but I'm sticking to my guns. Graham can't come in here.

"Let me see that you're okay to be left by yourself and then I'll leave," Graham yells.

"I look like shit. Just leave the medicine and go, please," I plead from my spot on the couch. I'm not even sure I can make it to the door to get the pills once he leaves. If I look half as bad as I feel Graham will take one glance at me and I'll never see him again.

He waits on the other side of the door for what feels like an eternity. He's at least as stubborn as me—maybe more so —and I fully expect him to argue with me. Instead he surprises me. "I got you some soup and some Gatorade. Make sure you eat something and stay hydrated. The antibiotics are here and you're supposed to take them twice a day. Got it?"

"Got it," I answer, relieved that he's giving in so quickly. I don't have the energy to fight him. "Just leave them."

I listen for the sound of his shoes on the steps and the opening and closing of the hallway door and then I lie on the couch until I can talk myself into making an attempt for the front door. I'm wobbly on my feet and consider crawling. Graham really has saved me here because if I can hardly walk there's no way I could drive. I have to lean against the wall to unbolt the door but when I go to pull the door it flies toward me. And then Graham's torso falls in, his head landing right in front of my feet. Sneaky three hundred pound bastard must have crept back up here on his tiptoes after pretending to leave. If I had more energy I'd say something snarky about it, but right now it's taking all my strength to stay upright.

Graham takes one look at me and hops to his feet. *Baby,* is the only thing that comes out of his mouth before he's scooping me up and bringing me deeper inside my apartment. He's changing me out of my scrubs and smoothing the sweaty hair away from my forehead as he slips me between the sheets. "Do you have a thermometer? You're burning up." He's scurrying around to grab the pharmacy bag from the hallway and get me to take one of the pills before he slides in next to me.

I want to be angry, but the look of concern on Graham's face takes all the fight out of me. "You shouldn't be in here," I whisper. "You'll catch something."

Graham only scoffs as he pulls his T-shirt over his head and slides out of his jeans. He makes himself into a human pillow and props me up against him, kissing the top of my head. "Go to sleep," he orders and instead of arguing I shut my eyes. He pulls me closer, rubbing one big hand up and down my back and I drift off, dreaming of Graham's lips at my temple and the slow rise and fall of his chest.

Graham

"Nice sash, princess."

The next person who comments is getting a fist to the face. I watch as Cassie tries unsuccessfully to hold her laughter in as the most recent smart ass retreats into the crowd. If it wasn't making her and Julia extremely happy, I'd have taken the damn thing off hours ago. I'm expecting to collect on about a million good sport points for this. Can you trade those in for sexual favors? At least that gives me something to look forward to because, as it stands, me wearing this stupid, sparkly Maid of Honor sash is basically the best thing at this party.

And this party really blows. Whoever suggested having a coed bachelor party really didn't think things through. Technically this is Julia's bachelorette party too so it isn't just the guys who are missing out on a good time. At least we're all suffering together, I guess.

Cassie's hand on my thigh reminds me of one slight perk to this joint celebration. No one's going to get too wild tonight, but I get to look at Cassie as much as I want. We're packed up against the bar in this nightclub and for once I'm happy the place is crowded; it gives me an excuse to bump up against her. I slide unnecessarily close to order us another round of drinks and Cassie doesn't move away. She pretends she's getting pushed from the other side and rams her chest up against my bicep. When I look down at her she looks up at me and shrugs. Well played, Cassie. Well played. I make sure to jostle her when I make a show of reaching for my wallet, let my finger brush her chest as I pretend to straighten her matching sash.

"Who chose this place anyway?" I yell over the music. It doesn't seem like either Julia or Zach's scene.

"Who do you think?" Cassie hums into my ear as she looks over at Zach's sisters. The twins are occupied with Jaeger shots and a handful of bro dudes from Zach's gym. "They wanted a party, I guess, and Julia let them plan it."

"So the rest of us have to suffer?" I ask, only half joking.

"Poor baby," Cassie croons into my ear, taking full advantage of the need to get close to be heard. "Are you suffering?" Her hand skims the front of my jeans.

"I am now," I confess, wishing I could take her hand and put it back on my crotch.

"Maybe we can figure something out." Cassie raises an eyebrow. "I was thinking about checking out the ladies' room."

My cock twitches. The thought of cornering Cassie in another public restroom should not make me this excited. "Here?"

"Give me a two minute head start to scope it out." She slithers past me, making sure her entire body makes contact with mine. Goosebumps break out all over my exposed skin. These next two minutes are going to feel like an eternity.

I'm just about to give up hope and order another drink when my phone buzzes in my pocket.

3rd door on the left...

I try not to knock anyone over in my rush to get to Cassie, try not to make eye contact with any of the other guests at this ridiculous party. I'm almost to the hallway and getting ready to count doors when I run—almost literally— into a pack of Zach's gym buddies. A hand claps down on my shoulder and I stiffen. Cassie won't wait forever.

"Hey G, time for shots. You in?" One of the guys shouts at me as he turns me back toward the bar. I resist getting pulled into their scrum and plant my feet.

"In a minute, maybe. I've gotta hit the head." I jerk a thumb in the direction of the hallway. "I'll catch up with you guys in a bit." My phone buzzes again in my pocket and I fish it out, forgetting to tilt the screen, giving my friend a full view of my texts. He gives me a puzzled look before releasing my shoulder.

"I see you've got something more important to do."

I look at my phone and cringe.

What the hell is taking so long? Get in here and fuck me.

Only the fact that I've changed Cassie's name in my contacts is saving me from a major disaster. I'm going to have to count on the fact that Zach's friend won't be able to guess who it is I'm calling "firecracker." I shrug and push past him, not even responding when he yells something about the men's room being the other direction. It's not like I need to explain myself. He's got a pretty good idea of what I'm up to and it has nothing to do with my earlier excuse.

One, two, three doors. I turn the knob and find myself in a dark supply closet. It isn't a bathroom, but we haven't exactly gone up a notch in the ambience category. The space smells of disinfectant and I can almost make out the outlines of some industrial shelves pushed against the far wall. A warm hand slips into mine and gives me a tug, pulling me tight against a body that can only belong to Cassie. She wraps herself around me like a vine, stealing all the oxygen from my lungs. I haul her up against me, press her against the door, and try to ignore the fact that I'm desperately making out with my not-really-girlfriend in the world's least sexy place.

Cassie pulls her mouth from mine and sighs against my neck. Immediately I go into mother hen mode. She's still not one hundred percent recovered from whatever it was that knocked her on her ass last week and I've been trying my best to baby her without getting on her nerves. I slide a hand up to her forehead. She's warm, but not feverish, but when I move to kiss her again Cassie pulls back.

"Did you just feel my forehead?" she asks, shaking her head.

"No," I deny.

"Are you trying to see if I have a fever? Because I don't think that counts as foreplay."

I scowl down at her in the dark. "I just don't want you to relapse. You probably shouldn't even be out. You'll get run down and then you'll be sick again. Are you even supposed to be drinking on those antibiotics?"

Cassie laughs. "I'm fine. You've kept me trapped at home for almost a week. I'm not going to let you pretend I'm sick so you can drag me back to my bedroom."

"What's so bad about your bedroom?" I ask, kneading her ass in my hands. "I have plenty of fine memories from your bedroom."

"Not this past week. Unless you like snuggling up with a giant ball of snot."

In truth, I haven't minded being with Cassie while she

was sick. It didn't mean tons of hot, sweaty sex, but it meant sleeping tangled up with her every night and breakfast every morning. I watched more of her terrible '80s movies and TV shows just so I could spend more time on the couch with her. We got into a routine that seemed almost normal —domestic—and I liked it more than I should. Tonight, if Cassie decides to banish me back to my place, I'll have trouble being alone in my own bed.

"No more talking," Cassie orders and I obey if only so she doesn't decide to ditch me and go back to join the rest of the party. I'll take this closet with her over more time at the bar any day. I let her explore my body, run her hands all over me while I suck on the side of her neck. I breathe in the smell of her skin and block out everything else.

"Is there a lock on this door?" I ask and feel Cassie grin against the side of my face where she's nuzzling me.

"Afraid of getting caught?" she teases even though she's the one who wants to keep us a secret.

"*I'm* not."

Cassie stiffens in my arms before she reaches down to fumble with the doorknob. Once I hear the telltale *click* I know we're slightly safer, although we're still taking a chance. Everyone's here, it isn't some random club where no one knows us.

"We could save this for later," I suggest. "Not that I'm complaining, but we can wait until we're home." *Home.* Which doesn't mean what I want it to, not even close.

"Who knows how long this party's going to last? I don't want to waste my Saturday night watching Zach's sisters hit on random dudes." She goes back to running a hand over my chest.

"Then we could leave. Tell Julia you're not feeling great and I'll save the day by offering to make sure you get home safe." I groan a little as Cassie lets her thumb hit my nipple.

"Or we could stay and do *this*." Cassie lets go of my neck and glides south, pulling free from my grasp. She slips a hand under the waistband of my pants and I suck in a breath. Just like that I'm hard which pleases Cassie to no end. "That's what I thought," she purrs as she works on the button. In a flash she's got my pants down over my hips and my dick in her hand. When she takes me in her mouth all thought of ever leaving this closet flies out of my head.

"Cassie?"

"Hmmm?" Her humming nearly does me in. She looks up at me, her eyes glittering in the darkness of the closet.

"Nothing." Now isn't the time for talking, not when Cassie's giving me every reason to shut up. Her answering chuckle has my whole body shaking. I run a hand through her hair and wrap the silky strands around my palm, pulling tight. She looks up at me again but doesn't stop, taking my cock deep into her mouth. As one hand glides along my shaft, the other skates up my belly, making my skin prickle. I lean my free hand against the door, aware that people are moving around on the other side, but I can't make myself care about that right now. All I care about are the sounds Cassie's making, the tiny hums and soft sucking sounds that threaten to drive me over the edge.

When I haul her up the length of my body she protests. "Hey! I wasn't finished yet." I silence her by crushing my mouth to hers and pushing her dress up over her hips. When I line the wet fabric of her panties up with my already throbbing cock we both groan. The friction is almost unbearable and I hate to shift Cassie to the side to try to grab for my wallet and the condoms I now never leave home without.

"What are you doing?" Cassie hisses, impatiently trying to get our bodies aligned again.

"Condom," I tell her, nearly whacking her head on the edge of a shelf as I dance around with my pants around my ankles and Cassie wrapped around the rest of me.

I can feel the moment when Cassie makes the decision. There's a split second of hesitation before she announces, "Forget the condom."

I'm panting, pressing my forehead to hers. "Are you sure? This seems like a big decision for this closet." Cassie's offering to let me fuck her bare, something that speaks to me of commitment and exclusivity. Something that I was sure she'd never give me.

Cassie answers me by sliding her panties to the side and impaling herself on me. If I had reservations or misgivings I've forgotten them now as I'm wrapped in Cassie's tight heat, my only thought that I need to get deeper, move my hips, convince Cassie to scream my name until it bounces off the walls.

We're both frantic as we start to move, Cassie's legs wrapped around my hips, boot-clad feet hooked against my bare ass. I pull at the lacy panties wedged between us until the fabric gives way and there's nothing but skin. The door wiggles on its hinges as I press her against it again and again and between the sounds we're making and the bottles and cans falling from the wire shelf next to us we're putting on quite a show for whoever might be walking down the hallway. But neither of us stops, neither of us even slows down. I keep pumping in and out of her and Cassie keeps urging me on, her mouth fused to mine and her hands tangled in my hair. I come with her name on my lips, shouting loud enough for anyone to hear, as she shudders against me.

As we catch our breath, I push the tangled hair away

from her face. I kiss her mouth, her eyelids, her cheeks and keep her body pressed against mine, not wanting to break the contact. I softly chant her name, the whispered *Cassie, Cassie, Cassie* standing in for all the things I want to tell her. She doesn't push me away like she would have before, but I know she doesn't want any of my declarations even if she's letting me stay close.

"Cassie, I—" The words are almost out of my mouth when she cuts me off.

"We should clean up and get back to the party." Cassie untangles herself from my hold and looks around for her purse. "We kind of destroyed this place."

"We did," I admit. "Should we talk about..." This isn't a conversation I want to have here, but with Cassie I have to take my chances when they come. "I mean are we..."

"Well, these are a lost cause," Cassie tells me as she looks at her ruined panties. She's avoiding the question.

"I'll buy you a new pair. Look at me."

She turns in the dark and I can see the panic on her face. Cassie's scared, and pushing this issue tonight won't get me anywhere, so I wrap her in my arms and hold her for as long as she'll let me. Then before I let her go, I just go ahead and say it.

"I love you."

This closet is full of monumental moments. I see Cassie's face twist and her mouth gape open.

"You don't have to say it back. I just can't hold it in anymore." I kiss the top of her head. "We should get back."

Wordlessly we do what we can to smooth our wrinkled clothes and make ourselves look less like we've been screwing in a supply closet and more like we were just caught in a passing hurricane. Cassie's lack of underwear makes me unhappy but there's not much I can do about that. "I'll go first," she says. "I could use a trip to the ladies' room." Cassie slips out though the door and into the hallway.

I notice her sash on the floor as soon as the door shuts and instinctively I reach for the knob. "Cass, don't forget this." She's right outside and my outstretched hand bumps her back. She jumps when my fingers brush her shoulder and turns to me with eyes wide. Standing not two feet from her are Zach's sisters, both smiling at the sight of us, obviously up to something we shouldn't be.

"You owe me twenty dollars," one twin says to the other as Cassie and I stand like guilty statues in front of them.

Great. Now we're really fucked.

26

Cassie

I huddle in the bathroom stall, trying to get my breathing under control. This isn't the best place to try to assume the fetal position or put your head between your knees, but it's the only place I could reasonably flee to once Kat and Amy caught me with Graham. It's obvious that they figured out what we've been up to. If they had any lingering doubts, my running away like my hair was on fire probably only cemented the fact that their suspicions were right. So, so right.

And now they're probably out there sharing what they know with everybody else.

Breathe, Cassie. In and out. This isn't the end of the world.

Only it is. If Julia finds out that Graham and I have been seeing each other behind her back, that we've been having a secret *relationship*—how in the hell did we ever end up in a relationship?—our friendship will be different. How can she trust me again when I've kept something like this from her? When I've kept the *someone* of this from her? Graham doesn't seem worried, but what does he know? He doesn't have to follow the girl code. The code that pretty explicitly states exes are off limits, especially to best friends. He's a man and he doesn't have to play by those rules.

A man who just told me he loves me.

I groan into the empty space above me in the stall. Hopefully I'm alone. Not that I've cared about making noise tonight. Sneaking into a closet full of cleaning supplies and having loud sex for anyone to hear? What was I thinking?

That you couldn't wait even one more minute. That you couldn't keep your hands off Graham even if it meant people finding out. That maybe you hoped you'd get caught.

Fine. I can admit it to myself. When it comes to Graham I want more and more and more. It's why I let him keep coming around, it's why I can't tell him no, it's why he's broken down so many of the barriers I've meticulously put in place to keep my heart safe. I even told him not to use a condom—something I have never, ever in my life, in all my hook ups thought about suggesting. That's the kind of thing that gives Graham hope. He's probably out there seeing hearts and flowers and all that crap. Unless he's out there running interference with Julia and the rest of our friends. Which brings me back to the matter at hand.

I can't hide in this bathroom all night. I stand up and pull the metal door open with enough force to have it crack on its hinges. Alone in the bathroom I square my shoulders in the mirror and give myself a silent pep talk. Whatever's happening outside these doors isn't going away so I march myself back out into the club.

It's way less eventful than I imagine. Graham's leaned up against the bar, sipping on a beer. If he's battling some internal demon, he certainly doesn't show it. The look I give him keeps him there at the bar even though his face tells me he'd prefer to come over and make sure everything's okay.

Julia's on the dance floor with Zach's sisters, but she's not in the middle of having some sort of emotional moment about how I've ruined our friendship. When she sees me, she squeals and runs from their group over to where I'm standing.

"There you are! Where've you been hiding? You're missing all the dancing!" Julia tugs me out onto the dance floor where the twins act like nothing interesting has happened in the past few minutes. No sideways glances, no knowing smirks, not even one of those telepathic twin moments. I wait for the other shoe to drop because, let's get real here, it has to, doesn't it? There's no way Amy and Kat watched me sneaking away from Graham and said nothing to Julia. Right?

But no one's acting like anything has changed. The twins are enjoying the company of some dudes with questionable dance moves and Julia's urging me to quit standing around like a lump and shake my booty. It's like I'm in a *Twilight Zone* rerun. Am I the only one who remembers what just happened out in the hall? I guess so because Zach and Graham are shoulder to shoulder at the bar, laughing at something one of the dude bros has said and Julia's with me like our best friend status isn't in jeopardy.

Screw it. If everyone else can act like nothing's wrong, then so can I.

I throw my head back and shimmy my hips. Julia's right there with me as we dance like two high schoolers who've snuck out for the night. Julia motions for the boys to join us, but Graham and Zach just shake their heads and stay where they're parked at the bar. Their loss because Julia and I are having a fabulous time without them. We dance until we're both out of breath and in need of drinks.

We throw ourselves up against the bar and try to make

eye contact with the bartender. "It's gotten really crowded in here!" Julia shouts over the music. We're both sweaty in that post-dancing kind of way and she pushes several strands of her glossy brown hair back from her forehead. "Definitely need something cold after that." She laughs and I'm still keeping my fingers crossed that this isn't the last time we can be together like this. The threat of what Kat and Amy know keeps pinging in the back of my mind.

When we finally get the bartender's attention, I rattle off our order like the pro I am, making sure to include two glasses of ice water. He's a heavily tattooed guy with an unfortunate goatee who would normally be under consideration if I hadn't been bitten by the Graham bug. As is, I'm suffering from some unfortunate virus that makes all other men almost invisible. I try not to look at Graham down at the other end of the bar where he's still deep in conversation with some of Zach's friends. Locking eyes with him is the worst thing to do when I'm trying to pretend he means nothing to me.

"I'll get those," a voice croons close to my ear and a credit card materializes out of nowhere. I turn and find myself up close and personal with a mystery stranger. He's handsome and gives me a smile that tells me he knows it. I smile back, but can't muster the interest I'd normally be able to, even with the free drinks.

"Thank you," I tell him. "But you didn't have to do that. We've got a tab going."

"I can't let two pretty ladies pay for their own drinks." He moves closer. "Not after I've had such a good time watching you dance." He rakes his eyes up and down my body and then turns to get a better look at Julia. When he sees the ring on her finger, I can actually see his mouth twitch but he doesn't stop leering.

"Well, thank you again for the drinks. I think we're going back out." I raise my glass to him in a little mock toast and go to steer Julia back out on the dance floor or at least closer to it. Definitely away from this guy.

Four fingers and a thumb clamped around my elbow make me stop. "You're leaving? I'd think buying drinks would get me at least two minutes of conversation."

"It's a little loud for conversation, don't you think?" I give my arm a tug, but he holds fast. I glare down the place where his fingers are digging into my skin.

"Then maybe we could move somewhere quieter. You never even told me your name." He smiles again and his fingers relax a little on my arm. "We haven't even gotten to the introductions."

I narrow my eyes at him. If this fucker thinks buying me a drink entitles him to quality time, he's got another thing coming. Julia's still beside me and she's giving him the death glare but this guy can't seem to take a hint, and we're way beyond hinting now. I set the drinks back down on the bar and prepare to rip this guy to shreds when a familiar voice booms over my shoulder.

"Don't touch her."

Graham towers over this guy, the veins in his neck already starting to bulge. Shit, shit, shit.

"Graham, I've got this," I try to reassure him.

"Yeah, we're fine here. My friend and I were just having a conversation." Again, this man is an idiot. Anyone can see Graham's not in any mood to be talking. The fingers on his right hand clench into a fist that seems to be having a hard time staying by his side. If this guy keeps it up, he's going to get that fist right in the mouth.

Graham looks down at my elbow. "I don't want you touching her." I've always made fun of him for being like a big, threatening Thor impersonator when anyone would so much as look at Julia, but there is nothing funny about Graham right now. Right now, if he could, he'd spit fire at this man who has his hands on me.

"What's the problem here?" Thank God for Zach. He's over by us in an instant, putting Julia behind him and trying to figure out why the hell Graham's gone from chatting at one end of the bar to getting ready to pummel someone at the other end. He looks at my elbow and sees the place where my unsuspecting suitor has really dug his fingers in and Zach's suddenly all business too. "Let go of her arm," he tells him. "Right now."

He looks ready to argue, this man who is most certainly in the wrong place at the wrong time. He's caught up in this thing between me and Graham while also at a party where the main invite list involves a bunch of guys who hit each other for fun. Even if he wanted to, he couldn't handle the eight pairs of fists that have gathered around our group. He lets go of my arm and dramatically pulls his hand back.

"There!" he announces. "I'm not touching her. You should tell your girlfriend not to let other guys buy her drinks."

"He's not my boyfriend!" I shout which only raises Graham's ire. "And I didn't let you buy me a drink. You didn't exactly give me a choice." I root around in my purse until I find my wallet and then I slam a twenty down on the bar top. "There. Debt paid. And for the record, buying a woman a drink doesn't entitle you to shit, you asshole." With that I stomp off, not even caring that Graham's still standing there ready to rip someone's head off.

I walk straight out of the club and out to the street. Too late I remember that I've left my coat. It's not freezing out here, but it's cold enough that I consider going back in.

Screw that. Going back in will only give people more of a chance to stare, more of a chance for Graham and me to cause a scene. I get to work finding the nearest Uber and start walking.

"Cassie! Cassie, wait!"

I sigh. Of course he followed me out here.

Graham's long legs easily catch up to me. "Where are you going? It's freezing out here. Where's your coat?" He reaches for me, but I don't let him pull me in. His hand drops to his side and we stand on the sidewalk, our frozen breath filling the space between us.

"I'm going home," I tell him and go back to walking. I want to get as far away from this bar and this night as possible.

"Let me text Julia to tell her we're leaving." He fumbles around for his phone.

"No, Graham. *We* aren't going anywhere. Go back inside." I'm firm. I can do this. I can keep Graham at arm's length.

"What? Can I come over later?" He's genuinely baffled.

"No, no you can't."

"Is this about what happened at the bar? I'm sorry I got so angry. I saw him pulling on you, touching you, and I just lost it." Graham runs his fingers through his hair. "Can we at least talk about this?"

"There's nothing to talk about. It isn't just the guy at the bar. It's everything. This whole night..." I look at Graham's confused face. "I think we need to take a break. At least until after the wedding."

Graham looks like I've hit him, the shock on his face making my heart seize in my chest. "No."

"No?"

"No, Cassie. That isn't what I want." He shakes his head.

"I want to go back into that bar and tell everyone the truth. I think that's what you want, too. You just can't admit it."

"This has gotten too complicated." I try to keep my voice even, no emotion or I'll back down. "We have to take a step back from this. If this all blows up now it will ruin Julia's wedding."

"You think I give a fuck about Julia's wedding? I care about what's happening with *us*, Cassie. Nothing else." Graham paces in front of me, blocking the sidewalk.

"There's no *us*, Graham."

"The hell there isn't."

The gods of the gig economy smile down on me and deliver my Uber before Graham has a chance to get another word in. I hurriedly pull the door open and throw myself inside.

"Cassie, do not do this." Graham's pleading with me through the glass of the window, his face furrowed. "Do not drive away from me right now."

"I'll see you in Mexico," I say. "Please let me go."

When Graham backs away from the car, I feel relief wash over me. He's not going to fight; he's going to walk away. From me. From whatever this was that was growing between us. He stands on the sidewalk as the driver pulls away from the curb.

He lets me go. What the fuck? *He just lets me go.* He doesn't jump in front of the car or try to wrench the door open. Suddenly, I find it hard to catch my breath, the implication of what I've done making me gasp. I'm getting what I wanted, right?

"Is everything okay back there?" my driver asks.

"Yes," I gulp out. "Everything's fine. I'm going to be fine."

Eventually.

27

Cassie

"So, there's been a little bit of a mix up with the rooms."

I let out a giant sigh and give my neck a good roll. I have had the travel day from hell so it would be only natural for it to continue here at the resort. After having flight delays and weather issues I finally ended up in the very last row of a plane bound for Mexico after barely making my connection. Prime spot next to the bathroom? Check. Screaming toddler with no sense of personal space? Check. A middle seat that didn't recline? Check and check. I'm exhausted and want nothing more than a hot shower, tropical drink, and then my bed. Apparently, the universe has other ideas.

Julia's at the front desk to intercept me before I can try to check in and she's got her apology face on so I'm sure this is going to be good.

"Are you trying to tell me I don't have a room? I made the reservation the second you told me the details." I start to make my mental list of all the ways I'm going to yell at the poor guy at the check-in desk. He's about to wish he'd stayed in bed today. I know I'm already wishing I'd done the same.

"No, no. You have a room," Julia assures me, taking me by the arm and steering me back toward the middle of the lobby. "It just isn't in the main part of the resort. It isn't in the hotel."

"Isn't in the hotel? What does that even mean?" I look at her suspiciously. "Am I in some cardboard box out on the beach or something?"

"Oh, no, no, no." Julia keeps patting my arm as she gets someone to load us into a golf cart. My bags are hoisted into the back and Julia prods me onto the imitation leather seat. "It isn't a cardboard box. It's actually better than a regular room."

"Then why are you acting all shifty?" I ask. "What's the problem, Julia? You might as well tell me."

"Well, they ran out of regular rooms over at the hotel. They were overbooked so they offered us some upgrades. Free of charge, of course! You won't have to pay extra or anything." The words spill out of Julia's mouth in rapid-fire succession.

"If I'm getting some great upgrade then why are you all jittery?" Julia's not the world's best liar. It got us in trouble countless times growing up. Even as an adult she has no poker face. I don't know how she manages to convince her kids that the tooth fairy leaves that money under their pillows without just confessing to the whole thing. Now she's twisting her fingers and sweating underneath her swim suit and sarong.

"I'm not jittery!" Julia yelps. "It's just that they gave us these villas—which are beautiful, really beautiful—but they're big so..."

I can see where this is going. "So, I'm sharing. Is that it? I'm in some amazing villa with Zach's sisters or something?"

"Noooo," Julia says as the golf cart comes to a stop. The

driver works to free my bag from the back while Julia scurries over to the front door. The villa is lovely, with bright pink flowers hanging from a vine over the entry. The breeze from the ocean blows back some of the hair from my neck and I can't help but feel a little more relaxed. Julia pulls a key card out to slide it through the lock, still giving me glances over her shoulder. She pushes the heavy wooden door open and I'm thrilled with what I see. This is definitely an upgrade from the room I booked.

As I drag my suitcase over the threshold, I can see the beach through the giant wall of windows along the back. There are fresh flowers everywhere in the living room. With its pristine white couches and gorgeous view, it looks like something out of a travel magazine. I won't have a problem spending the next few days here.

"It's got this living area and a little kitchen in case you want to whip up a pitcher of margaritas or something." Julia's nervous laugh has me coming back to reality. There's some sort of catch to staying in this beautiful house and she's getting ready to come clean. "There are two bedrooms. Each one has its own bathroom so you won't need to share a bathroom, don't worry about that." She's barreling on with all the features of the house, really selling it. Julia should be a real estate agent, not a photographer.

"You've even got your own little pool out back," Julia tells me as she points out the plunge pool in the tiny little yard. Even that is gorgeous with the greenest palm trees against the bluest sky I've ever seen. "And there's your roomie!"

I look past the pool to the beach beyond and see the man I've been working so hard to avoid these past few days. Walking up to the back door is a slightly sweaty and completely shirtless Graham. He's breathing hard, probably back from a beach run, unaware that Julia and I are watching him from the window.

"Graham?" I sputter. "I'm not sharing with Graham."

"Come on, Cassie," Julia pleads. "I couldn't exactly put Amy or Kat over here. I needed someone immune to his, well, to that." Julia points out the window to Graham rinsing off under the outdoor shower. I shudder as I watch the water run down his chest. When he's done he positions himself in one of the lounge chairs by the pool, still glistening all over.

"I can't believe you're asking me to do this." In truth Julia has no idea exactly how much she's asking of me. Avoiding Graham was hard enough when we were home. I ignored his texts and calls, pretended not to be home when he unexpectedly dropped by. After he let me leave the club alone, I was surprisingly relieved to find he was still tenacious about getting in touch with me, even if it was just to curse me out. Not that I'd know that was his intention—I didn't listen to any of his messages and deleted every text with surgical precision. But I couldn't bring myself to block him, couldn't sever things completely. If ignoring Graham then was hard, this is going to be impossible. Resisting him when we are basically living together will be torture.

But Julia doesn't even wait for me to argue. She just walks out the back door and makes a beeline for Graham. He shades his eyes with his hand as he looks up to hear whatever she's saying. He flicks his eyes toward the villa and then back again, but other than that there's no change in his posture, no tensing of his shoulders. When Julia's finished she doesn't come back inside; she goes straight back to the golf cart and speeds off to do whatever wedding business she's got going on now. I secretly wish I had some urgent place to be because as Graham sits outside for what seems like an eternity, I start to get pretty antsy. He knows I'm in here. What the hell is he waiting for?

Graham lounges in the sun like a giant blond lizard, only getting up to dunk himself in the pool and lay back down on the lounge chair. I'm left standing in the middle of the living room, not even sure which bedroom is mine. I consider marching outside to demand that Graham tell Julia we can't share this space, or at least tell me which room is his, do something other than look all relaxed. Do something other than looking like he doesn't care I'm here.

By the time Graham decides to grace me with his presence, I'm beyond irritated. I've looked in both bedrooms and found his suitcase, all of his perfectly tailored pants hanging in the closet, the room already smelling like him. I keep myself from running my fingers over the shirts folded in the drawers and taking one for myself before I stomp across the hall to the room that must be mine. I'm shoving things on hangers and throwing my shoes into the closet when I hear the back door open. I anticipate Graham's shoulders coming through my door but instead he heads across the hall, closing his door behind him. I hear the shower come on and fume some more.

When Graham finally comes out of his bedroom he's looking handsome and smelling fabulous. I ignore him from my spot on the couch where I've been camped out for the past forty-five minutes. I debated walking down to the beach or going to the hotel bar for a drink, but the lure of Graham naked in close proximity kept me here in the living room. I look out the window at the rolling surf and try to keep myself from running over to him and jumping into his arms.

Graham doesn't seem to even notice me as he walks through the villa to the kitchen. He grabs a bottle of water out of the fridge and unscrews the top. As he brings the bottle to his lips he spares me a glance.

"Aren't you going to get ready for the rehearsal?" he asks in between massive gulps of water.

Rehearsal? Shit. We've got nonstop events every day leading up to the wedding and tonight's no exception. That explains Graham's casual but confident outfit. He's wearing a pair of dress pants that perfectly accent the muscles in his ass along with a linen shirt that has me wishing I could touch it. *Hands off, Cassie.* After we practice Julia and Zach getting hitched, we'll have to endure dinner.

"I was just about to go and change," I lie. I'd forgotten all about the dinner, forgotten about pretty much anything after I saw Graham out by the pool. I'm still covered in traveling stink and now I probably won't have time to take a shower.

"Well, you'd better hurry. We're supposed to be there in twenty minutes." He doesn't spare me a smile, barely even looks at me as he finishes his water and crushes the bottle to put it in the recycling bin next to the counter. "I'm going to start walking up there but if you want the golf cart can pick you up. You can call the front desk and tell them."

"Oh, okay." Is all I can manage as I watch him move toward the front door.

"I'll see you up there."

And then he's gone.

The rehearsal dinner is gorgeous, of course. When the backdrop for your event is the beach you really can't go wrong. Most of the wedding guests have arrived and Julia and Zach are holding hands as they circulate through the crowd. The look on Julia's face whenever she looks up at Zach is enough to give me a sugar overdose. She really is crazy in love with him. From the way he keeps grinning down at her and pulling her in for sappy kisses, the feeling looks to be mutual.

Their happiness should be contagious, but instead of getting swept up in their warm and fuzzy feelings I find myself getting more and more unhappy. Watching Graham make his way through the party doesn't help. He looks relaxed, like he's enjoying talking to all the extended family and corralling Julia's boys. He even sits with Charlie and Noah, making sure they put their napkins in their laps and wipe their mouths. He's a natural with them which doesn't go unnoticed by Zach's sisters and the other female guests. There's a constant stream of pretty ladies clustered around Graham's table all vying for his attention. I bide my time over near the bar, watching all the exploding ovaries as I sip on my cocktail.

The clink of silverware against the side of a glass focuses me back on the reason I'm supposed to be here. We're supposed to be celebrating Julia and Zach, not wallowing in the misery of a torpedoed not-really-relationship. Plenty of Zach's friends from the gym have made the trip to Mexico so when Zach's dad stands to give the first toast, it's already getting a little rowdy. They love hearing the incriminating childhood stories and are more than happy to lift their glasses once Frank finishes warning Julia that it's too late to back out now. Julia's family doesn't shy away from a little roasting either and before I know it Graham's standing up to give the speech he and I worked on.

Really, I should probably be the one giving the toast. Anyone who knows anything about Graham and Julia's history is probably holding their breath right now as they wait for Graham to speak. The ex giving a speech at the rehearsal dinner? A definite opportunity for drama. But we had decided that the only thing worse than Graham making a toast now would be having him make one at the wedding. That's fallen to me and I've got the whole thing memorized, ready to go tomorrow. At least tonight he can make use of the possibility of humor because if people can't see the ridiculousness in this situation then there's no hope for them. Having him sit on the sidelines might look like he was still upset that Julia had moved on so he's standing in front of everyone and giving Zach his approval. Not that Zach needs it, but any doubt that Graham has some secret agenda when it comes to Julia is supposed to be excised with this toast.

And Graham is fantastic. He could be a stand-up comedian the way he has people laughing at the stories of Julia as a teenager—all G rated, of course. I spent an entire afternoon helping Graham make sure this toast was perfect. Well, not an *entire* afternoon since there was also plenty of break taking while we made ourselves into naked human pretzels. I try not to think of that part of the speech writing process as Graham starts to wrap things up.

"Most of you know me from football, but I do other things too." Graham pauses just long enough to let a few people call out their disagreement. "No really, like, I can read. I know it's surprising." He lets people laugh at him for a second before starting again. "And I read to try to figure things out. To get a better understanding of things I don't know much about. I'm going to admit that I don't know much about marriage. Never had the chance to try it. But Lao Tzu—he was a Chinese philosopher for those of you less educated than myself."

Here Graham takes a sip of his beer, letting everyone

groan. He's going off script and my palms start to sweat. This isn't the speech we worked on. "Lao Tzu said that loving someone deeply gives you strength and being loved by someone gives you courage. These two obviously love each other enough to have the courage to try this marriage thing again and the strength to deal with everything that comes with it." Graham's eyes flick over to me. It's barely a look, but my entire body reacts, tingling at even this slight hint of attention. "That gives me hope that one day I'll be able to have the same courage and strength. That maybe someone will have that courage and strength because of the love I have for her." My bottom lip starts to shake. I want that for Graham, too. Even worse, I realize I want to be able to give that to him.

"I'm also a movie guy. I know, I know, you had no idea I was so versatile. I'm going to end this with a quote from a movie that I have been forced to watch several times against my will." Graham looks over at me and raises an eyebrow. A few heads turn my way. Again, he's not using what we worked on and my stomach starts to churn. "Once the main characters realize they're meant to be together in *When Harry Met Sally*, the main character Harry gives this great speech I think is relevant here. He says when you realize you want to spend the rest of your life with some-body, you want the rest of your life to start as soon as possible. So, let's hurry up and get this wedding out of the way so Julia and Zach can start the rest of their lives together."

I cover my sudden burst of emotion with my vigorous clapping and watch Graham sit back down and high five Noah and Charlie's little hands. When I beg off early, rushing back to the safety of my bedroom, no one questions my motives. Tomorrow's a big day and we all need to rest up, so no one notices that I can hardly keep my hands still or that I'm on the verge of tears.

Back at the villa I douse myself under the scalding water of a too long shower and try to get some sleep but knowing Graham's just across the hall has me tossing and turning. I could go and knock on his door, but what for? To tell him again I can't give him what he wants even though I'm realizing I might want to?

I get up to grab a bottle of water out of the kitchen fridge. The lights are out which confirms Graham's returned. I left a few lights on so it wouldn't be pitch black when he came back from dinner. Now the villa's dark and quiet as I slink down the hallway. Graham's door is closed as I rush past it, reminding myself not to linger there to try to hear him on the other side.

The light from the refrigerator casts a greenish glow all around me when I reach in to get my water. A cup of tea or something would probably be better at getting me to sleep. Actually, a shot of whiskey might do the trick but I'm trying to make as little noise as possible so those options are out.

"You can turn on the light if you need to." Graham's voice cuts through the darkness, startling me. I nearly hit my head on the handle of the freezer when I jerk out of the fridge. He's sitting on the couch, long legs extended, bare feet resting on the top of the coffee table. He's changed into a T-shirt and athletic shorts and the moonlight coming in through the bank of windows lets me see just enough of his face to know he isn't happy.

"I'm just getting water," I tell him unnecessarily. If the past few hours are any indication, he doesn't care what I'm doing.

He grunts and goes back to looking out the window.

I unscrew the top of the plastic bottle and start to walk

back to my room. I'm never going to sleep now, but what are my other options? Graham wants nothing to do with me—a situation I orchestrated to keep myself from feeling, well, anything—so I can't exactly plop down on the couch next to him. His rejection is something I never actually allowed myself to think about and it hurts more than I ever could have imagined.

"Your speech was great tonight."

Graham grunts again. He's not even bothering to answer me with words, let alone complete sentences.

"How long are you going to do this?" I whisper and Graham turns his head.

"Do what?"

"How long are you going to ignore me?" I'm close to tears and I know he can hear it.

"I'm only doing what you asked me to do."

"I didn't ask you to be mean."

Graham turns his body toward me and I can feel the anger pouring off him. "Mean? You think I'm being fucking mean? The last time I saw you I told you I love you and you left me standing in the middle of the goddamned street, Cassie. You haven't answered my texts or taken any of my calls. Have you even listened to any of the messages I left you?"

I shift uncomfortably from one foot to the other.

"That's what I thought. You want me to leave you alone so I'm leaving you alone. I can't help it if we're forced to stay here together, but I am so fucking pissed at you right now and you have the nerve to complain about me doing *exactly what you asked me to do*."

Graham isn't yelling, but that almost makes it worse. He's right; this is exactly what I told him I wanted. I'm getting exactly what I asked for.

"This is killing me, Cassie, but I'm doing it because I'll always give you what you want. Which makes me a pussy, I guess, and now I'm here and I can't look at you, or talk to you, or touch you. Congratulations for getting your way. Turns out we both hate it." I can see the muscle in his jaw working as he tries to calm himself down. He closes his eyes and rests his head against the couch cushions. "Go back to bed."

But I don't. I can't. I can't walk away even though I know I should. I should let that anger fester, give Graham the chance to hate me so he'll realize he should be with someone else. I know what's best for him in the long run and it isn't me. I'm a terrible bet for a man who wants the white picket fence and a house full of babies. An awful choice for a man who thinks people can stay in love forever. I should turn around and go back down the hall, close my bedroom door behind me, and leave Graham sitting out here alone. But my feet refuse to listen to my brain and instead I walk into the living room and stand in front of him.

"I'm serious, Cassie," he warns as he looks up at me. The hardness on his face almost scares me a little. I want him to look at me the way he usually does, not like this, with disappointment and resentment in his eyes. If I walk away now this is how he'll look at me always. This is who he'll be to me forever.

I climb into his lap, straddling him. Graham stiffens. The fury on his face is still there, but there's enough confusion to muddy it up. He's not sure what I'm doing.

Neither am I.

I take his face in my hands, expecting him to fight me. He doesn't resist but the hurt in his eyes is enough to have me treading lightly. This pain is all me, I can't blame it on anyone else, and in this moment I want it to go away more than I want to protect myself.

"I'm sorry," I whisper.

Graham shakes his head, trying to pull away from me.

"I'm so, so sorry," I tell him again and I mean it. I'm sorry for everything, for making him feel this way, for starting this in the first place, for not being strong enough to let him go. For being so scared that I can't let him love me. "You deserve someone who doesn't make you feel like this. You deserve someone who can be what you need."

"No," Graham says, finally pulling his face from my hands. "You don't get to decide that. You don't get to decide for me."

I rest my hands on his chest as it rises and falls. We sit there staring at each other, unsure what to do. He shifts underneath me and my knees dig into the fabric of the couch. His hands slide to my hips and he holds me there, still breathing like he's run a marathon.

"I get to decide what I want," Graham whispers. It's more forceful than I expect, possessive, and when one of his hands moves up to cup the back of my head, I know I welcome what's coming next.

Graham presses his forehead to mine, breathing still ragged, and closes his eyes. He slides his nose against mine but still doesn't kiss me. I whimper, and the side of his mouth twitches. I feel him growing hard underneath me, the fabric of his athletic shorts and the thin cotton of my pajama bottoms barely separating us. I angle my mouth toward his, but Graham avoids me, dragging his lips along my jaw line and then down the column of my neck. He nips and sucks there, holding my head in place with one hand and using the other to force my hips down against him.

I grind against him, panting, as he reaches for the hem

of my T-shirt and pulls it over my head. He pops a nipple into his mouth, dragging his teeth along the nub, and I arch my back to get closer to him, pulling at the short hairs on the back of his neck. When I move to get his shirt off he bats my hand away, a muffled *"nu huh"* escaping from his lips as he trails his tongue over to my other breast. He lets me wiggle my fingers under the cotton but makes no move to pull the fabric over his head.

Graham's hand darting down the front of my pants surprises me. He barely grazes the skin and I'm writhing around looking for relief. Normally Graham would laugh at this, tease me for being so eager, but tonight he's not joking. The anger from earlier's just below the surface as he pulls his fingers through my wetness, working me into a quivering pile of nerves. He raises up just enough to slide his shorts down over his hips before he forces my pants down over the back of my ass. They stick around the tops of my thighs, keeping me from opening my legs any farther. He pulls his head back to look me in the eye before I feel him position himself at my opening and drive himself in.

The sudden thrust has me gasping, but Graham's eyes never leave my face. My bare chest slides against his still covered one as he uses his hands on my hips to control the tempo. He takes his hands off me only to rip his shirt off and throw it into the darkness of the living room. Again I tilt my face toward his to kiss him, but he turns away, frustrating me.

"It sucks not to get to make the decision for yourself, doesn't it?" he asks me as he lifts his hips again and again. When he finally turns his face toward me and slams his lips against mine there's nothing gentle about the way he kisses me. I answer back with the same intensity and ride him like it would kill me to stop. We're frantic, rocking against each other, unable to get close enough. He presses me hard to his chest, his fingers digging into my back. We're fused together as tightly as possible, every movement making me more and more certain that Graham's body fits mine like no one else's ever will.

We finish like animals, biting and clawing at each other, crying out loud enough for the neighbors to hear. I wrap my arms around Graham's sweaty torso and try to catch my breath with my head on his shoulder. He breathes into my ear, as affected as I am.

"What do we do now?" he asks me and already I can hear the hesitation in his voice.

"We try to make it through this wedding." I don't lift my head. I don't want to see his reaction to my non-answer.

Graham lifts me off his lap and sets me down next to him. Without a word he stands, pulls his shorts back up over his hips, and walks to his bedroom.

"You do know that once this wedding's over you're going to have to come up with a new excuse to push me away."

He slams the door behind him and leaves me half-naked on the couch.

28

Graham

I'm sitting in the living room staring at the floor between my feet. I've been waiting out here for what feels like forever, hearing Cassie getting ready in her room across the hall. I've thought about knocking at least a million times, but every time I manage to convince myself to move closer to her door, I lose my nerve. What if she answered the door in her underwear or wrapped in a towel? As it is I can barely keep myself from pawing all over her. She came back from having her hair and make-up done with Julia and immediately locked herself in her bedroom. The sound of the bolt turning gave me a clear signal that she doesn't want to be bothered, but now we're running late. The wedding party is supposed to be on the beach for photos at three and it's nearly ten till now. If I don't get Cassie out the door in the next two minutes we'll be holding everything up and I don't want to be accused of doing anything to ruin Julia's wedding. After last night I'm dangerously close to doing something that's sure to make things less than perfect on Julia's perfect day. A day that I'd always hoped would include me meeting her at the altar although for the life of me I can't remember why.

I pull myself up and out of the chair, dragging my feet all the way to her bedroom door. I can already smell her spicy perfume; the whole villa is starting to smell like her and I know when she opens the door, I'll get a cloud of Cassie right in the face. I take a deep breath and let my knuckles hit the door. One, two, three taps. I wait, hearing her scurrying around on the other side.

"Just a second!" Cassie calls out. She curses softly as I stand rooted to the spot. I imagine her naked on the other side, imagine her waiting for me instead of avoiding me. When the door flies open she's surprised to see me still standing there, closer to the door than any normal person should be, my hand still resting in the spot where my knuckles landed.

"Uh." I sound like an idiot but it's all I can get to come out of my mouth. Cassie's standing in front of me in a bright purple dress, her legs on full display. The dress hugs her curves and highlights the freckles on her shoulders, now even more noticeable with a hint of suntan. My eyes follow the tiny straps down to the deep V that's barely containing her breasts. Cassie clears her throat and I will my eyes back up to her face. "You look…"

"Crazy, I know. The flower in the hair is too much, but Julia's making us all wear one. I told her it looked ridiculous but she's the boss today, I guess."

I try to interrupt, but I'm so distracted by Cassie's mouth that I have a hard time formulating a reasonable thought. Other parts of me are starting to have a hard time as well and I hope Cassie doesn't notice the growing bulge in the front of my pants.

"And I'm regretting the dress. We're all in purple, but I

think maybe I should have chosen something more conservative. Zach's sisters chose more, I don't know, they're showing less skin. Now I look—"

"Beautiful. I was going to say you look beautiful."

She freezes. If there's one thing I've learned about Cassie it's that if you give her a chance, she'll always find a way to disparage her looks. But she's beautiful. All the time, but especially right now with the sun coming in through the bedroom window and her cheeks flushed from my compliment. I reach my hand out and trace the line of her jaw. She stays still, hands at her sides. I slide my thumb over her lips, careful not to smudge her lipstick. I'd like to be able to get her messy, but I know there's no time for that even if she'd let me. She parts her lips and I let my thumb rest there for a split second, our gazes locked. "You look perfect."

Cassie blinks, breaking the spell. She takes a step back and lets out a ragged breath. "We're going to be late," she says, eyeing me like a rabbit about to run.

"Yeah, we should get going so we don't mess up the photo schedule," I agree. "Are you ready?"

Cassie closes her eyes. "I need you to zip me," she tells me, her voice barely a whisper, and when she turns around, I can see an open expanse of her creamy skin between the teeth of the zipper. "I can't reach all the way to the top and I can't get the hook by myself."

I step closer to her and she flinches before I even touch her. "Relax," I murmur even as my own heart starts beating wildly in my chest. I reach for the zipper and let my fingers linger on her back. Her skin is soft and warm just the way I knew it would be, just the way it always is. I fight the instinct to move the zipper south and let my fingertips graze her back as I watch the metal teeth close against her. Once I get to the top it takes me a minute to successfully close the tiny hook, my fingers too big to handle the little pieces with much skill. I let my eyes wander down her back to the outline of her ass and I wonder what she'd do if I pressed myself up against her. My cock responds to the thought of Cassie warm and willing, and I have to remind myself that now isn't the time or the place to push my luck. I lean forward and plant a kiss on her shoulder, feeling her twitch at the unexpected contact. Cassie waits, barely breathing until I finally finish and remove my hands from her back.

"Cassie…" My hands itch to be back on her skin, and I flex them open and closed at my sides.

When she turns her eyes are wide. "You can't do that," she tells me, her voice hard and serious. "Not today."

"Sorry," I apologize even though we both know I don't mean it.

"Let's just get through this, okay?" She's pleading with me. Begging me not to let everyone in on our secret. Sassy Cassie's terrified of me blowing our cover with my roaming hands. But more than that she's just plain terrified, afraid of whatever's keeping her from letting herself be with me. "Today's supposed to be about Julia and Zach; I don't want this stuff with us to interfere with that."

"Okay." It comes out flat. "So that's the angle now? That we don't want to ruin their day?" I sigh. Cassie's got a new excuse. "We should go."

Cassie nods and moves to grab her bag, a tiny little thing that can't have room for much more than our villa key.

"Why do you need a bag?" I ask her. "I've got a key in my pocket. You don't want to keep up with that all night." I don't know why I'm discussing her purse with her, acting like we're a couple. She can do what she likes, obviously.

"There's lipstick in here too." She opens the bag to let me see inside. "I'll need that, especially for the pictures."

I reach out my hand. "Give it to me. I can put it in my pocket." Cassie stares at my outstretched hand but then slides the tube of lipstick in it. I don't know why I'm asking for it or why she's giving it. Now she'll have to find me all night when she wants to touch up her make-up. She'll have to find me when she wants to come home.

"You look nice." Cassie reaches out to straighten my jacket. I'm not wearing a tie and she lets her pinky finger skim the open edge of my shirt collar. "I like these suits for a beach wedding."

I grunt. "Kind of ridiculous to have to wear a suit but then take off our shoes." The spot where Cassie's finger touched me burns.

Cassie smiles. "We can't stand in our shoes in the sand."

I shrug. "Let's go, gorgeous." I hold out my hand to her. Cassie frowns down at it until I clench my fingers into a fist and shove it into my pocket. Her lipstick rolls around between my fingers. "Fine. After you." I gesture toward the front door and she moves toward it giving me a view of her swaying hips and her muscular calves. I follow after her, her heels clicking on the hardwood floor. Getting ready to spend all day not being able to touch her the way I want to, trying not to look at her *that way*. This is going to be torture.

29

Cassie

"How about another one of just Cassie and Graham?"

For a day that's supposed to be all about Zach and Julia there sure are a lot of photos of the wedding party going on here. I try to send a telepathic signal to the bride that this might be taking things a little too far, but Julia doesn't get the message. She stands behind the photographer, back-seat driving his attempts to do his job. So far she's criticized the lighting, his choice of lens, and the fact that his camera's a Nikon. She prefers Cannon. You would think it was a divide that would rival the East coast versus West coast rap feud from the way she keeps bringing it up. Julia should be taking her own photos if she's going to micro-manage him. I'm sure having to be the photographer at another photographer's wedding is one of the circles of hell.

All this posing with Graham is pretty hellish as well, truth be told. After last night we're even less sure how to act. He's apologized for every single accidental touch and twice for looking at me, so standing impossibly close and pretending to smile over and over again is uncomfortable for both of us.

"How about this one with the beach in the background?" Julia confers with the photographer again and while they argue about specifics, I try to work some of the kinks out of my neck. I barely slept at all last night and had to be up early for wedding stuff with Julia. Not even the sound of the waves outside could drown out the angry silence of having Graham fuming one room away. At least he's speaking to me this morning even if it is somewhat monosyllabic.

"Your neck hurt?" he asks without looking at me.

"A little."

"Did you sleep on it funny?" He keeps his eyes trained on the surf.

"Maybe. I didn't get much sleep."

At that Graham turns his head, a flash of anger passing over his face before he goes back to calm and collected neutral. "Sorry to hear that."

I almost expect him to offer to rub my neck for me as inappropriate as that would be. I close my eyes and imagine his strong hand on the back of my neck, long fingers working out the knots there. But Graham's hands stay at his sides until he crosses his arms over his chest, huffing a little in impatience.

"I fucking hate this," he says under his breath just as Julia comes walking back to us. It would be easy to interpret that to mean seeing her in her wedding dress or any other thing about having his ex get married off again, but for once I know that's not what he's talking about. The jealous part of me would love to believe that he's still wanting Julia, then I could be angry or sad and blame Graham for the way things are right now. But he's not even looking at her, he's still focused on the water, the muscles in his jaw ticking away.

I fucking hate this, too.

"Okay, guys, move over here," Julia orders and I groan like I'm in kindergarten and about to throw myself on the floor for a tantrum.

"Haven't we done enough of these already?" I whine.

"Last one, I promise," Julia tells me unconvincingly and starts to set us up like Graham's my prom date.

"You have to get closer to her," the photographer yells. "Come on, she won't bite."

The strangled sound that comes out of Graham's mouth keeps me from looking at his face. I do bite and he knows it. In fact, under his shirt right now are several marks that might prove it. My face flames as he goes into a coughing fit.

"Do you need water?" Julia asks as Graham bends at the waist and catches his breath.

He waves her off. "I'm fine. Just got a little choked up, I guess." He straightens back up and wipes the tears from his eyes, muttering, *"Doesn't bite, my ass"* under his breath.

"I've never bitten your ass," I whisper back at him and he actually almost smiles before he remembers he's busy hating me today.

"Now put your arm around her."

Graham's arm comes woodenly around my waist.

"Not like that," Julia coaches from behind the photographer. "Like you like each other, not like someone asked you to give your great aunt a kiss on the mouth. Good lord, Graham, this shouldn't be so difficult."

Graham moves closer and lets his arm relax. His fingers slide along my hip as he pulls me up beside him. I'm close enough to be able to smell him, if I turn my head my nose'll be in the crook of his neck.

"Now turn a little toward him, Cass."

That's the last thing I want to do.

"And then put one hand on his chest. That looks great."

Under my palm Graham's heart beats steady and strong, the warmth of his chest making my fingers relax. I tilt my face up toward his and he grunts down at me, his lips twitching just enough to let me know he's thinking about kissing me. It would be so easy to lean forward on my tiptoes just enough to put my lips on his. But I won't, not here. And Graham won't either, not in front of everyone and not with almost certain photographic evidence. I give him the tiniest smile and he lets the corners of his mouth shoot up just long enough for everyone else to think he returned it. Then we turn our faces toward the camera to endure the longest thirty seconds ever.

When we're done Graham slides his arm back around, letting his fingers graze the top of my ass. I don't protest so he slides them down lower until he's able to give me a squeeze. Then he stalks off without a word.

30

Graham

Keeping my distance like Cassie asked isn't easy. There's the excruciating photo shoot that requires us to pose with the rest of the bridal party. Then we're forced to stand next to each other for the entire ceremony. I stare at her shoulder and focus on breathing in and out, keeping my hands at my sides so I don't accidentally reach out to run my fingers along the little patch of freckles positioned next to the strap of her dress. Noah and Charlie provide a welcome distraction after they fidget their way down the aisle and come to stand between us. When they move to stand with Zach and Julia for the vows I go back to my fixation on Cassie's shoulder.

At the reception I don't ask her to dance. There's no way I could keep my hands to myself and there's no way everyone here wouldn't know how I feel about her. Everyone except Cassie, that is, since she never lets me tell her. I spend most of my time entertaining Charlie and Noah, dancing with the contingent of moms, and hanging around the bar. I'm getting another refill when I notice Cassie sitting with one of Zach's buddies. I linger at my end of the bar, watching them, trying not to let the burning ember of jealousy get the better of me. She's laughing at whatever stupid thing he's saying, tipping her head back enough that I can see him peering down the front of her dress. Inside I seethe, but I stay where I am.

"How's it going over here? Having a good time holding up the bar?" Julia's father appears at my elbow. You would never guess he's as stealthy as he is, but he's managed to surprise me in many compromising situations since I was a teenager. It no longer catches me off guard that he can materialize out of nowhere, especially when I'm in danger of making a bad decision.

"Sure," I tell him, never taking my eyes off Cassie. "Do you need drinks?" I motion for the bartender closest to us as Cassie's buddy orders a round of shots from the bartender at the other end. They throw them back, Cassie in good time girl mode, her hair spilling over her shoulder. When her sidekick's hand comes out to brush a curl back from her neck, I have to grip the bar top to keep from moving over to them and ripping his arm off.

"I do need to keep Frannie in Old Fashioneds," Steve tells me, taking one look at my face and turning to see what's got me annoyed. "Which one is that?" he asks before ordering his drinks.

"Hmm?" I act like I have no idea what he's talking about, but Steve's no fool. He follows my line of sight and tips his chin in the direction of Cassie and her new friend.

"That's one of Zach's friends over there with Cassie, right? Which one is he?" Steve leans against the bar as the bartender works behind him, mixing and shaking before sliding two glasses over.

"That one's Travis," I grind out, still working to be the

good boy I've promised I'd be. It's getting harder and harder the longer I watch Cassie flirt with someone I know is a horrible choice.

"That's Travis?" Steve lets out a low whistle. "I thought we weren't too fond of him."

That's the understatement of the year, especially right now as Travis scoots his bar stool closer to her, effectively caging Cassie in with his legs. "We don't like him at all," I concede, staying where I am, digging my fingers into the edge of the bar so tightly I'm surprised there aren't permanent marks.

"Then you should probably go and get your girl." Steve sips on his drink.

I turn my face toward him. "Cassie's not my girl."

"Well, she could be if you'd stop waiting around for her to make the decision. Don't act so surprised. Anyone can see you mooning over her. If angry looks could kill, Travis'd be dead ten times over. And your agent is terrible at keeping secrets."

I sigh. Fucking sigh. Obviously I've got it bad. There's no use trying to hide it from the man who's been the most stable male figure in my life. Steve knows. And if Steve knows then other people know too even if Cassie wants to pretend this is all still a big secret. "She asked me to leave her alone, at least until after the wedding."

"And how do you feel about that?" he asks over the rim of his glass.

"Not great, but I get it. She doesn't want to add drama to Julia's wedding."

"And how do you feel about *that*?" Steve gestures toward Cassie and Travis and the ever-shrinking space between them.

"Also not great." I take a gulp of my drink. The whiskey

scorches as it heads down my throat, but even that's a welcome feeling compared to the anger slowly building in my chest. I watch as Travis orders them another round of shots and then lets his hand slide to the spot where Cassie's dress leaves the creamy skin of her back exposed. When he does that, I feel my hands release the bar.

"Graham," Steve calls after me. "No fist fights at this wedding." I give him a nod as he raises his glass toward me. I'll try to settle this without punching Travis in the face.

I'm next to them in two seconds, frowning at the offending hand. Cassie looks up, her face clouding when she sees me. I know what I've promised her, but I can't keep myself from grabbing her bar stool and yanking it back to put a little space between them. Travis' hand falls back into his lap where it belongs. I put my hand on Cassie's shoulder and leave it there despite the annoyed look she gives me.

"Hey, Graham," Travis slurs at me. He's three sheets to the wind. What the hell is Cassie doing over here with this jerk?

"You two know each other?" Cassie asks, turning in her seat to give me another pointed look. She's not happy I've interrupted and keeps trying to wiggle out of my grasp. I keep my hand on her. There's no fucking way I'm going to give Travis another opportunity to touch her again.

"Yeah, Graham comes to the gym sometimes when we have open sparring and stuff. He's not half bad." Travis' explanation has Cassie raising an eyebrow.

"You go to Zach's gym? *To spar*?" She doesn't seem convinced. It doesn't help that I've never mentioned this to her. I'm going to have to explain myself later. That's a conversation I dread having, but for now I've got to get her away from Travis and back where she belongs.

"I used to. I haven't gone in a while." It's the truth, but Cassie scoffs, reaching for her drink.

"We miss you, man," Travis tells me as he clamps a hand on my shoulder. "You should stop by when we get back. Now that you and Zach are like brothers-in-law or something."

I ignore Travis and his inane comments. Cassie at least has the good sense to roll her eyes at his stupid attempt at a joke. "You two look cozy over here," I say. "I didn't know you knew each other."

"We met at the engagement party," Cassie volunteers and slides her hand over to squeeze Travis' knee. I all but lurch forward to remove her hand. *Cool it, Graham. No fist fights.* Another promise getting harder and harder to keep.

"We're just hanging out. I'm trying to convince Cassie that this is the perfect night for skinny dipping." Travis gives Cassie a suggestive glance and her cheeks pink up a bit. "We were just about to head down to the beach."

"To go skinny dipping?" I can barely get the words out. The idea of Cassie slithering out of her dress and running into the surf naked with Travis has me clenching my jaw hard enough to crack a tooth.

I'm pretty sure Cassie's not up for a skinny dipping adventure, but she stays silent. Maybe she's as shocked as I am that Travis is playing the douche card so early in the evening. Maybe she's thinking about taking him up on his offer. Regardless, it's time for this shit to be finished.

"Actually, I just came over to see if Cassie was ready to go home." I give her shoulder a squeeze. "I'm pretty beat."

Cassie swivels to face me. "You're *beat*?" she asks me, narrowing her eyes.

"Yep. Really beat," I tell her and watch her head tilt,

considering what I'm telling her. "And since I've got the only key..." I leave that there for Travis to consider.

"You guys are rooming together?" He's beginning to catch on.

"Not really," Cassie clarifies. "We're sharing a villa but we've got separate bedrooms and bathrooms." She glares at me.

"Well, if you're tired, I can make sure Cassie gets home safe," Travis volunteers. "I'll take good care of her. Scout's honor."

I'm pretty sure this asshole was never a boy scout. "Thanks, but I think I'd feel better if Cassie came with me. You ready to go, baby?"

She bristles at this, as expected. I wait for her snappy retort about how she's not my baby, bracing for a possible punch in the gut and the opportunity to watch her leave the bar hand-in-hand with Travis. He's waiting too, unsure how Cassie will decide to play things. I know she's weighing her options, considering how best to handle me and the testosterone I've brought over here. If she goes with him, I'll be right behind them even though I know better. Steve never stipulated that there couldn't be a fight on the beach. If Travis so much as touches her again—or if he mentions the naked swimming—I won't be able to control my fists. Already, the hand I'm not using to mark Cassie as my territory is balled dangerously tight. Travis might spend plenty of time learning tricks from Zach at the gym, but I've got a good thirty pounds on him, all of it muscle. And I have the added advantage of not being so drunk as not to understand that I've stepped in a hornets' nest. Which Travis doesn't seem to understand. At all.

As if reading my mind, Cassie shifts gears. She slides her

hand in mine and fakes a huge yawn. "I am pretty tired," she concedes. "Not *beat*, exactly, but I could sleep." She gives me an eye roll. "Zach and Julia are gone already so I guess we're off the clock."

"Yeah, we are," I agree. "But we still have to get up tomorrow for the brunch in the morning. Can't miss that."

"That is pretty early." Cassie's suddenly amenable to whatever I suggest. "We should probably get back to the villa. And I'd hate to have to wake you to get in."

We're the most reasonable people on the planet. Cassie stands, keeping her fingers laced in mine. "Thanks for hanging out, Travis. It was good to see you again."

"Sure. We should do it again once we're back in town," Travis tells her, glassy-eyed and red-cheeked from the alcohol. Of course he could be sunburned. He seems like the kind of guy to forget the sunscreen.

"I don't know about that, buddy." It comes out more forcefully than it should and I wait for Cassie to react. When she doesn't even flinch, I take that as permission to plow on ahead. "Cassie doesn't have too much free time these days." I stare him down, hoping that he gets the hint.

It takes a minute, but then Travis' face nearly explodes in recognition. "Ah, dude. I... I didn't know. I wouldn't have... I mean, shit." He squirms a little in his seat and I enjoy every second of it.

"No problem," I tell him. The not-so-subtle subtext being *stay the fuck away from her*. "We'll see you tomorrow." Then I all but drag Cassie out into the night.

The walk back to our villa isn't a long one, but as I wait for Cassie to speak it feels like an eternity. I count the waves crashing on the beach to keep myself from blurting out something stupid, but I'm only delaying the inevitable.

Cassie won't want to hear anything but an apology and I'm not about to tell her I'm sorry for getting her away from Travis or for letting him in on our secret. Shockingly she leaves her hand wrapped up with mine until we reach our front door. It's still warm enough that we could leave the windows open tonight if we wanted to, could even maybe jump in our little pool out back. But those are things a real couple would think about, not two people who are pretending not to even care if the other one exists.

I pull the key card from my pocket and my fingers hit the tube of lipstick Cassie gave me earlier. The one she needed repeatedly throughout the day, ensuring I knew where she was all the time. I couldn't have dreamed up a better excuse to follow her around. "I should give this back before I forget," I say and hand it over. She reaches for the silver tube and her fingertips scrape my outstretched palm. Now we're facing each other under the light of the porch, both hands touching.

"Why did you do that back there?" Cassie asks, her hand still lingering with mine.

"Do what?" There are so many possible things she could object to or question about what just happened that I'm afraid to volunteer too much too soon.

"Why did you use the safe word?"

"The safe word?" I feign ignorance.

"Yes, the safe word. The word Julia and I use as our S.O.S. You told me you were *beat*. You know that's the safe word."

"Is it?"

"Don't play dumb, Graham. I know Julia told you, since you're all safety first. But it's for emergencies, not just to get your way."

"That was an emergency!" Cassie has no idea how much of an emergency it was about to become if she had run off to get naked on the beach with that douche. "You were about to go skinny dipping with that asshole."

"He's not that bad. Nothing would have happened." She removes her hand and palms the lipstick.

"You don't know him the way I know him." There's no way to get her to understand without spelling it out. "He is the worst womanizer of the bunch. You should hear how he talks about the women he sleeps with. Total dick."

"And you know this from the times you went to Zach's gym, right? To spar? Is that what they call it?" Cassie glares. "You never told me you were doing that."

"I haven't done it in a while." I stall. "And it isn't like it was some big secret."

"Does Julia know you were doing that?"

It's a reasonable question, one I could easily deflect, but instead I quickly give Cassie more ammunition. "No, but Steve knew."

"Steve? What does Julia's dad have to do with any of this?" Her other hand retreats and finds its familiar spot on her hip.

"Nothing," I lie. "I'm just saying it wasn't a secret." This does nothing to make Cassie relax. She swats me away when I reach for her hand.

"You were going to Zach's gym and you were talking about it with Steve."

"Sure. I mean, not talking about it exactly. I'm sure Zach told Julia. Like I said, it wasn't a big thing." I'm starting to sweat.

"Were you and Steve spying on Zach?" Cassie asks with just a hint of disbelief.

"No," I sputter out. "Not exactly." It had been Steve's

idea. After Julia's first husband turned out to have a secret life, we both agreed it wouldn't hurt to check Zach out a little. Not spying exactly, but just getting to know his friends, seeing him away from Julia and her family. The gym was the logical choice. He'd invited me to the informal nights he put together. I'd always declined because hanging out with the guy who was sleeping with Julia? No thanks. But Steve had made the point that I was the best candidate for the job. If Zach was an ass, if he had any secrets, it'd all come out with that group of guys. So I had swallowed my aversion and joined them for a couple of sessions.

"What do you mean 'not exactly'? Either you were there to wrestle, which I already know is highly unlikely, or you were there to check up on Zach. I'm not an idiot. You and Steve wanted to keep tabs on him. Get to know his friends, right?"

"Something like that." I know I've basically just signed my death warrant here. Cassie will be furious at the deception on Julia's behalf. She'll rail against the way Steve and I inserted ourselves into Julia's private life, the way we took advantage of Zach's good nature.

"And?" Cassie asks, both hands on hips now.

"And what?" Again, she could be asking about anything and I know I'm already dangerously close to the edge here.

"And what did you find out?"

"They got married today, didn't they? If I'd found out something scandalous Steve never would have let her go through with it. Zach's a nice guy. Genuinely nice. I can't say the same for all of his friends."

"I'm sure you were disappointed." Cassie avoids eye contact and instead focuses on the still unopened door to our villa.

"Disappointed? Why would I be disappointed?"

"Because if there'd been a problem you could be with Julia now. That would have fixed everything for you."

"Cassie." I don't know what to say here. Can't seem to convince her all of that is in the past. I might have wanted to be with Julia before, but now all I see is Cassie. Only her.

"It's okay," she whispers before finding her voice again. "It's fine."

"No, it isn't. You aren't understanding. I was only trying to protect her from what happened last time. I had feelings for her, you know that and I can't change it, but I don't have those same feelings now."

Cassie looks unconvinced. "But even after she'd rejected you again. Even after she chose someone else, you still tried to protect her. You still went out of your way to make sure she was safe."

"Of course." This is what she's focused on? "She's my friend. Hell, she's my family. I'd do anything to make sure she and the boys are safe. That her parents are taken care of."

"It must be nice to have someone to look out for you like that." She says it sarcastically and I'm thrown.

"What are you talking about?"

"You and Steve cooked up some sort of FBI level plan to get information about her fiancé and his friends. You race over whenever she needs help—whenever her father needs help. I've never had anyone do that for me."

"Are you kidding me, Cassie?" I almost shout. "What do you think I just did? What do you think I've been doing for the past few months? I've been trying to get you to let me in —to let me take care of you. How can you not see that? I was ready to beat the shit out of that guy tonight. That's got nothing to do with Julia. That's got everything to do with you."

Cassie's eyes widen and her mouth flies open. She shakes her head. "No," she tells me. "No."

I take her face in my hands and look into her eyes. "Yes," is all I tell her. "Yes, Cassie." And then I kiss her right there on the porch where anyone can see.

31

Cassie

Have you ever had the feeling someone's watching you? Where you can feel their eyes boring into you, exposing whatever weakness you have? Welcome to my morning because when my eyes snap open, they catch Graham's blue eyes fixated on me.

"Holy shit, Graham!" I startle.

Graham laughs, propped up on one elbow.

"What are you doing? Watching me sleep?" I can't decide if it's creepy or endearing, but Graham shows no signs of self-consciousness.

"I was waiting for you to wake up so I could do this." He leans in and kisses the bridge of my nose. "I needed to taste those freckles right there."

"Oh, those particular freckles were the ones you want- ed," I tease and stretch my arms up over my head. Graham watches the movement, his eyes scanning over my nearly naked body. The sheet we're tangled up in does little to cover either of us up.

"I also like these over here," he murmurs as he moves to my shoulder, planting his lips there. "And these over here." He trails lower, moving across my collarbone and over to my breast. "There are a lot of freckles that I haven't gotten to sample yet."

I let Graham slide over me, enjoying the way his mouth feels on my skin, the slight tickle of his teeth when he nips at me, the feel of his tongue as he explores my body. "Don't get too carried away. We've got a brunch to get to."

Graham groans. "This wedding crap is seriously affecting my plans for this morning." His mouth's still pressed to my nipple.

I shift slightly to look at my phone. "We've got forty-five minutes to get up, get rid of our sex hair, and get to breakfast before we run the risk of having one of Zach's sisters come banging on the door." Or someone else. Julia. Her father.

"I don't have sex hair," Graham tells me as he continues to kiss every inch of my chest. "And I like you with sex hair."

I look down at his blond head. Even all mussed up he looks gorgeous. "It takes you five minutes to get ready. I'm going to need a little more time than that to tame what I've got going on over here." Even if that's the last thing I want to do. Even if I'd rather stay here in this bed with him all day.

"We don't have time to do this the way I would like, but I think I can finish what I have planned and still give you enough time to get ready. What do you say? Willing to see how well I work under a time constraint?" Graham lifts his head and gives me one of his dazzling smiles. I'm pretty sure no one says no to that.

I close my eyes and surrender to the feel of his body over mine, his hand sliding lower. It's thrilling and terrifying to discover how well he knows my body. His fingers drag down my belly and settle between my legs.

"I actually have an idea," he says.

"Mmhm," I manage because whatever he's going to suggest I'm going to agree to right now.

"What if we don't leave this afternoon?"

I open one eye and look at him. "What do you mean 'don't leave'?"

"What if we stay for a few more days? Just you and me?" He's serious.

"Here? In Mexico?"

"I can move our flights if you can organize your shifts. I'll check with the front desk and see if we can keep the villa. If not, I'll find another place for us to stay."

I imagine staying longer, staying with Graham like we're a real couple, and I feel that terrible little flutter in my belly. "I don't think I can answer that question with your hand where it is," I tell him, but his fingers don't stop and the idea of taking a few extra days starts to get all mixed up with the physical feeling of Graham and how he's working my body.

"I'm hoping to distract you into saying yes," he whispers, his mouth moving to my other breast.

"Could we actually do that?"

"Sure. And we could do all the things we can't do at home. We can go out in public, we can stay in bed all day, I can kiss you in front of whoever I want whenever I want." I feel him smile against my skin and I want to feel that over and over again. I want to be able to say yes and see him smile because I've been able to give him what he wants. Just this once.

My orgasm surprises me, scattering any thought of telling Graham no. I fist the sheets and writhe against his hand, addicted to the way he makes me feel, the way he takes care of me. As I come down, his mouth meets mine and I open to him, letting his tongue slide against mine. When we break apart he gives me another peck on the nose.

"I'll take that as a yes."

I start to have doubts as soon as we walk onto the patio. Graham insisted on holding my hand on the walk over even as I pointed out the obvious questions we'd have to deal with if anyone saw us. I could feel the bliss from this morning seeping out with every step we took. The closer we got to the pavilion with its heaping trays of food and the sound of chatter from the other guests, the less secure I felt in the decision to try this Mexican vacation idea with Graham.

When he finally gave in and dropped my hand, I was surprised by the wave of regret that almost knocked me over. Would it have been so terrible to walk in together and just face everyone? Would Graham have done it if I had a little more confidence in us? In him? I've been avoiding relationships so I can keep from feeling this confusion so why am I even entertaining the idea of being with him?

Zach's sisters look a little worse for wear along with the rest of the under forty set. Everyone must have been hitting the bar pretty hard last night. Some of the older guests could have used a few extra hours of sleep as well. Tell me again why there are all these events scheduled that no one really gives a flip about? We should all still be in bed, myself included, especially if I could get back to this morning again with Graham's arms wrapped tightly around me.

Julia runs up to hug me still buzzing from yesterday's adrenaline. "Good morning!" she yells. "Thanks for making it to this. Zach and I had bets on whether you'd be able to get out of bed. I had faith in you, of course." She pauses and zeroes in on the skin near my collarbone. "Is that a hickey?"

My hand flies to the spot where her eyes are resting and I pull my hair forward to cover the offending section of skin. How did I not notice that this morning? Oh yeah, maybe I missed it because I was rushing to get ready after prolonging my morning activities with Graham. It's hard to take a really fast shower when someone keeps convincing you to help them soap up just one more time.

"It's sunburn," I lie, not very convincingly.

"Sure it is." Julia smirks. "I'd love to tell you I had a bet on that too, but I don't think anyone would have taken me up on that one."

I scowl at her.

"So..."

"So what?" I ask, still trying to keep my alleged hickey covered.

"You aren't going to give me any details?" Julia waits patiently.

Luckily, or unluckily I suppose, Graham chooses this moment to come back from wherever he's been hiding. "Details about what?" he asks, shoving his big hands in his pockets.

"Cassie has a hickey," Julia announces with a little too much enthusiasm.

I have to give Graham a little credit; he doesn't flinch. "A hickey? Let me see." He meets my eyes and gives me that look that begs me to trust him and even though I'm still getting used to it, I do. I pull my hair back to expose the skin, giving both Graham and Julia the chance to look the spot over. Graham reaches a hand forward and rubs his thumb over my collarbone. Our eyes lock and I forget that Julia's even there, forget that we're in public as the rough skin of his hand skates over the place his mouth had been less than an hour ago.

"Looks like sunburn to me," he tells Julia, pulling his hand back before looking at me again. "We should find you some aloe and make sure you keep some sunscreen on. We don't want more of that, do we?" And then he cocks one horribly suggestive eyebrow at me.

I feel my entire body heat from the suggestion of having *more of that*. Every inch of me screeches *please, please* even as I keep my hands clenched by my sides, my breathing becoming a little ragged.

"Can I steal Cassie for a minute?" Graham asks Julia like it's the most innocent thing in the world. "We've got last minute wedding party stuff to iron out." He gives her a wink and she gives his upper arm a punch.

"Whatever. If you want to rescue Cassie, I'll let you. Maybe she'll tell you who she spent last night cuddled up with. I've got to get back to hitting all these tables anyway. I'll try to catch you guys before Zach and I leave." And then Julia's off again, fluttering between the tables like a butterfly, catching Zach's hand as he comes over to land a kiss on her neck.

"Should I have told her there wasn't much cuddling?" Graham asks, moving in a bit too close to keep up our just friends charade. Not that we'll be able to keep that up much longer if Graham keeps telling everyone who gets too close to me that he has some sort of claim. I see Travis from across the room and wonder if he's told anyone about last night.

"Earth to Cassie. Focus, baby."

"I'm listening."

"But you're looking at Travis. Now I'm regretting not

breaking his nose last night." Graham's voice is teasing, but there's an edge there. He's still not over it.

"Well, now you've got my full attention." I bat my eyelashes up at him. I'm no good at acting sweet and attentive. Graham's mouth twists into a smirk.

"I checked on the villa and we can keep it if we want to stay," he tells me with just a hint of trepidation. "And I looked at changing the flights. All doable. Are you in?"

I've got two choices here: I can give into the fear or I can ignore it. As Graham waits for my answer, I can feel the part of me that wants to keep my heart safe try to claw its way out of my throat. Saying no should be easy. Watching Graham's disappointment should be something I'm used to by now. I've done it over and over since he made the mistake of hooking up with me.

I surprise us both when I give Graham an enthusiastic nod.

Graham looks like I've given him the best present ever and manages to restrict his celebratory moves to one small fist pump. "You won't regret this, Cassie. I promise."

That's what I'm afraid of.

32

Graham

"Where are we going?" The slight hesitation in Cassie's voice has me tugging a little harder on her hand.

"If I tell you it'll ruin the surprise."

"I hate surprises." Cassie stops walking so I stop too, looking at her scowling face.

"But *I* like surprising people and I think you'll like this one." I give her hand a yank and pull her up against me. "As much as I'd like to drag you back to bed, we should at least leave the room once or twice, don't you think?" Cassie melts against me and tips her face up, sticking her bottom lip out. I lean down and take her pouting lip between my teeth and give it a nip. "Better put that back where it belongs."

Cassie sighs and rubs her nose against my chest. "Fine. Let's get this over with," she says into the cotton of my T-shirt before untangling herself from my arms.

I lead her down the wooden dock in front of us, scanning the back ends of the first few boats we pass. When I find the one I'm looking for I pull Cassie along behind me until we're flush with the side. "Here we go," I announce and make a move to lift Cassie to deposit her on the boat's deck.

Cassie squirms in my arms. "You can't just climb on someone else's boat, Graham," she protests, twisting to keep me from taking her off the dock.

"This isn't someone else's boat. This is our boat. Well, for today." A tall man chooses this moment to appear from inside the boat. I wave and he waves back, coming toward us.

"Mr. Stevens?" He extends a hand for me to shake. I take it and give it a few firm pumps.

"You can call me Graham," I say as I position Cassie in front of me. "And this is Cassie. You must be our captain."

"Yes, you can call me Diego. Come aboard and I'll introduce you to the rest of the crew. We'll get started in a few minutes."

As he turns, Cassie shoots me a look. "A sailboat?"

"Sure." I shrug. "You don't want to go on a sailboat?"

"I've never been on one."

"Then this'll be a first." I can barely keep from puffing up my chest a little at the idea of showing Cassie something new. When I had the idea to rent a boat, I thought it might be something she'd like, but with Cassie you can never tell. She's a little hesitant, but if the flush on her cheeks tells me anything, she's also a little excited. "Let me help you climb aboard." I extend my hand and she takes it willingly. Once I have her safely on the deck I follow right behind.

"When did you arrange this?" Cassie asks as she looks the sailboat over.

"You're not exactly a light sleeper." This earns me a punch in the arm. "And I had a little time this morning when I let you sleep in." In truth it was the only way to keep myself from waking her up. I was desperate to run my hands all over sleeping Cassie. She'd been tangled in the sheets, her hair fanned out over the pillow and if I hadn't come up with something else to do, I would have woken her in a more creative way.

"It's beautiful," Cassie whispers.

"It is," I agree although I'm less concerned with looking at the boat and more interested in focusing on Cassie's face. The boat's too big for just two people, but now that we're here I'm glad I decided on this one. It's a catamaran with teak decks and shiny blue paint. Everything's polished to gleaming. "Let's go find Diego and we can get a tour."

It turns out Cassie loves sailing. Once we're out on the water she's full of questions. I'd be jealous of Diego and all the attention he's getting if it wasn't so fun to watch her animated reactions to everything he's telling her. And the most amazing thing of all? Cassie speaks Spanish.

When she busted out her perfect pronunciation with the crew, my eyes nearly bulged out of my head. Her reaction was one I could have anticipated. After a quick eye roll and a shrug, she played it off like nothing. "What? I'm a nurse."

She's gorgeous and smart and those two attributes combined with her sassy mouth are going to be the death of me. As I watch her move along the deck, salt water spraying her as the boat cuts through the waves, I feel a sudden rush of pride. She's here with me—really here with me—and there's no reason to hide it. I want to hold onto this feeling for as long as I can.

I follow her to the front of the boat where she's stretching herself out like a cat in the sun. She's stripped down to the bikini I suggested she wear and she smiles when she sees me picking my way along the side of the boat toward her. I'm way less agile on a boat than dry land. I keep waiting for the inevitable moment when I'll end up bobbing alongside it.

"Come sit with me," Cassie calls and even if I wasn't planning on it, I would be doing whatever she asked. She pats the space next to her. "Guess what this part's called?" I try to settle myself down on the net strung over the front of the boat. She doesn't wait for me to answer; she knows I have no idea. "The trampoline. Isn't that funny? It isn't a real trampoline, but this is the most amazing place to sit."

I couldn't care less what the parts of this boat are called, but I do agree that this is an amazing place to sit because as soon as my ass hits the net, Cassie's curled up against me, her head on my bare chest. I breathe in the smell of her hair and the suntan lotion she's been slathering all over herself. Redheads need to constantly reapply, I've been told, and that's given me plenty of opportunities to suggest that she let me help her. I've taken more time than is strictly necessary getting underneath the straps of her bathing suit.

Cassie relaxes against me and I let my hand wander up her arm, my thumb stroking over her skin. "Don't let me fall asleep out here," she murmurs as she closes her eyes. Her breath tickles my nipple as she dozes. I tell myself I'm letting her sleep because I've kept her up for the past few nights, but I know why I'm really doing it. This is the only way she'll let me hold her, the only way I can whisper how I feel without her freaking out. I spend the next few minutes feeling her body pressed against mine, telling her I love her. When Diego pops his head up front to tell us lunch is ready, I'm sad to have to wake her.

When we stop in a cove, Diego hauls out the snorkeling equipment. Expecting Cassie to be less than enthusiastic,

I'm surprised to hear her jump into the water the second the boat stops moving. She paddles around, diving back under several times before wiping the water from her face. "Come in here!" she shouts to me as she treads water.

"Do you want a snorkel?" I shout back. Cassie's exaggerated nod has me laughing, scrambling to launch myself off the deck of the boat to join her. I cannonball off the back and hope I manage to splash her.

The water's warmer than I expect and when I come back up to the surface, I'm face-to-face with Cassie's exuberant grin. She leans in to give me a kiss before taking one of the masks and snorkels I've brought along with me. She slides the mask over her face and positions the snorkel in her mouth like Diego demonstrated to her earlier. She's never done this before, but you'd never know it. She's fearless.

Cassie squeals through her snorkel as a school of fish swim underneath her. She chases after them and I follow along, caring more about watching Cassie's body slice through the water than looking at any fish. Her pink toenails flash in front of me as she kicks her feet, the curve of her ass bobbing just above the water line. I resist the urge to put my hand out and pull her back toward me by one of her ankles. I dive down deeper, holding my breath, and turn to look back up at Cassie floating above me. She gives me a wave as she keeps exploring, looking for more fish. There's plenty to look at even just in this little cove—fan coral and all sorts of other plants sway in the water—but nothing catches my eye like this girl. I resurface and blow the water back out of my snorkel just in time to see a large sea turtle cruise near Cassie's arm. I wait to see her reaction, hoping she doesn't die of excitement. She sputters and flails, causing the turtle to rush off in the opposite direction.

"Holy shit!" Cassie's back on the surface, her face

obscured by the giant plastic mask. She spits out her snorkel and leaves it hanging on the side of her head. "Did you see that?"

"I saw you almost drown," I tease.

Cassie slaps the water in front of her, trying to splash me. I pull the mask off my face and give her a grin. "Come over here, that mask is making me crazy."

"Too sexy to resist?"

"Exactly."

She swims over, sliding into my arms. My attempts at reaching her mouth are thwarted by the plastic. "This mask is a good deterrent. I'll have to remember that." Cassie laughs. Her eyes are magnified behind the lens, glittering green orbs with just enough mischief to keep me trying.

"You'll have to take it off eventually," I taunt. "I can be very patient."

"You're the most patient man I know," Cassie tells me. "Blessing and a curse." She pulls the mask off her face and lets me put my lips on hers. "Thanks for this."

"For kissing you? No need to thank me for that." I go in for another, but Cassie pulls back, tilting her head back to look me square in the eye.

"No, for today. Best day ever." She smiles at me and I have to bite my tongue to keep from asking her to marry me on the spot. The look on her face is one I want to see every day for the rest of my life. That's a thought guaranteed to send Cassie swimming back to the boat like a shark's after her, and since I want her to stay right where she is, I keep my big mouth shut.

"Know what would make this day even better?" I give a little push with my hips.

"Are you kidding?" Cassie yelps. "Put that away. You're going to scare the fish."

I tilt my head back and laugh, still keeping Cassie pressed against me. She laughs too, putting her lips against my neck and I wish we could keep this moment forever—the easiness of it. Even more than keeping it I want to have it again and again, over and over, at home in front of everyone. Again, I push that sentiment down and try to focus on right now. "Fine. I'll just use some of that patience we were talking about, but when we get back to the villa..." I cock an eyebrow to go with my threat and Cassie shivers.

"I'll keep that in mind," she tells me before slithering out of my grasp and swimming off, leaving me treading water. I'll think about this moment later, the way she looks with the sun reflecting off her hair and just a kiss of pink on her shoulders. I'll wish I had a photo of this instead of the selfie I take of the two of us on the bow of the boat with the sun setting behind us.

Best day ever.

33

Cassie

On our last afternoon together we walk along the beach. From the villa it's easy to pick our way over the rocks until we're back on the sand closer to one of the resorts. Graham holds my hand in his and I let him instead of pulling it back like I would at home. He's right—here there's no one to see us, no one to look at us touching and think twice about it. I let my arm press against his as we walk along, the hot sand beginning to burn the bottom of my feet. He pulls me closer to the surf and the water splashes up against my calves.

"Let's go in." He gives me a grin.

"We are in."

"No, let's swim out. Last chance to enjoy the ocean."

He's right. We've been so busy with the wedding and trying to keep our relationship a secret and then after that with spending every minute naked that we've ignored the beach. His sailboat trip is the only time we've really been in the water since we decided to extend our stay. He tugs me against him and I can feel the sunshine on his skin. I know that if I lean forward and brush my lips against his chest, he'll be even warmer than usual. "Come on. One swim."

Graham lets go of my hand, turns to the water, and jogs out. He looks back over his shoulder and calls to me again. "Hustle up, Firecracker!"

I groan. "We don't have any towels!" I yell after him, but he's already waist deep. He jumps a little to avoid a wave and then dives under. When he comes up a few feet farther away, I give up and follow him into the water. I don't dive under, but try to walk out, feeling the sandy bottom with my feet. I hate the surprise of stepping on something unexpected and so I poke along until the water begins to splash against my belly.

"What are you doing?" Graham laughs. "Just swim out here. It's not like you can't swim."

"I have to ease in," I protest. "The water's cold!"

Graham laughs again, leaning his head back. Water droplets hang on his shoulders and chest and he looks like an ad in a surfing magazine—all blond hair and tan skin. "It makes it worse to go slow. Just dunk yourself under."

I think about this, if I can just dunk myself under. Part of me wants to, just to throw myself into this, but part of me also wants to run back to the beach. I keep the same slow pace until the water is just hitting my chest. My nipples harden as the icy water splashes them and I take in a sharp breath. Graham comes back toward me, looking amused.

"For someone so fearless, you sure are taking a long time." Once he's close to me he holds out his hand again. "I thought you'd beat me out here. Should've made it a race or something."

I take his hand with scowl. Graham pulls me out to deeper water and I feel for the bottom with my toes.

"I don't think I can stand here."

"I can. Just hold on to me." He pulls again and brings me in front of him. I float a few inches away from him until he wraps his arms around my waist and slides me up against him. I watch his face change as he feels my nipples press into his chest.

"I told you it was cold," I whisper. Our faces are so close I can see flecks of sand along his jaw line, see when his lips open just enough for his tongue to dart out. He runs a hand to the nape of my neck and presses his lips against mine. Automatically I open for him, letting him possess my mouth, eagerly kissing him back. His other hand cruises along the exposed skin on my stomach, moving higher until he finds my breast. He eases his fingers under the triangle of fabric and tweaks my nipple.

"Graham." My voice is a warning.

"What?" He's the picture of innocence.

"We can't do this here."

"Do what?" He puts his lips on the side of my neck and gives the skin there an open-mouthed kiss.

"You know what. We can't. People will see."

Graham keeps kneading my breast as he scans the beach. "There's hardly anyone out and they aren't paying attention to us anyway."

He turns us so I have a view of the beach. It's late afternoon and the place has cleared out. Only one family remains near the edge of the water. The two small children run back and forth between the surf and their parents.

"And we're up to our necks in the water," Graham adds. "No one will see." He keeps his voice even, soothing me, but when the movement of the ocean bumps our bodies together, I feel his erection. He kisses me again and I can feel his hand moving slowly south. When his fingers dip into the top of my bikini bottom, I narrow my eyes at him.

"Graham, I swear if we get arrested or something I will fucking kill you."

"There's my adventurous girl," he growls into my ear. "I knew you were still in there somewhere. We won't get arrested. I promise." He looks in my eyes, his face serious. "I won't let anything bad happen to you."

His girl? It's a throwaway line but my heart lurches in my chest. He's not Prince Charming. He's not here to protect me. I put on my best annoyed face and raise an eyebrow. Graham just grins again and makes a move to bite my bottom lip. We're bobbing up and down now with the water and when he slides his hand lower and his fingers graze my pussy, I have to stifle a groan. He finds my clit and uses his thumb to work in a slow circle as he eases one long finger inside me. He's gotten good at knowing what I like and he's using that to his advantage now. If he keeps this up for much longer, I'll be begging him to fuck me and not caring who hears me.

"Wrap your legs around my waist."

I do it without hesitation as he forces the top of his swim trunks down, freeing himself. He moans as I rub myself against him, the only thing between us is the flimsy fabric of my swimsuit. He yanks that aside and positions the head of his cock against my opening. Even though I know what's coming, I gasp a little when he enters me.

He fills me with a grunt and waits for me to adjust. I work my legs more tightly against him and he lets out a little half laugh like he can't believe we're doing this either. There's the combination of the water and the sunshine, the salty air and our bodies making me forget everything else.

Graham presses his forehead against mine and thrusts up into me. I force myself back down and we get into a rhythm, slow and steady, almost languorous. The water laps up around us and I wrap my arms around his neck. His hands tighten on my waist and he slides me up and down over his shaft until I'm breathless. He's making soft, measured little murmurs and I open my eyes to find him looking directly at me. We stare at each other, him slowly fucking me as I try to keep quiet. I can feel myself tightening, my orgasm building and as much as I want to, I know I can't come if I'm looking at him. Already this closeness is too much. Tomorrow we're back to reality and that means no more Graham. I can't get any more attached than I already am. Looking at him now doesn't feel like an easy fling. Looking at him now feels like something real so I wrench my face away from his and bite down hard into the muscle of his shoulder. He hisses, but doesn't stop thrusting into me. I know I'm hurting him, but it only makes him fuck me harder until we both shatter around each other, fighting not to call attention to ourselves.

I release my teeth from Graham's shoulder, panting. I can feel him still pulsing inside me, his breathing fast and hard against my neck. From where we are I can see the family on the beach, oblivious to what we're up to in the water. They remind me of Julia and Zach with her boys— smiles and sunburned noses. The kids are piling buckets of sand on the feet of their father, laughing as he tries to free himself over and over again. My eyes well up with tears as jealousy bubbles up inside me. I'm jealous. Jealous of that family and how happy they are. Suddenly I want that for myself. And the best shot I have of getting that is right now tangled up with me, his cock still deep inside me. My best shot at that is Graham.

Which means I can never have it. I will fuck this up six ways from Sunday and ruin him in the process. We'll both lose Julia and he'll never forgive me.

I have to let him go.

34

Graham

She's pulling away.

Before we even make it to the airport Cassie's distant. Sure, she's still holding my hand, still smiling up at me when I look down into her green eyes, but the connection's not there. After all we've done these past few days, after how close we've gotten, it hurts more than any tackle I've ever made. I'd rather have my face pushed into the turf than watch Cassie pretend everything's normal. I thought she'd see how good we are together but she's going back to the way we were before.

"What's wrong?" I ask as we settle into our seats.

"Nothing." She gives me a big smile. A big, fake smile. Not the carefree grin she's been giving me. "First class, huh? That's a little much, don't you think?"

"I'm too big for the seats in economy. That's my excuse," I try to joke. I upgraded Cassie's seat without asking her because I already knew how she'd react. She'd probably prefer economy. And not to be sitting anywhere near me.

"It's expensive," Cassie tells me as she pulls her airline

blanket up to her chin. "It'll take me a while to pay you back."

"You aren't paying me back." I bristle. "Consider it a gift."

Cassie rolls her eyes.

"What? I can't buy nice things for my girl?" I lean over and kiss the top of her head and try not to get angry when she tenses. Maybe she just needs more time to get used to us being out in public. Mexico was like our own little universe. Our own perfect little world where I had Cassie all to myself. I can't expect her to be the same at home. I try to tamp down the anxiety I feel taking over. I have to be realistic. Mexico was a vacation and now we're back to real life. Real life that I thought would include telling everyone we know we're together.

"I'm going to try to sleep." Cassie rolls away from me to face the window.

"I tired you out, did I?"

Again she barely gives me a flash of teeth. "A little. I need to be back at work early tomorrow and I don't want to show up dead on my feet." Cassie tosses this over her shoulder as she curls up. She can't really spread out much with her seat upright but apparently she can't wait to postpone her nap until after takeoff.

"Do you want a drink? They'll come through in a second with drink service. That's another perk of being up here instead of in the back. No waiting and real glasses."

"No thanks."

"Don't you at least want to wait until you can put the seat a little flatter?" I sound like my grandmother. Nag, nag, nag.

"I'm fine like this. I really don't want to talk, okay?" Cassie lets out a deep breath.

Pin pricks of uncertainty have me wanting to reach over

and give Cassie a shake. I want to pull her into my lap and kiss her until she remembers that we're on the same side here, that she doesn't need to protect herself from me. I make a move to haul her over the armrest but I'm saved from that terrible decision by the arrival of the flight attendant. By the time she gets my drink order and moves on to the next customer Cassie's fast asleep.

35

Graham

When we landed and Cassie pretended to be too exhausted to come back to my place and too busy to have me come to hers, I tried not to let the bruise on my heart get the best of me. I've usually got a few default options for dealing with disappointment, but it's been a while since I've had to use them for losses that weren't about football. The first week of radio silence burns, but I keep from chasing after her. I allow myself two calls. Both go straight to voicemail. The second week doesn't feel much better and I try a few tentative texts which she ignores. Halfway through week three I'm going crazy, the urge to show up at her apartment or to stalk her at work becoming too difficult to resist. Christmas comes and goes without a word. I punish myself at the gym and up my running schedule knowing neither of those will fix things long term. Just when I feel like I've made some progress with Cassie I always find myself taking two steps back. I need a different perspective so I decide to try an old tactic I haven't tried in a while.

"Mom!" I yell as I turn the knob to let myself into the

front hallway of my childhood home. I'm instantly trans-
ported back to middle school. Old photos line the walls—
me in my pee wee football uniform, Julia and I as prom king
and queen, my mother and father on their wedding day. I've
been passing these photos all my life and right now I need
all this nostalgia. I let the smell of homemade meatloaf and
the sound of my mother making dinner in the kitchen wash
over me.

"In the kitchen," my mother calls and I follow her voice
through the living room to find her mixing something with
a wooden spoon in her newly remodeled kitchen. Last year I
finally convinced her to get new appliances after years of
cajoling. Could I help it if the new fridge didn't fit with the
old cabinets? My mother hates to spend money unnecessarily and resisted letting me buy her anything when what
she had was "perfectly fine." No amount of professional
success would change her mind. I ended up surprising her
while she was away on a trip with her girlfriends and just
hoped that she'd be able to forgive me. She loves the new
stove, so luckily, I was saved.

"Come in and help me. I've made too much food! I got
all excited when you said you were coming over." She leans
over so I can plant a kiss on her cheek. I get a whiff of my
mother's perfume and know that coming home tonight for
dinner was the right choice.

"You didn't have to make anything. We could have
ordered in." I always say this, but my mother knows better.
When I come home I love having my mom make me dinner.
Nothing beats Jackie's meatloaf—it's basically the reason I
made it to the pros.

"Well, I wasn't sure if you were bringing someone..." She
doesn't make eye contact and for that I'm grateful. I think

the hurt would be so obvious on my face I'd be unable to hide it.

"Not tonight."

"Maybe another time?" my mother asks, still not looking at me.

"I'm not sure if that's ever going to happen, Ma." Admitting it pokes at that soft spot I've been trying to protect.

"No?" Jackie's head snaps up. "What happened?"

I haven't told my mother anything about Cassie, but apparently she knows all about it. I could blame Steve or my agent, but in the end I appreciate not having to start from the beginning. "Nothing. She just isn't ready, I guess."

"Well, can you blame her? After meeting her mother I can see why she'd be a little gun shy. You need to give her time."

"That's what I've been doing, but it doesn't seem to be working. She's..."

"She's tougher than you're used to." Leave it to my mother to get right to the point.

I laugh. "That's true, I guess."

"There's nothing wrong with having to work a little." She's back to moving around the kitchen before I can argue. "Sometimes that makes you appreciate things more when you get them."

"I keep trying to give her space. I just don't know how long to keep working on it. Eventually I have to give up, right? I can't make her change her mind."

"Is that your pride talking or your heart?"

Ouch.

"I'm not sure I can tell the difference."

My mother gives me the look that has always told me she's on to my bullshit. After my father passed away, it was just me and my mom. She never remarried and I can barely remember her dating. My life was always her main priority. As an adult I feel guilty about that but as a kid I loved knowing I had someone in my corner no matter what. My mom worked hard to be the best mother and father she could be and I'm grateful for that, even more so now when I see what that might have cost her.

"Do you ever wish you'd gotten married again?"

"Don't change the subject."

"That's the same subject," I protest even though she's right to think I'm taking the heat off myself for a minute.

"I never found anyone worth making the commitment to." She shrugs like that settles that.

"But you never even went out on dates."

"I dated." My mouth falls open at my mother's admission. "I just never made it your business. Don't look so surprised." She gives me an eye roll before going back to the potatoes.

"I don't remember you going on dates." I'm sure that would have been seared into my brain. The thought of my mom going out with someone other than my father makes my chest burn a little. I rub the spot to try push the feeling away and notice my mother watching.

"That right there is why I didn't make it your business. If there'd been anyone worth mentioning I'd have told you, but there was no reason to get you upset for nothing."

"But didn't you want to have…"

"Love?" my mother asks. "Or are you asking about sex?"

"God no, not sex. I'm not asking about sex," I blurt out. I'm not as grown-up as I think and I could live the rest of my life without thinking of my mother and anything sexual.

"Calm down, Graham. I'm not going to scandalize you with any stories." She smiles. "So, you're asking about love?"

"I guess."

"I had that. I still have that. I had that with your father for twelve years. Five before you were born and then seven more after. I never found anyone to compare."

"But it was hard being on your own, raising me." I know this already, but I feel the need to say it out loud. She could have been like Julia, could have found a partner to help her. Instead she stayed single.

"Oh, it was hard. You were so little when Connor died. It seemed overwhelming. He'd helped you pick out that suit for your first communion the week before and then you had to wear it to his funeral."

I'd forgotten about that—the gray suit and blue tie, the shoes that pinched just enough to keep me from crying. I'd focused on my feet and on holding my mother's hand until the service had been over and then cried myself to sleep with my face pressed into my pillow.

"I thought I'd die from the grief and they'd have to bury me with him. But we got stronger, you and I. If I'd found somebody I loved as much as I loved your father then I might have married again. But we weren't talking about me. We were talking about you."

"Were we?" I hedge.

"We were. Are you in love with Cassie?"

"Yeah." There's no use in denying it, especially to my mother.

"And you told her that?"

"Yes, ma'am."

"And she doesn't feel the same way?" I can see the little ridge of concern come across my mother's forehead.

"I don't know."

The furrow in my mother's brow deepens. "What do you mean? You told her and she didn't say it back?"

"There were extenuating circumstances. There *are* extenuating circumstances."

"Well, it's not like you to let a few obstacles get in your way." She's right. Normally I'd push and push until I got what I wanted. If one way didn't work, I'd regroup and try again. I haven't been like that with Cassie; I've been letting her call the shots, afraid too much pressure would make her run. Nervous that the Graham she remembers from before —the headstrong, selfish one—would never be able to convince her to try. But that tactic didn't make things any easier. She's hiding anyway, avoiding me. Maybe it's time for the more stubborn Graham to try things his way.

"What was that quote your high school coach always used to drill into your head?"

I groan. "You're pulling out the big guns here. High school football *and* Vince Lombardi?"

"I know you remember it. Something about heart power? I think it's time to go visit the poster."

Of course I remember it. It's something I've said to myself constantly in my career when it looked like the odds were going to be against me. I know my mother remembers it too, because that damn poster's still hanging on the wall of my childhood bedroom. I trudge down the hall because there's no use arguing with my mother. Once I crack the door open, the words taunt me from underneath the cheesy graphic. The poster's nothing to look at, really, but I've left it on the wall for years because the quote is.

Once a man has made a commitment to a way of life, he puts the greatest strength in the world behind him. It's something we call heart power. Once a man has made this commitment, nothing will stop him short of success.

. . .

My mother waits for me in the kitchen, as I turn the words over in my head. I hear plates clanking together and know dinner's almost ready. "Always loved that poster," she calls down the hall to me. "Having that ratty thing on the wall means I can save my breath for other things." I march back down the hall and she slides two plates into my hands. "The question is, I guess, how committed are you to this? To Cassie?"

I don't even have to think about it before I answer. "One hundred percent."

"Then come and help me set the table and we can work on getting you to success."

36

Cassie

If the way I feel right now is karma then I have a newfound respect for the universe. After waking up with yet another sickly stomach I nearly lose my breakfast all over a patient after dealing with his rolly veins. Trying to put that IV in his arm was like watching a horror movie and now as I bend over the toilet in the hospital bathroom and actually throw up, I don't find myself feeling much better. I run through the list of things I've eaten trying to figure out what's got me feeling so queasy, but there isn't much. Nothing has sounded good to me since I've been home and I've been forcing myself to put food in my mouth so I won't be too weak to work out.

I've been blaming my lack of appetite on the situation with Graham. After Mexico I've ghosted him again and the pain of missing him has me crying on the couch every night. I've picked up extra shifts at the hospital and tried to put myself back together by going back to my old routine, but the giant Graham-shaped hole in my life keeps derailing me. I know it's for the best. He needs to find someone who can give him what he wants—someone who can be with him here the way we were in Mexico. Someone who isn't terrified to at least try.

I'm splashing water on my face when Delia comes into the bathroom. She gives me the once over and shakes her head. "Did you just throw up?"

I don't answer, but my shaking hands and sweaty neck give me away.

"If you're sick you should go home. What is it with you and germs this year? You're never sick and suddenly you're sick all the time." She watches me wash my hands like she's monitoring a kindergartener.

"I'm not sick, really. I think it's probably food poisoning. It'll pass."

"What have you eaten that could possibly give you food poisoning? I've seen you picking at those salads you keep buying. You aren't eating enough to actually get food poisoning, Cassie." Delia leans against the sink. "I'm getting worried here. The no cupcakes and the moping around having me thinking you've messed things up with that boyfriend of yours." Delia's missing her weekly cupcake delivery. Those have stopped now that I've given Graham the cold shoulder.

"For the last time, he wasn't my boyfriend."

"But he wanted to be." Delia's too smart for her own good. "And you were too scared to let him, so you ran him off. Am I getting close?"

"I didn't run him off. I just ignored him until he stopped trying." It sounds even more stupid when I say it out loud.

"Well, that is just fabulous, Cassie. Are you really so afraid of turning into your mother that you'd waste something good just to prove your point?"

"What point do you think I'm trying to prove?" I turn to face Delia, ready to argue.

"That you're unlovable or undeserving, I don't know. That you can't trust a man to stay. That you can't have nice things. That you're supposed to end up alone."

I open my mouth to disagree but find myself clamping my hand over it instead. I run back into the stall just as another wave of nausea crashes over me and vomit forces its way out of my already empty belly. Delia's over in a flash with a paper towel to wipe my mouth and a hand on my forehead. It makes me think of Graham and the last time I was sick enough to have someone else take care of me like this.

"You're not warm. I don't think you have a fever." Delia's touching me all over, putting her cool hands on the back of my neck. "How long have you been feeling sick like this?"

"A week, maybe," I confess as Delia's eyes widen.

"Touch your boob," she orders out of nowhere.

"I'm not really up for that right now, Delia. Maybe when I stop puking we can talk about your little fantasy." I manage a half-hearted grin.

"This isn't me getting sexy with you, Cassie. Just humor me here. Grab one of your boobs." Delia's back over by the sink wetting paper towels for my neck.

"Fine." I reach under my scrub top to tweak my own nipple. "But I don't think that this is a great way to calm an upset stomach or else everybody'd be doing it. Ow!" My breast is surprisingly tender.

"Did that hurt?'

"A little. It's just really sensitive, I guess."

Delia looks at me in the bathroom mirror. "Cassie could you be..."

"Could I be what?"

"Could you be pregnant?"

"No." I'm adamant. "I'm on the pill and I always use condoms." Except with Graham at the bachelor party. And that time in the ocean. And the shower. Basically all over our Mexican villa.

My mouth pops open.

"You should take the rest of the day off and get to the pharmacy," Delia tells me, her voice full of concern. "We can call someone in to cover for you."

I stand there blinking, letting my brain catch up with this possible situation.

Pregnant?

Two hours and thirty pregnancy tests later I am dehydrated from all the peeing I've done. After the first positive test I'd needed two more trips to the pharmacy and two gallons of Gatorade only to confirm what I could have just accepted with that first set of double lines.

I'm pregnant.

I arrange the tests on my bathroom counter and settle myself on the tile floor. A baby?

My brain blips like I'm watching the cursor on a computer screen. What comes next? I have no idea so I do the only logical thing I can think of and grab my phone.

Can you come over? It's an emergency. Use the key.

I hit send before I can take it back and go back to stretching out on the bathroom floor. I let my hand rest on my belly, testing out how it feels, but my stomach still feels the same as it always does. I try to imagine a bump there, but my imagination fails me. If I can't even picture my body changing how can I get to the part where I imagine myself raising a baby? I haul in a ragged breath and try not to let the tears come. I can't spend any more time crying; I need to stay focused.

The sound of my apartment door opening and closing has me rolling over onto one elbow. Time to put on my big girl panties and figure this out.

Julia comes around the corner holding a grocery bag. "I brought ice cream. And vodka. I wasn't sure what kind of an emergency this was."

"I don't think I'm allowed to have the vodka." I motion to the counter.

Julia's eyes widen as she takes in the long line of white plastic sticks. Then a huge grin spreads across her face. "Cassie?" She looks at me. "Are you pregnant?"

"You tell me. I was hoping you might tell me those could all be false positives." I keep my metaphorical fingers crossed.

"I'm not an expert, but I don't think you get false positives. And that would be a whole lot of faulty product. How many tests did you take?" Julia marvels at the display on the counter.

"I bought two of every brand."

"I see."

I cover my eyes with my arm. Julia's done this a few times. She'll know what to do. Although, I think whenever she got a positive pregnancy test it was always fantastic news.

"What did he say when you told him?" Julia asks. "He must be so excited."

"Who?"

"Graham. Is he over the moon? He's wanted to be a dad for so long." Julia pauses. "Unless... it is Graham's, isn't it?"

My arm shoots away from my face. "Graham?" Normally

I would try to play it cooler here, try to pretend like I have no idea what Julia's talking about, but in my current state of distress I have a hard time hiding anything. Julia knows about Graham? About *me* and Graham?

Julia looks more guilty than she should for someone with absolutely no knowledge of my secret relationship. "You have been seeing Graham, right? I thought..."

I sit up. "How did you know about Graham?"

Julia shrugs. "It would be hard not to notice how you two look at each other, Cassie. And after Kat and Amy caught you guys in that closet or wherever it was, well, that confirmed it."

"They told you about the closet?" Kill me now.

"Sure. Why do you think I put you and Graham in that villa together? I'm not sure why you two have been hiding it, but anyone could see that you two are together. Unless you aren't?" Uncertainty creeps into Julia's voice. "Maybe we should go and sit on the couch." She extends a hand and moves to help pull me up.

"I'm not seeing Graham. We were just sleeping together." I dig my heels in.

"Cassie," Julia says in that voice she reserves for her children. "How many classic movies have you watched in the last six months?"

I frown. I've actually lost count.

"How much of that disgusting protein powder does he like in his shake in the morning?"

A scoop and a half.

"If I go in your bedroom right now how many of his T-shirts are going to be in your top drawer?"

Three. Not counting the one I've been using as a pillowcase. Not that any of that proves anything.

"You're dating Graham, Cassie."

"You've known all this time?" I croak, not sure if I feel like crying because of my predicament or the fact that my friend has discovered my betrayal.

"Let's not talk about it in the bathroom. Come on." Julia herds me into the living room and plops my crying ass on the couch. "Ice cream?"

"Honestly, I don't think I can hold it down." I reach for a tissue from the box on the coffee table. I've got Kleenex positioned strategically around the apartment for the frequent teary moments I've been having.

"It's the hormones," Julia confides. "It'll get better." She gives me a pat on the leg.

"I'm sorry about Graham." I wait for her to give me the friendship beat down that I so deserve. Julia has to be angry about what's happened and now a baby makes things not only messy but difficult to deny.

"Why would you be sorry?" Julia seems genuinely perplexed.

"He's your ex, Jules, and a big part of your life. You have every right to be mad at me for getting involved with him."

"Cassie, you can't think that I still have some claim over Graham? That was more than a decade ago. I've been married twice since he and I were together. I don't have any say in who Graham dates or what he does."

I blink. "I thought you'd be upset."

"That you and Graham were happy? Cassie, I love you and I love Graham and you two are perfect for each other. Why would it make me sad to see that?" Julia reaches for my hand. "We could double date."

I'm speechless. I've been giving myself an ulcer over something that barely registers for Julia. I've been avoiding Graham in order to preserve something that never needed protecting in the first place.

"But we both know that you worrying about me is just an excuse," Julia says like it's common knowledge.

"What do you mean? I've been terrified that you would find out. Why else would I keep pushing Graham away?" I wipe my eyes with the back of my free hand.

"Because you're terrified of commitment?"

"No, I'm not."

"Then explain to me why you've never managed to get this far in a relationship before." Julia waits like she's my therapist. "Should I open the vodka and make myself a drink while you think about it?"

I consider asking for a drink myself, before I remember the reason I called Julia over in the first place.

"Are you talking about how I've never managed to get myself knocked up before?" I ask. I know this isn't what Julia's talking about at all and she lets that crack slide right off.

"Very funny. I'm talking about the warm and fuzzy part. Although, the G-rated version of how you ended up pregnant would also be interesting."

"Antibiotics," I tell her and then confess the part that will only confirm everything I've been denying. "And no condoms."

Julia's eyebrows shoot up. "How did the queen of condoms end up in a no condom situation?"

"I told him not to wear one. Several times." Could Julia's eyebrows get any higher? I slide lower on the couch. "He thinks he's in love with me."

I expect Julia to show some emotion, wince or something, but she does nothing but squeeze my hand. "I think you're in love with him, too."

"But I don't know how to do love, Julia. And I don't think this is exactly how Graham pictured his happily ever after."

"I don't think he'll mind, actually. He's not the kind to run even if the situation isn't perfect. You just have to tell him. Give him the chance to show you that all the stuff you're afraid of doesn't scare him at all."

I shake my head. It isn't Graham I'm worried about. "What if I can't do this, Julia? What if I can't work out the staying part? I don't exactly have the best track record and Graham deserves someone who can be sure."

Julia hands me another tissue. "Cassie, no one's ever one hundred percent sure and nothing ever goes exactly according to plan. Look at me; I'm on my second marriage! If you'd asked me a few years ago how I thought things would work out there'd be no way I'd tell you any of this would happen. Hell, I moved down the street from my parents. Don't try to tell me about plans."

Julia might be right, but that doesn't make the lump in my throat go away.

"And you should give yourself a little credit; you've just never tried this before. You're not your mother and Graham's not your dad. Have you told Graham anything at all? Did you tell him you were late?"

Julia's about to be very disappointed in me.

"I haven't spoken to him since Mexico." Julia's mouth sets into a hard line. "I thought it was better to let things fizzle out."

"You have to tell him. Even if you aren't sure what you want, you have to let him know. He won't be able to forgive you if he finds out about it later, Cassie. He'll be so hurt."

Graham will be hurt, no matter what I decide to do. And I've hurt him so much already.

"I know. But after all the times I've pulled away I can't expect him to be waiting around. And now with a baby? I don't want to make him feel obligated, like I've trapped him into being with me. I'm a walking cliché."

"God, Cassie, you've really been thinking about this." Julia laughs. "Just give it a chance. It's not like you went after him for his status. A real gold digger would've been trying to trap him years ago."

"Thanks for that helpful clarification." I sigh. "Look, anyone can see how perfect Graham is. How can he be so sure he's supposed to be with me?"

"Did you just call Graham 'perfect'? I think Hell must have just frozen over. Trust him. He might surprise you."

That's what I'm worried about.

37

Graham

Knocking on Cassie's front door is one of the hardest things I've ever had to do. Is my hand made of concrete or something? It takes all my strength to lift it. I know she's home because her car's in the parking lot, but that doesn't mean she's going to be happy to see me. But there's no turning back now. I'm already letting my knuckles hit the place where the paint's been worn away from years of knocking. And if she doesn't let me in, I'm prepared to sit out here all night. I'm in it for the duration.

I hear Cassie shuffling around on the other side of the door. I didn't call first because what would be the point? She wouldn't have answered the phone anyway. Short of hiring a sky writer, this is the only way to get her attention. I hear the click of the lock and watch as one green eye becomes visible though the tiny crack between the door and the jamb. She doesn't have a peep hole and this suddenly makes me irrationally annoyed.

"Hi," she squeaks.

"You just opened the door without asking who it was?"

It's out before I can stop it. Not the best first line under the circumstances.

"I knew it was you." Cassie doesn't open the door any farther.

"Can I come in?" I don't want to say what I need to say out in the hall. The flowers I've brought like some high school kid crinkle in my hand. Cassie glares down at them through the sliver of space.

"Maybe. Did Julia send you over here?" Cassie's eye flits back and forth between my face and the flowers.

"Why would Julia send me over here?"

Cassie opens the door a little wider. She's in a baggy pair of sweats with her hair in a messy bun, the bags under her eyes alarmingly dark. At the sight of her I immediately go into panic mode. "Are you sick?" I reach out for her but, she takes a step back, drawing me into the apartment. "You look..." She looks exhausted. Beautiful but exhausted. Maybe these past few weeks have been hard on her too.

Cassie blinks up at me and runs a hand over a few errant strands of hair. "If I'd known I was going to have company, I'd have cleaned up a bit," she bites out.

"I've tried to call you. Tried to text. The only way to get you to see me is to show up." I shift uncomfortably. "So here I am. I miss you, Cassie."

Cassie moves to the couch and I follow, aware of every noise in the room. "There's something I need to talk to you about," I begin, but I'm silenced by a raised hand from Cassie. "Damn it, Cassie. I came here to say something and you need to let me say it."

"I have something to tell you first." Her voice is shaky. I'm sure this is going to be something I have no interest in hearing. Something that's going to derail my plan.

"Just let me say what I want to say," I keep pushing.

"Graham, don't make this any harder than it already is."

I'm starting to sweat. I thought Cassie'd be difficult, but not like this. "What I have to say is important."

"Not nearly important as what I have to say." Cassie stands and puts her hands on her hips.

"What I have to say is life altering," I nearly shout. This is not going the way I planned it at all. Even in my wildest imagination I did not see things going off the rails like this.

"Life altering?" Cassie shouts. "You have no idea." She stomps away from me toward the bathroom and I watch her rummage through the top drawer. She pulls out a handful of white plastic sticks and flings them in my direction. "I'm pregnant."

As the sticks ping me in the chest I consider what Cassie's saying. What is she saying? My brain tries to process, but it's pretty damn hard over the sound of my heart pounding and the blood rushing through my ears. Pregnant? Cassie bursts into tears and I'm slapped back into reality.

Cassie's pregnant.

I scoop her up and she lets me, her head falling on my chest as she sobs. She's a wet snotty mess by the time I make it back to the couch and get her all tucked in. I grab a handful of tissues which she takes reluctantly. "Don't look at me," she orders but I can't stop staring.

Cassie's pregnant.

"How..." I have questions but I'm not even sure where to start.

"The antibiotics," Cassie wails. "So stupid. I know that antibiotics can interfere with birth control pills. I'm a nurse, for fuck's sake!" She wipes her nose again. "But I guess the no condoms..." Cassie looks at me sheepishly and shakes her head. "I'm so sorry."

"It's not your fault. I was more than happy to help you get... Mama's going to be a mama." Cassie glares at me. "Sorry, it just slipped out." I'm mentally giving myself a kick in the ass when it dawns on me. "I'm going to be a dad. Right? I mean unless..." I can't even bring myself to say it out loud. But if Cassie doesn't want to have this baby it's her decision. My brain knows this even if my heart has already started painting the nursery.

"Unless what?" Cassie snarls. "Don't even tell me you're doubting it's yours?"

"No, no, nothing like that." The thought hadn't even occurred to me, actually. "I just didn't want to assume you were planning on having it." Even if she doesn't want me, I want her to want this baby. *My* baby.

Cassie relaxes a little. "I'm having it."

I let out a shaky breath.

"When I found out I wasn't sure, but I was up all night thinking about what to do. I'm not sure if I'm ready to raise a baby by myself, but I think I can do it."

"Why would you be doing it by yourself?" I'm afraid to hear Cassie's answer, my stomach already doing threatening somersaults.

"Come on, Graham."

"Come on what? I love you. We're having a baby. You think I'd what? Run?" I'm feeling some serious damage to my pride right about now. Cassie doesn't want me in this? Screw that. I slide off the couch onto one knee on the hardwood floor. I reach for Cassie's hand and watch her terrified eyes get as big as saucers.

"Marry me."

"No, no, no," Cassie whispers. "You're only asking because you feel obligated. Graham, you'd regret this. I don't want you to think you have to be the good guy here and ask the pregnant girl to marry you because it's the right thing to do."

"I'm not asking because of the baby," I protest. Shit. I'm going about this all wrong. I straighten a little and dig around in my pants pocket, finally finding what I'm looking for. I take a deep breath and try again.

"Cassidy Blake, I am crazy in love with you and I'm tired of pretending. I want to show you off to the whole world. No more hiding. I want you to be my wife. Please say yes."

The ring isn't fancy, but it still glitters. Cassie's confused face lifts to meet mine. "You have a ring?"

"It's my mom's. The one my dad gave her when he asked her to marry him. She gave it to me so I could ask you. Baby or no baby I was coming over here to convince you to give me a shot."

"You planned to ask me?" Cassie's voice is tiny. "And your mom knows?"

I pull out my phone and give it a few swipes then hand it to Cassie. "What are those?" I ask her as she stares at the screen.

"Plane tickets?"

"To Vegas. For tomorrow morning. I've got your dress in the car."

"My dress?"

"*The* dress. And my mom knows. She's hoping I'm unavailable for dinner tomorrow night. She'll be sad if I show up. And Delia can cover your shifts if you decide we're going."

Cassie sits shell-shocked on the couch. "Delia's in on this too?"

"It turns out we aren't so great at keeping things secret." I shrug. "Delia knows, Steve knows, now my mom. Zach's sisters know, obviously. Probably everyone else, too."

"Julia knows," Cassie says. "She said you'd be happy about the baby." She says it so tentatively my heart breaks a little. I climb up on the couch and pull her into my lap.

"Happy doesn't even begin to describe how I feel about the baby," I whisper into her hair. "But you're leaving me hanging here. You haven't answered my question and you're making me a little nervous. No matter what, I'm sticking. Whatever you and the baby need, I'm here. But I didn't ask you to marry me because you're pregnant. If you don't love me, say no, but don't chicken out because you're afraid."

"It isn't about loving you," Cassie whispers into my shirt. "It's about you eventually realizing that you don't want me. I don't have a great roadmap for this marriage and family thing. No matter how much I love you I'm going to fuck this up. I can't do that to you. I can't do that to a helpless baby."

I take Cassie's face in my hands. She's red and puffy from crying but to me she's never looked more beautiful. I kiss her forehead, her eyes, her nose, her cheeks—memorizing her. "Cassie, did you just kind of say you love me?"

She smiles. "I guess."

I smile back because right now I can feel how close I am to winning this thing. My team's at the one yard line about to run it in for the touchdown. "Baby, nobody has a roadmap for this. We make it up as we go along. Okay, you weren't raised by the world's best mother." Cassie snorts. "But you know what *not* to do. And I *was* raised by the world's best mother so we have that going for us. And we've got other people to help us out while we figure out the parenting thing. The marriage part? I'm not worried. We're both stubborn and not afraid to put the work in. I've been waiting so long for you, Cassie, there's no way I'm letting you get away."

Cassie straightens in my arms. "You bought me that wedding dress?"

"Fran helped me," I confess. "She knows, too."

Cassie gives me a punch in the arm. "You really want to do this?"

"More than anything."

"Put the ring on me, then."

When I slide the ring on her finger I almost expect the universe to provide blaring trumpets. Cassie holds her hand out and I marvel at the fact she's said yes.

"It's beautiful," Cassie whispers. "Perfect. It actually fits."

I close my eyes and wrap my arms tighter around her, one hand splaying over her belly. *There's a baby in there.* The thought snaps my eyes open. *My baby's in there.*

"Why are we waiting until tomorrow to go to Vegas?" Cassie asks. "Why aren't we going tonight?"

"Now you can't wait?" I laugh but I'm just as impatient to make this thing official. "I haven't seen you in weeks and I've made a lot of decisions. I thought we'd have things to talk about. Looks like I missed some big things happening over here, too." My thumb moves over her stomach. We have plenty to catch up on, but that wasn't my real reason for booking the tickets for the morning. There was the possibility of rejection, sure, but I went into this convinced I could pull it off. Waiting until morning gives me the chance to be a little selfish. "That, and the fact I haven't seen you in forever and, if you said yes, I would want to celebrate by ripping your clothes off. I figured we'd need until tomorrow morning."

Remembering the last part of my surprise I stand up. "I got you another present," I tell Cassie as I start to unbutton my pants.

"Whoa there, cowboy." Cassie laughs, scooting away from me. "Think I've unwrapped that present before."

"Mind out of the gutter, Cassie," I tease. "You can have that present in a minute." I slide the edge of my pants and boxer briefs down giving her a look at the sliver of skin on my hip. "Check it out."

Cassie leans forward, the tiniest hint of a smile playing on her lips. "Is that what I think it is?" she asks and then tilts her puzzled face up toward mine.

"What? You need to get closer to get a better look? I could take my pants completely off," I suggest and Cassie waves her hands in front of her face.

"I think I can see fine with you right where you are. I just can't believe... When did you do that?"

"Right after Mexico."

She runs her fingertips over my new tattoo. Just having her touch my skin makes it almost unbearable to be this close to her and not pull her up against me.

"You do realize this is permanent."

"Wouldn't have it any other way."

"A firecracker?" Cassie asks, laughing. "You got a cartoon firecracker tattooed on your body."

I shrug. When I'd thought about what to do about my old ink, nothing had seemed as perfect as this. Sure it looks like something Yosemite Sam would be shooting off for the Fourth of July, but it covers the reminder of my past and there's no mistaking who's there now. I put a bright red fire-cracker there to prove it to her. This isn't fooling around. This is forever.

"Thanks for that," Cassie whispers and I know this time I've really got her. Tomorrow I'm going to marry the shit out of her.

I have Cassie on her back in record time, kissing up her

neck to find her mouth. I slide my hand under the fabric of her shirt but stop when I reach her chest.

"Are your boobs bigger than they used to be?"

Cassie groans. "Yes, and you have to be gentle with them. It's pregnancy stuff."

This is going to be so much fun.

38

Cassie

I can't stop humming. Who would have thought *Viva Las Vegas* would be the most romantic song in the world? But I guess if one of your best wedding memories is dancing back down the aisle with your gorgeous new husband while an Elvis impersonator serenades you then the song might get stuck in your head.

Husband.

That's going to take some getting used to.

But I've got a ring on my finger and so does Graham after our perfect non-wedding wedding.

I was worried he'd be disappointed later, maybe regret eloping just the two of us. I've never had dreams of my wedding—never thought I'd ever have one—so Vegas is more than fine with me. But Graham probably wanted his mother there and all his football buddies, Julia and her family.

"Nope," he'd told me for the millionth time. "This is just us, Cassie. When we get home we'll have a party to celebrate with everyone else, mainly so all my friends can see you in that dress."

I do rock this dress.

The way Graham looked at me when I walked down that aisle made me forget any of the reservations I'd had about being a bride. Standing there in his suit, ready to take my hand from Elvis and promise forever... Why did I fight so hard to keep from having this?

And "just us" is different from top secret, which I'm trying to get used to. The second the deed was done Graham was posting a photo of us with our Elvis officiant all over social media. He just ripped the Band-Aid right off and I surprised us both by not dying. Not even a little bit. Because the way Graham and I are looking at each other in that photo? It makes my heart want to come right out of my chest.

We've called everyone we love to let them know, and hearing how excited they are that we've gone ahead and jumped in the deep end makes me even surer that I've made the right decision. Even my mother was happy for us. Begrudgingly happy, but I still count it. She was more angry that I hadn't worked faster so she could have had season tickets when Graham was still playing pro ball. Once Graham promised her she could still have them she was right as rain.

"What are you smiling about?" Graham asks me as he rolls over onto his elbow. He's sporting some serious sex hair. We are never leaving this bed.

"Nothing. Everything." I slide my hand over to tangle up with his.

That makes Graham smile back and we lay there just grinning at each other until my mouth almost hurts.

"Are you hungry? We should eat. You should definitely

eat." He rolls over to grab the room service menu. This will be our fourth time to call down there since we got back to the hotel. After announcing to the entire lobby, "This is my wife!" to a nice round of applause, Graham's been content to stay right here. We ordered in dinner, then ice cream around midnight, and breakfast this morning. That makes this lunch, I guess, but I have no idea what time it is or how long we've been cocooned up here. The only thing I care about is being wrapped up with Graham.

"What sounds good to you two?" Graham asks. *You two* because really there's three of us in this room right now. "Will Bruiser let you eat a cheeseburger?"

I gag a little at the thought of that. "No, he doesn't want a cheeseburger," I tell him. "Bruiser could be a she, you know."

"I know." Graham puts his face close to my stomach. "Either way is fine by me as long as I can put him or *her*," he raises his eyes to mine, "in my jersey."

"Your jersey's going to be a little big at first, don't you think?"

"They make onesies." Graham tells me this like it's the most reasonable thing in the world. "And small sizes."

"Let me guess, you've got a box of those somewhere in the house already." Of course Graham's got a stash of baby gear with his number on it.

"College and pro," he tells me with absolutely no shame. He's been waiting for this for forever.

"I love you." I say it first now. Without any fear. Without any hesitation.

"I know," he answers me back with his lips against my belly. "I know."

"Wait, isn't that..."

"From *Star Wars*?"

"Seriously, Graham?"

"What? That's a great movie." And then he rolls me over, pinning me underneath that massive body that I get to keep forever. "I love you, too."

I feel myself relax into his touch, relax into the way things are now.

Yeah, I could get used to this.

EPILOGUE

.

Graham

"Here, hand him to me."

"You have to go up and give your speech. You can't hold him while you talk."

"I'll put him in the front pack. We'll be fine." I reach for my son and lift him up high.

"Don't do it," Cassie warns me.

"Don't do what?" I pretend I have no idea what she's talking about.

"Don't do the *Lion King* thing."

"But he loves it!" I protest. He really does like it. His blue eyes shine down at me, waiting for me to start singing. It's one way I can always guarantee he'll laugh. The laughing is new and I can't get enough of it. I make a fool of myself daily just so I can hear Connor's crazy belly laugh.

Connor. Named after my father.

It was Cassie's suggestion because she gets me, knows exactly what I need before I even know it myself. Like today. She's been right there with me helping to organize this event —the first fundraiser for my new charity. Cassie's the one who originally gave me the idea to help kids and now here we are putting our money—and all the money I could coax out of my friends—where our mouths are. We're walking to raise money, but really this is more about getting people excited, letting people know what we're all about. And we're at the zoo because Connor loves the zoo.

Cassie claims Connor's too young to know much about what he's looking at, but he knows what he likes. When we go by the monkey house he kicks his legs like crazy and makes these spitty bubbles with his lips. You can't tell me that isn't excitement.

"Come here, buddy." I pull him close to me and work him into the baby carrier I've got attached to my torso. I've gotten pretty good at figuring out this baby thing, especially since I'm home so much. I never thought I'd be happy not to be traveling with the team, but if I was still playing I'd be missing so much. Being retired means being here and being a hands-on dad. I don't love changing diapers, but I wouldn't trade my nights rocking Connor to sleep for anything. Not even a Super Bowl win.

I could never have imagined I'd love anything the way I love football, but from the moment Cassie and I decided to make this thing official I've come to realize that my feelings for a game can't compete with the love I have for my family. The day Connor was born I had a high like I'd never had on the field. Watching the woman I love give birth to my son— there aren't words for that. Cassie was a champ, fighting her way through hours of labor to give me the greatest gift I've ever been given. When they put Connor in my arms, I thought my heart would explode and that feeling keeps coming back with every new thing he does. He and Cassie are my team now and I've been lobbying hard to get Cassie to expand our franchise. She's not ready yet, but as soon as she says the word, I'm going to be working on giving Connor a little brother or sister.

"You want him to face out like that?" Cassie asks. "No one's going to be paying attention to you with his little guy looking at them." She leans in to put a raspberry on Connor's cheek. He grabs a handful of her hair and holds on, turning his round little face to put it in his mouth.

"Easy there, killer, let go of Mom." I untangle them and smooth Cassie's curls back down, letting my hand rest on the back of her neck. She smiles up at me and I lean down to kiss her, careful not to squish the baby between us. "He likes to face out," I tell her, adjusting the straps that keep my son attached firmly to my chest. "So he can see everything."

"Let me know if you change your mind and want to hand him off." Cassie moves back into the crowd. She's spent the morning greeting people as they come in, helping with the registration table, and corralling stragglers into the main area in front of the stage. She hasn't stopped since we got here. In a few minutes I'll need to get things started and then we'll do a loop around the zoo.

But first I take a few minutes to look around. Julia and Zach are here with Charlie and Noah. Her parents are right next to them with my mother. All of them in their matching T-shirts, Julia's fitting a little snug around the middle. I give the boys a wave and they both give me two thumbs up. It's all the encouragement I need to go ahead and get started. I take the mic I'm handed and wait for the crowd to settle down. My old teammates are the last ones to get the message, of course, and I can still hear my agent blabbering long after everyone else is quiet. When Andre gives him an elbow he finally shuts up.

"Thank you all for being here today," I start, looking out over more people than I ever imagined would come out on a not quite spring day. There's still a chill in the air, but you'd never know it from the smiles on people's faces. "It means a lot to me to have so many friends here to help kick things off. And I consider all of you friends now because anyone who gives their time and money to help out kids who've suffered the loss of a parent is a friend in my book. The money we raise today will help those families get counseling and support."

I scan the crowd to find Cassie. "And I'd like to take a minute to thank my beautiful wife Cassie. She was the one who pushed me to start this foundation. The original seed for this idea was hers." Cassie dips her head, blushing. "If you want something done, you go to the boss. She's the smartest person I know. She's the best thing that's ever happened to me. Thanks for always believing in me, baby."

Connor squawks and I bounce a little to keep him quiet. "I guess that's my cue to wrap things up," I joke. "Let's have fun today!" I walk off the stage to more applause than my speech deserves and head straight for Cassie. I take her hand in mine and we move to the front of the crowd. Having her next to me makes me feel ten feet tall, and having Connor strapped to the front of me makes me realize all that I've been missing. But I have it now.

And I'm never letting it go.

ACKNOWLEDGMENTS

Thank you for reading Cassie and Graham's story! From the moment Cassie appeared on the page in *Fight For It*, I knew she needed her own book. That she ended up with Graham was a surprise to even me.

Obviously there are some people to mention here that helped immensely in the early stages of this book. Special thanks to Austin Ryan and Jessica Devlin who read early versions. Their suggestions made the story stronger.

Thanks to Tamara Mataya for her editing skills and her suggestion that maybe Graham and Cassie need a bit more "bubble." You were right.

And, as always, thanks to my crack team of live-in teenagers. How would I pick a cover model without you and your friends? How would I be able to determine if a blurb was about a book you "definitely didn't want to read" but were confident "some other people might"? Kudos to the three of you for helping support your mom as she continues to embarrass you with her writing.

ABOUT THE AUTHOR

Jessie Harper writes steamy, contemporary romance with a slightly Southern flavor. Originally from Nashville, Tennessee, she has lived all over the world—from Europe to Asia. She currently resides in Park City, Utah with her husband, three children, and more rescue animals than she ever intended. She appreciates a nice glass of whiskey, homegrown tomatoes, and well-delivered sarcasm. She hopes to never have to "bless your heart."

For updates and more visit www.jessieharper.com.

facebook.com/JessieHarperAuthor

twitter.com/jessiehromance

instagram.com/jessieharperromance

amazon.com/author/jessieharper

www.ingramcontent.com/pod-product-compliance
Lightning Source LLC
Chambersburg PA
CBHW030314200626
46816CB00006BA/1778